D0977262

IN A SPLIT SECOND

SOPHIE MCKENZIE

SIMON & SCHUSTER BFYR

New York   London   Toronto   Sydney   New Delhi

SIMON & SCHUSTER BFYR

An imprint of Simon & Schuster Children's Publishing Division
1230 Avenue of the Americas, New York, New York 10020
For information about special discounts for bulk purchases, please contact Simon &
Schuster Special Sales at 1-866-506-1949 or business@simonandschuster.com.
The Simon & Schuster Speakers Bureau can bring authors to your live event.
For more information or to book an event, contact the Simon & Schuster Speakers
Bureau at 1-866-248-3049 or visit our website at www.simonspeakers.com.
Book design by Tom Daly
The text for this book is set in Weiss Std.
10 9 8 7 6 5 4 3 2 1
Library of Congress Cataloging-in-Publication Data:
McKenzie, Sophie.
[Split Second]
In a split second / Sophie McKenzie.—1st edition.
pages cm
First published in Great Britain in 2013 by Simon and Schuster UK Ltd, as Split Second.
Summary: Told in their two voices, Nat, who believes his brother set a
bomb in a London market, and Charlie, whose mother was killed in the
explosion, team up to infiltrate and stop the organization responsible
for the act of terrorism.
ISBN 978-1-4814-1394-7 (hardcover)—ISBN 978-1-4814-1396-1 (ebook)
[1. Terrorism—Fiction. 2. Bombings—Fiction. 3. Deception—Fiction.
4. Private schools—Fiction. 5. Schools—Fiction. 6. Orphans—Fiction.
7. London (England)—Fiction. 8. England—Fiction.] I. Title.
PZ7.M47867617Spl 2015
[Fic]—dc23
2013040880

FIRST
EDITION

For Joe. And the time that is given.

LONDON,
THE NEAR FUTURE

NAT

I glanced at my phone. It was almost 3 p.m.

Three p.m. was when the bomb would go off.

I raced along the street, my heart banging against my ribs. I *had* to find Lucas. *Canal Street market.* That's what the text had said. That was where Lucas would be. My lungs burned as I gasped at the cold air. I ran faster, pushing through the crowds.

The covered market was packed with shoppers, most of whom were heading for the food stall run by the Future Party. Since the cutbacks had really set in last year, unemployment had risen fast. Now people who would once never have dreamed of taking a handout lined up for free food from the only political party in the country that seemed to care. I hurtled past the line. Most people were staring at the ground as they shuffled along, avoiding eye contact.

There was no sign of Lucas.

I kept running. The bomb wouldn't be here, anyway. Why would anyone want to bomb people so poor they had to line up for food? The next few stalls all sold ethnic clothes—a mix of bold African prints and soft Thai silks. I turned the corner, past the section of the market specializing in baby stuff. No. No way. Neither Lucas nor the bomb would be here. Not where there were *babies,* for goodness' sake. I ran on, panting, past the market clock. It was just four minutes to three. There was hardly any time left. I looked up. The market had a second floor full of cheap toiletries and household goods. Should I go up there or check more of the ground floor?

A security guard strode past. I stared at the radio that hung from his belt. I'd been so focused on finding Lucas I hadn't thought about everyone else in the market. There were lots of people milling about. Lots of children with their mums and dads.

I chased after the security guard. Grabbed his arm. "Listen," I said. "You need to clear the market. Get everyone out."

The man turned. His face filled with suspicion. "What did you say?"

"There's a bomb," I said. "I don't know exactly where, but it's in the market and it's going to go off in a few minutes."

The security guard frowned, a look of disbelief on his face. "What makes you think that, kid?" he said.

"I just do. You have to believe me. *Please.*" Heart pounding, I caught sight of my reflection in the shiny Future Party sign that pointed the way to their free food stall. My hair was messed up, my eyes wild and staring. No wonder the security guard was looking at me like I was crazy. "You have to clear the whole place."

"Wait here," the guard said with a sigh. "I'll go and get the site manager."

"No, there's no time."

But the security guard was already striding away, heading toward the stalls I had just passed. As I turned to the next aisle, intending to run on, I caught a glimpse of a black leather jacket on the stairs up to the second floor. Was that Lucas? I strained my eyes, but the jacket had disappeared, lost in the crowds.

I swerved to the left and raced toward the stairs. I sped past a stall promising fifty percent off piercings and tattoos. A girl about my age stood in front, arguing with a woman. She was gesticulating wildly, her face flushed.

"Why *not*, Mum?" she was shouting.

Even racing past at top speed I could see the girl was pretty, with a mass of wild, honey-colored curls cascading over her shoulders. But there wasn't time to take a second look. I took the stairs up to the second floor, two steps at a time. It was two minutes to three. And I still hadn't found Lucas.

CHARLIE

Mum shook her head. She reached out to smooth a curl off my face. I backed away, furious.

"Come on, sweetheart. We've been over the reasons," she said, lowering her voice.

"It's just a tattoo," I insisted. "I'm not going to get anything outrageous. Or big. Maybe a butterfly, or that yin-yang symbol thing."

Mum pursed her lips and shook her head again. "You don't even know what that symbol *means*, Lottie."

"Don't call me that," I snapped. "You said I could *choose* what I did with my money. I've been saving forever."

Mum sighed. I turned away, so angry I wanted to scream.

It wasn't just the tattoo or Mum using her old name for me. It was *everything*: all the ways that Mum tried to stop me growing up. Dad died when I was very small and Mum and I had been on our own for years. This was great when I was little and had all her attention. But I would be sixteen in a few months and she needed to let me make my own decisions.

"As I've already explained . . . , " Mum said with another sigh.

"You can't have a tattoo because it's permanent—you're basically mutilating yourself for life. And it's a waste of money we don't have."

"It's *half price* here," I hissed. I know I sounded like a spoiled brat, but I was so fed up with us having to count every penny, every day. On my last birthday we hadn't even had a cake. "And it's just a fashion thing. I'm not going to have one anywhere obvious. Maybe on my shoulder or—"

"And it's *painful*," Mum added. "It will really hurt."

"So what?" I said. "Childbirth's painful. That's what you always say. But you put up with that. I can—"

"Childbirth was worth it," Mum said. "A tattoo isn't. Come on, sweetheart. There are lots of better things you could do with that money. A tattoo isn't exactly a practical choice."

"*Please*, Mum?" Tears sprang into my eyes. Just a few years ago, when Mum still had a job, before her benefit payments were stopped in the Government cuts, there had been plenty of money for impractical things. Mum reached for my arm. Her hands were red and rough from her part-time work at the factory. She worked nights but had gotten up this morning to come to the market for the free food bags. Her face was lined and worn. Once she had used eye makeup and nail polish. Now she looked old and dowdy.

Out of the corner of my eye I glimpsed the Asian woman running the tattoo stall watching us. She saw me looking and turned back to the TV, on which the mayor of London was speaking directly to camera—another appeal for support for the austerity cuts. I was filled with loathing at the sight of his fat face and sleek, dark hair. He looked like an overfed rat. Just like the last mayor—and the past two prime ministers—he kept telling the country that we were "all in it together," that more cuts were necessary.

I turned back to Mum. It was obvious from her expression that she wasn't going to change her mind.

"I hate you." The words shot out of me. I wish I could say that I didn't really mean them, but in that moment I did.

Mum fixed me with an unhappy look. I've often thought back to that moment, the last time I saw her for real. In my memory I can still hear the drone of the mayor of London's voice behind us, but what I remember most is Mum's expression: part disappointment, part hurt, part weariness.

"I'm sorry, Charlie," she said, her voice low and even. "You can have a tattoo when you're eighteen, when you're free to make your own decisions. But as long as I'm responsible for you it's not going to happen." She paused. We were still looking at each other. I remember the slant of her eyes, just like my own; the curve of her lips, pressed together. "Now, let's go down to the free food stall. There's already a line and the meat always runs out fast. I was hoping they might have some lamb. We haven't had that for ages."

"We haven't had *anything* for ages."

Mum bit her lip. "I know, but—"

"I'm not coming." I folded my arms. I knew I was being childish but I couldn't stop myself. I was too hurt, too angry. "I'm going to look at the clothes stalls."

"Okay," Mum said. "I'll come and find you when I'm done.

Don't go far. And don't buy anything until I get back."

She walked away. Her coat—long and leaf green—swung around her as she headed to the Future Party's stall where a large crowd of people was already lining up for the free food bags that were handed out every Saturday. A second later Mum disappeared into the crowd.

I glanced over at the tattoo woman. She was still watching the TV. The Future Party's leader, Roman Riley, was speaking now, his handsome face alive with conviction.

"Youth unemployment is now running at sixty percent and the government has the audacity to—"

I moved away. I wasn't interested in politicians and their talk, though at least Roman Riley's party organized handouts. The Government only ever took things away.

Still furious with Mum, I wandered to the far corner of the market, idly looking at a rack of cheap sweaters, then a big display of discounted jackets. They were all hideous. I sighed. Mum wanted me to wait nearby. Well, tough. I headed toward the exit, passing a stall selling African-print T-shirts, then another steaming with the scent of coconut curry. I stopped at a sign advertising free noodle soup—ONE PERSON, ONE CUP—hesitating as I wondered whether to get some.

WHAM! The blast knocked me off my feet. I slammed down hard on my back, onto the floor. Winded, I lay there, stunned. What was happening?

Voices rose up around me, shouts and screams. An alarm. Footsteps pounded past me as I struggled up onto my elbows.

An elderly woman had been knocked over too. We stared at each other, then turned to look across the market. Smoke was pouring up above the stalls two or three aisles away.

"What *was* that?" I said.

The elderly woman was struggling to her feet. I jumped up. *Mum.* I raced back through the market. People were staggering past, going in the opposite direction. Thick clouds of dust swirled around us. Jackets and sweaters from the stalls I'd passed before were scattered across the floor, blackened and ripped. I headed for the section of the market where the smoke was coming from. My head throbbed. Was the explosion gas? An accident? A bomb?

"Did you see what happened?"

"Call an ambulance!"

"Help me!"

People all around me were yelling. Screaming. I raced toward the smoke. I had to get back to the free food stall. Find Mum. Rubble was all around, counters from stalls splintered and on their sides, clothes and food strewn across the dirt-streaked floor. A man staggered out of the smoke, blood pouring from his face. Another man followed, holding a little boy in his arms, his jacket covered in dust, his eyes wide with shock. Two women held another up between them. More people, blocking my way. I pushed past them into the next aisle.

Mum had been right there, exactly where the smoke was coming from. Terror tightened my throat. I had to find her. My eyes were watering from the thick air. It was hard to breathe. I pushed through the crowds. People were rushing past me, desperate to get out of the market. Injured people, terrified people.

I forced my way past them. The smoke was even thicker as I passed the tattoo stall. The TV was smashed on the ground, the woman from the stall bent over, groaning. I held my hand over my mouth, choking on the dust. I stumbled, unable to see anything through the smoke. I stopped for a second, trying to make myself focus. The thin, piercing alarm stopped. An announcement sounded, telling everyone to leave the market.

"Make your way to the nearest exit. Make your way to the nearest exit."

I headed left, toward the free food stall. A small fire was burning out of a pile of cables. Shards of plastic crunched under my feet. Everywhere was blood and dust and metal. Hell. A shoe on its side with a broken heel. A torn poster showing just one side of Roman Riley's face above the words: FUTURE PA—

The smoke cleared slightly. I saw the leaf green of Mum's coat. Her arm flung out behind her head.

And I knew.

I knew but I couldn't face it.

"Mum!" I yelled, and time slowed down as I moved toward her. *"Mum!"*

NAT

I felt the bomb as much as I heard it, the ground shaking under my feet as I ran. I was on the second floor, at the far end of the market. The explosion had come from below. Two women on the other side of a trestle table stacked with bottles of half-price toilet cleaner looked up as I passed, their faces echoing my own shock and fear.

Was I too late?

"Lucas." His name came out in a whisper as an alarm pierced the air. I raced to the stairs. A security guard—a different man from the one I spoke to before—was stopping people from going down. Everyone was shouting. It was pandemonium.

"I think my brother's down there," I yelled, trying to shove the security guard out of the way.

"It's too dangerous," he said, pushing me back.

I swore, forcing my way past him and onto the stairs. I sped down the steps. Smoke rose up from the ground floor. Had Lucas been there when the bomb went off? Fear gripped me. It was impossible to think. All I knew was that I *had* to find him. I reached the ground floor. Smoke swirled everywhere. People staggered past, covered in dust. Screams echoed in the air, as the alarm switched to a P.A. system announcement urging everyone to leave the market.

I ran past the clothing stalls on the ground floor. The smoke was coming up from the middle aisle near the tattoo stall where I'd seen the girl arguing with her mother. People were shrieking and moaning, rising like ghosts through the smoke. I elbowed my way through the crowds, past the tattoo stall and around the corner, past splintered wood and twisted metal. A bag of potatoes lay on its side, the food spilling out. Two middle-aged women were on their knees, scrabbling around in the dirt, picking up potatoes. I reached the Future Party's food stall and stopped. A ripped poster of Roman Riley had fallen to the ground. Just beyond it the security guard I'd spoken to earlier lay spread-eagled, faceup. The man was motionless, his eyes open but unseeing. I shuddered.

Please let Lucas not be here.

And then I saw him, just a few feet away. He was lying on his back, his legs twisted awkwardly under him. A woman was bent over his body. I ran over, choking on the acrid smoke that rose up around me, filling my lungs. The woman pressed her fingers against Lucas's neck. She was feeling for a pulse.

I dropped to my knees. Around me the PA announcement, the shouts, the screams, the smoke all faded away.

"Lucas?" I leaned closer. There were no marks on Lucas's face, but his eyes were shut. *"Lucas?"* I turned to the woman. "He's my brother."

"He's alive. Unconscious, but alive." The woman looked at me. "I'm a nurse. He's alive."

I nodded, trying to take it all in. It was like a scene from a film. Terror and noise everywhere. But Lucas was alive.

A man in a suit was trying to usher people away through the smoke and the dust and the rubble. The nurse shook my arm. "I'm going to check on the others," she said. "Stay with your brother." She hurried away.

An empty plastic bag lay on the ground beside Lucas. I stared down at its ripped handles. I hadn't found Lucas in time. His eyes were still closed. Around us the dust swirled through the air. Across the market the girl with the wild, honey-colored hair was crouched over the woman she'd been arguing with just moments before. Her mouth was open in an agonizing scream.

"Mum!" she was crying. "*Mum!*"

I couldn't bear to see her face.

The nurse was with the girl's mother now. She was shaking her head. I glanced at the girl again. Her hands were over her mouth.

Firemen appeared. Paramedics. I had no idea how much time had passed since the bomb. My brain seemed to have stopped working.

The shock settled with the dust. A paramedic knelt down beside Lucas and I leaned back to give him room.

I looked around.

Blood in the dust. The air full of death.

And Lucas there, in the middle of it.

Lucas. My brother. The terrorist.

SIX MONTHS LATER . . .

PART ONE

INVESTIGATION

(n. a searching inquiry for ascertaining facts)

CHARLIE

I slammed the door and stomped away, into my bedroom. Outside, I could hear Aunt Karen sobbing. I felt like crying myself. Just for a moment. Then I forced the impulse away. I never cried. Not anymore. After months when I did nothing but shed whole rivers of tears, I had finally realized that it made no difference.

Mum was dead. She was never coming back.

And no one was going to face justice for murdering her. A little-known far-right group—the League of Iron—had claimed responsibility but no one had been arrested for the crime. The police insisted that they were still investigating but Aunt Karen was certain the officers in charge had turned a blind eye because so many of them actually supported the League of Iron's nasty, racist views. I thought it was more likely the police were just very busy. There were riots in the cities every few weeks and, since the latest round of cuts, fewer officers to deal with them. The bomb that killed Mum wasn't even the only explosion in recent months—though it had been the worst, leaving four dead and seventeen seriously injured.

Afterward, Aunt Karen had brought me to live with her despite the fact that she was even worse off than Mum had been. We survived on a series of tiny benefits and the kindness of our landlord.

A timid tap on the door. I turned to face Karen as she peered into my bedroom. I hated that room. It was basically a storage area that I had to share with the landlord's spare china and lots of Karen's clothes. Racks of these filled the long wardrobe—ancient dresses and tops that she never wore but couldn't bear to throw away.

"What?" I said.

Karen wiped her tear-stained face. "I can't cope with you anymore, Charlie," she said. "I'm at the end of my rope."

"What, because I ditched you and your stupid friends before?" I could hear how harsh my voice sounded and, inside, I felt bad for being mean. But I couldn't seem to stop myself.

Karen's lip trembled. "Please don't talk about my friends like that," she said. "And I had them over for *you*. Because it was Friday and the weekend and *last* weekend you didn't leave your room."

"So what?"

She was right, of course. I hardly ever went out. Losing Mum hadn't just meant moving to Karen's tiny apartment in Leeds but also leaving my old school and friends behind. Not that I missed anyone much. My friends all treated me differently after Mum died, like they were scared to come near me. The girls at my new school in Leeds, on the other hand, delighted in taunting me.

I'd never been to a single-sex school before and I hated how bitchy it was. The girls here teased me constantly about my

London accent, the way I'd use a long 'a' when they said it short and flat. They didn't even know I was called Charlie instead of Charlotte. Not that I cared. I didn't care about anything.

"I cut back on cigs this week to make sure I could afford that dessert." Karen's mouth trembled again. "I think the least you could do is say you're sorry."

I peered past her, out to the tiny kitchen, where the remnants of the chocolate trifle Karen had bought lay where I'd thrown it onto the grubby floor. Mum would have *made* a trifle. Mum would have kept her kitchen floor clean.

It suddenly struck me that of all the many reasons I felt angry with Karen, by far the biggest was that she simply wasn't Mum. It was ironic, really. Karen and I had gotten along well once, when Mum and I used to visit her. Karen was Mum's younger sister, with no kids of her own. She had been fun back then, at least I'd always thought so. But Karen was also kind of forgetful. Not about big emotional stuff, but the small things that make life easy, like paying bills on time and not losing cell phones and remembering when someone's told you ten times already they need new shoes for school.

Mum had been great at all that stuff.

Not that I'd ever appreciated it.

An image of her unhappy face, just before she'd turned away from me in the market, flashed into my head. I hadn't even really wanted that stupid tattoo we'd been arguing over.

A miserable fury filled me again.

"Charlie?"

"I just didn't want to join in before," I said, struggling to keep my temper. I knew that the rage I felt was all out of proportion. Karen had only been trying to be nice. But, again, I couldn't stop myself. "They're your friends, not mine."

Karen gazed at me and, though she doesn't look anything like Mum, for a moment I saw Mum's sorrowful expression in her eyes.

It hurt too much to look at her.

"Go away," I said. And I slammed the door in her face.

The next day was Saturday. I spent the whole morning asleep and then the whole afternoon reading in my room, coming out only for some toast and a cup of tea. The kitchen was in chaos, as usual: a huge mess of trifle still lay on the floor, dirty plates from last night were stacked in the sink, and an ashtray overflowing with cigarette butts sat on the table. It was funny, I thought as I wiped up the trifle, how Karen was always complaining about being poor, yet spent masses of money every week on her "cigs," as she called them. I expected her to come in and talk to me again at some point during the afternoon but she didn't appear until the evening. I was truly bored by then, with another whole day stretching ahead of me before school on Monday morning— and nothing to do.

I was just poring over my bookshelves, trying to pick another book to reread. I used to have an e-reader with loads of more grown-up novels on it but Mum had pawned it just before she died—so I was left with just the childhood books I'd loved from years ago. Right now I was rereading *The Suitcase Kid* by Jacqueline Wilson.

I heard the doorbell, then voices. A minute later Karen knocked on my bedroom door. She didn't smile as she asked me to come with her into the living room.

"There are some people here to see you," she said.

"What?" Who on earth could be here to see me? I felt like refusing, but Karen was already heading for the living room. Anyway, I was curious.

A man and a woman were sitting on the sofa. They stood up as I walked in. The man looked vaguely familiar, the woman less so, but I couldn't place either of them. They smiled at me. I glared back and the woman looked down at the threadbare carpet. Karen cleared her throat.

"This is Brian and Gail," she said. "Your uncle and his wife."

My mouth fell open. Dad was a soldier who died in action when I was a baby, and I'd met his brother, my uncle, only once or twice when I was younger. Brian looked different from how I remembered him, more fleshy in the face with a definite paunch under his sharp suit. I glanced at Gail. She was thin with a timid smile. I couldn't remember her at all. Brian had gone to work abroad when I was still very little. Mum had told me that he and my dad disliked each other and had hardly seen each other in years.

"Hello, Charlotte." Brian strode toward me and gripped my hand. He pumped it up and down. "It's a pleasure to see you again."

"Is it?" I withdrew my hand. "If it's such a pleasure, how come I haven't seen you for, like, a million years?"

Beside me, Karen gasped. Across the room, Gail's eyes widened. She looked horrified. I folded my arms, filling up with anger. How dare she looked so shocked? She and Brian hadn't even come to Mum's funeral.

And then Brian laughed. A big belly laugh. It transformed his face, softening all his features. I'd heard that laugh before. It sounded just like my dad's in the videos Mum used to play of him. Of them together. When they always seemed to be laughing. I'd grown up watching those videos, hearing the sound of Dad's guffaws, seeing his eyes shining with love for Mum.

I hated Brian for reminding me. Tears filled my eyes and I turned my face away from him, not wanting him to see how much losing Mum hurt.

Brian stopped laughing. There was a pause, and then he spoke in a low, gruff voice, quite different from the formal tone he'd used before.

"I deserve that, Charlotte," he said. "I'm truly sorry for all that you've been through. My mother died when I was younger. I know how hard it is and I can't imagine how impossible it must be for you losing your mum at such a young age."

I looked back at him. "I'm doing fine," I said, "and it's Charlie, not Charlotte."

"Okay." Brian nodded. He beckoned his wife, who drifted nervously to his side, eyeing me as if I were a wild dog that might bite her if she wasn't careful. "Gail and I would like to help."

I stared at them. "Help?"

"Why don't we all sit down?" Karen tugged me onto the chair next to her. Brian and Gail sat opposite.

"It's been difficult, as you *know*, Charlie," Karen said. She laid her hand over mine. "I love you very much but I don't think its really working out. We've both said as much, so . . ." She trailed off, not meeting my eyes.

"You're kicking me out?" I said.

"No." That was Brian. He leaned forward. "I'm back in London for work and living with the family full time instead of only on weekends. Gail and I *want* to have you. We have a large house and I've got a great job at ViaTech—and a good job is a big deal these days, as you'll know. Rosa's your age. Well, she's nearly ten months younger, but you're the same grade at school. We're your family. And I think it's time we stepped in."

"We just want to help, Charlie," Gail said. Her eyes were round and soft. "I only met your mother a few times but I liked her. It's a shame we lost touch. And I know we should have done more over the past few months but with Brian spending so much time out of the country it's been hard."

I looked from her to Brian. "You want me to come and live with you?" I turned to Karen. "You want me to go?"

Karen looked down. "It's not that, exactly."

Something twisted in my guts. It *was* that. Exactly.

"We'd treat it as a trial," Brian said. "Like a vacation, trying it out for a couple of weeks. There's no need to involve Social Services or do anything formal at this stage."

"Does that mean I won't have to go to school?" I looked up.

Brian chuckled. "I'm afraid school is nonnegotiable. This is an important year for you, with your tests coming up. Anyway, trying out Rosa's school is part of the reason for coming to stay for a couple of weeks."

"It's a great place, Charlie," Gail said. "Newbury Park. Rosa loves it. It's private, with lots of great facilities."

"A *private* school?" I sat back. Since the economy had gotten worse last year, lots of private schools had closed because parents couldn't afford tuition. You had to be really rich to go to one.

"We'd be happy to pay for your place there if you decide to stay. It's not a problem," Brian said.

I sat back, my head spinning. I'd never been to a private school before or mixed with private school kids. And I had no idea what Rosa would be like. On the other hand, the prospect of getting away from here was tempting.

"Where do you live?" I asked.

"North London," Gail said. "Near Hendon."

I nodded. Back to London then . . . not far from where Mum and I had lived and even closer to where my dad had grown up. Near, in fact, to the market where Mum had been killed. Still, I could avoid ever going there again. And no one would tease me about my accent in London, either.

Brian stood up. "Take some time to think about it. I know things haven't been easy for you this year. But Gail and I want to help, like we said." He sighed. "It's no secret that your dad and I didn't get along, but that's no reason you should suffer now. We're staying overnight in a hotel nearby. Call if you've got any questions. Karen has the number. We'll come back in the morning, you can tell us what you've decided then. If you need more time, that's fine."

"Right," I said. I looked at Karen. She was watching me carefully. I knew that if I refused to go she would let me stay with her. But was that what I really wanted?

"So . . . the school, me going there for a trial period, that's really okay too?"

"Absolutely. You can even join Rosa's house temporarily," Gail said.

I stared at her blankly.

"They divide the kids into houses, so they can have mentors and a real sense of identity. It's a great system."

"Will you think about it?" Brian asked.

I looked into his eyes. They were warm, strong, serious. Like my dad's had been. A sob welled up inside me. I swallowed it down. Karen didn't really want me. There was nothing to keep me here.

"I guess I could think about it," I said with a shrug. But inside I already knew I was going to say yes. After all, London was more my home than Leeds. And, in the end, it didn't matter where I was. Mum would never be there.

Wherever I went, I would always be alone.

NAT

I put my hand on Mum's shoulder. She leaned toward me for a moment, then shifted forward in her chair, her eyes fixed once again on Lucas. I let my hand drop.

There had been a time, before the bomb, when we were still a family: all five of us watching TV together or Mum insisting we sat down for meals or that last vacation in Spain when Jas got sunburn. But those memories belonged to another life. For the past six months Mum had spent most of her time in the hospital, as if somehow she could will Lucas back to consciousness simply by watching him. The doctors held out only the faintest hope that he would ever wake up. He had been in a coma since the bomb went off.

And I had kept his secret.

"Lucas looks better today, Nat, don't you think?" Mum glanced over her shoulder at me. "A bit more color in his cheeks."

"Mmm." I shrugged, feeling awkward. As far as I could see Lucas looked the same as he always did: pale and still and kept alive only by the wires and tubes that ran in and out of his body.

I walked to the door. Mum didn't seem to notice. Lucas had always been her favorite, her "golden boy," tragically left in a coma because he happened to be in the wrong place at the wrong time. But I knew the truth. I knew that Lucas had been part of the terrorist team who set off the bomb in the market.

I still didn't understand it. Lucas hadn't been a violent person with extreme views. He hadn't really been interested in politics at all. He'd admired the peaceful and democratic new Future Party— and its leader, Roman Riley—but then so did virtually everyone. It just didn't make sense that Lucas could have set off a bomb for the League of Iron, a nasty, far-right group that spouted vicious and racist propaganda.

Having said that, Lucas *had* changed a month or two before the bomb. Previously happy-go-lucky and disorganized, he had acquired a new sense of purpose. His grades improved. He made more effort around the house. He carried himself more proudly. And then, on the very day of the bomb, I'd overheard him on the phone, his voice tense and excited. I hadn't picked up much, but Lucas had definitely referred to an explosion that would happen "later today" and the resulting "blast radius." A few hours after the call, I'd screwed up enough courage to sneak a look in the pockets of his jacket and found the cell phone he'd used . . . a *second* cell that I hadn't even known he had. And I'd seen the text:

Take package—Canal St market, 3pm

I'd put the phone back in his jacket and psyched myself up to ask Lucas what was going on. But before I could say anything, Lucas had grabbed his jacket and left the house. I followed him to the market, but I was too late.

It ate away at me, not being able to tell anyone, but things at home were bad enough without me making them worse. The truth would destroy Mum and Dad—who would never understand how Lucas had gotten mixed up with a Nazi outfit like the League of Iron—and it would devastate my twin sister, Jas. She had idolized Lucas as much as I had.

After the blast, I found Lucas's phone with the incriminating text in his pocket. In a panic I'd thrown it away. For weeks I expected the police to come knocking at the door, but Lucas wasn't a suspect. He hadn't been right next to the bomb when it went off and there was no trace of explosives on his clothes, so no one connected him with the bombers. Perhaps the device had detonated sooner than it was meant to, before Lucas had time to get away. I had no idea. All I knew was that Lucas, with his easy manner and crooked smile, was the opposite of anyone's idea of a terrorist.

I stood at the door of the hospital room. "I'm going to school now, Mum," I said.

Mum didn't hear me. She was busy tucking Lucas's arm under the cover, her anxious fingers stroking the underside of his wrist with its tiny, strange tattoo in the shape of an open hand. None of us had even known it was there until after the bomb.

I dug my fists deep into my pockets as I walked away. I wanted to shout at Mum that there was no point fussing over Lucas, that he wasn't coming back. But of course I couldn't. There were no raised voices in my family anymore. Our house didn't even really feel like a home. It was just somewhere we all slept.

I dawdled along to school, seriously considering cutting the rest of the day. A couple of tramps shuffled past me. There were homeless people on practically every street now. I kicked an empty can of beer across the pavement. I couldn't cut again. It would just mean more stress for Mum and Dad.

It started to rain and I sped up, pulling my school blazer over my head. It was Lucas's old blazer—and slightly too big for me. Most of my school uniform was Lucas's now. It had felt weird at first putting on his clothes, but I had grown almost two inches in the past six months and my own stuff didn't fit anymore. It was obvious Mum wasn't up to replacing my uniform, even if we could have afforded new clothes, so I took Lucas's.

Out of habit, I checked the League of Iron forum as I hurried along the street. I had spent a long time trying to find out who Lucas had known in the League, hoping it would lead me to someone who could explain why my older brother had wanted to bomb the Canal Street market. But, so far, I'd discovered nothing. I checked a few threads. As usual there was plenty of anger against the Government and support for the League, now proposing that all black people should have their benefits stopped or their jobs taken away. Some forum users even wanted all non-whites and new immigrants rounded up into camps and killed.

I sighed. I understood how frustrating it was to see people on benefits when others, like Dad, worked sixteen-hour days. Still, a lot of people couldn't work through no fault of their own. And why did the League of Iron have to take their anger out on black people? It didn't make sense. Still, maybe I needed to get more involved, pretend to share the League's disgusting views. My tentative efforts to find out if anyone on the forum knew Lucas certainly hadn't worked so far. I logged in with my user name: *AngelOfFire*, then bent over my phone, writing in the "add your comment" box:

Killing people should be TARGETED. We need to destroy EVERYONE standing in our way: blacks, Muslims, corrupt politicians, bankers, scroungers. It means BOMBS, not talk. Not stupid politicians who wimp out from DOING anything.

I pressed the "post" button and my comment appeared live on the forum. I checked the time. I had already missed homeroom, which probably meant another detention. I trudged along as the rain poured down, matching my mood. Sometimes it felt that nothing had changed and that nothing was ever going to change.

CHARLIE

"We're here." Uncle Brian pointed out of the car window.

We had parked outside an enormous house. Wow, Brian and Gail must be really rich. Gail turned from the passenger seat and smiled at me.

"Rosa can't wait to see you," she said. "She's so excited."

"Don't worry, Charlie," Brian said softly. "This is just a trial period, remember? No pressure."

I nodded but inside I felt all churned up. Getting away at such short notice from a school I hated and leaving behind the constant fights with Aunt Karen was one thing, but now that I was actually on the verge of a new life the reality seemed overwhelming. For a moment I missed Mum so badly my stomach hurt. I gritted my teeth, refusing to give in to the pain. This was a fresh beginning, a chance to start over. *That's* what I had to focus on.

We got out of the car and walked up the path. The light was fading from a rather dreary Monday afternoon. Rosebushes—not in bloom of course—lined the edges of a crisply manicured lawn. I could hardly believe a lone family lived here—you could have fit ten of my old apartments into the place. I thought of Mum scrimping and saving to buy food all last year. It didn't seem fair that some people had so little while others had so much.

I caught a glimpse of a round, eager face at one of the ground-floor windows. That must be Rosa. If only I could have a few more days just with Brian and Gail to get used to the house before I met my cousin.

My whole body tensed as we reached the front door. Gail was fishing in her bag, reaching for a key, but before she could find it, the door opened. A girl stood there: shorter and plumper than me, with straight hair cut into thick bangs. She was wearing a lot of makeup, with glitter around her eyes and long blue earrings that matched her sweater.

"Hi, Charlie." She beamed. "I'm Rosa."

"No kidding." The words came out all harsh and disdainful. Inside, I winced. I hadn't meant to sound like that. Rosa blinked, her expression hurt and shocked. I wanted to say something nice, maybe ask how she was or whatever, but I couldn't figure out the right words to use. "Sorry," I mumbled.

There was an awkward pause then Gail bustled forward.

"Hiya, sweetie." She gave Rosa a kiss on the cheek. "How was your day at school?"

"Fine, thanks." Rosa stared at me.

Brian kissed Rosa too. "Come in, Charlie," he said. "Sorry, but I just need to do a bit of work before dinner. Still, it'll give you a chance to settle in, get to know Rosa, eh?"

"Charlie doesn't mind, do you?" Gail said, smiling anxiously at me.

I shook my head. "'Course not," I said, feeling awkward. Brian had taken the whole day off to collect me from Aunt Karen's and had spent most of our journey here from Leeds taking business calls on his cell. I watched him head across the hall, laptop in hand.

Gail cleared her throat. "Why don't you pop the kettle on, Rosa, make us a cup of tea. Charlie, would you like one?"

I shook my head, feeling more uncomfortable than ever. I followed Gail inside. The hall was large and square, with mosaic tiles on the floor and French windows opposite. Gail led me into the room on the right: a big, airy kitchen with shiny scarlet cupboard doors. A table stood at the far end. More French doors led onto what looked like a huge garden. For a second I felt disoriented; I hadn't anticipated a house so massive it would take me a while to find my way around. Then I realized Rosa was hovering beside me. I turned to face her, willing myself to say the right thing, though unsure what that was.

"Would you like me to show you around?" Rosa asked. She still had a smile on her face, but it was a little fixed now and there was a wary look in her eyes.

"Sure."

Rosa glanced at her mum. Gail nodded. "Go on then, I'll make the tea."

Rosa led me through the hall. Both the doors beyond the stairs were open. She stood back to let me peer into each room in turn. A gigantic living room, then a dining room with a polished wooden table and elegant, glass-fronted cupboards. I could feel

Rosa watching me as I took in both rooms. I felt hot and uncomfortable. I would so much rather have been left to wander around by myself. Rosa kept looking at me expectantly, but I had no idea what I was supposed to say. Everything seemed very grand and formal, the total opposite of Aunt Karen's mess and nothing like the cozy, comfortable home I'd shared with Mum. A sob twisted in my guts as I thought of her. I swallowed it down.

"Mum got our housekeeper to come in today so it would be nice for you." There was a slightly reproachful edge to Rosa's voice. I looked at her.

"She didn't need to do that," I said.

Rosa smiled her bright, fixed smile again. "We wanted everything to be just right. I helped with your room. Do you want to see?"

I nodded, wondering what Rosa meant by "helped." Privately, I hoped that the glittery eye shadow and harsh, bright blue of her sweater and earrings weren't an indication of the décor she'd chosen.

One flight up, Rosa pointed to all the doors that led off the landing, naming a study, her parents' bedroom, and at least two spare rooms and bathrooms.

"Our rooms are upstairs," Rosa said.

I followed her up the next flight of stairs to the landing. Rosa indicated the open door on the left. "That's mine," she said.

I peered inside. Every surface in the room overflowed with makeup and jewelry. Each wall was painted a different color: pale blue, dark blue, pink, and lilac. Clothes spilled out of the large wardrobe and onto the floor. It was all frills and bright colors . . . the opposite of my own, darker, simpler tastes.

Rosa surveyed her room proudly, then turned away. "The bathroom's opposite. You're there." She pointed to the only remaining door, next to the bathroom.

I crossed the landing, my heart in my mouth. What on earth was my room going to look like? I pushed the door open.

NAT

It was still raining when I got in from school on Monday evening. The house was empty but for once I was relieved. I was in no mood to chat. I dumped my school bag on the kitchen table—still covered with this morning's cereal bowls— then decided to check to see if anyone had responded to my League of Iron post. I opened the browser on my phone. The Internet connection was frustratingly slow, so I went to the bathroom while I waited. The floor was covered with damp towels. I kicked them into a corner, knowing that I should really take them all downstairs and put them in the washing machine. Maybe Mum would do it when she got in from the hospital.

Yeah, right. Even when Mum did come home, she was never really here. It was as if she left her brain at the hospital with Lucas and then simply drifted around the house, commenting that the boiler was overdue for a service or that Jas needed a haircut.

Back downstairs, I saw a note from Dad saying that he was working on a repair job at the garage and wouldn't be home until midnight. Shoving it to one side, I checked my phone. The

League of Iron forum had opened at last. Two other users had left supportive comments in response to my post. But there was nothing that directly picked up on my reference to the Canal Street market bomb.

And then I read the third post. It was a direct reply to my own words—an individual and specific invitation:

Saxon66 to AngelOfFire:

MEETING in London next week for all seeking answers. POWER watches. Be CAREFUL. Details to come. KEEP the FAITH.

Iron Right

Iron Might

Iron Will

I stood stock-still, the hairs on the back of my neck prickling. This was it. I had been personally invited to a meeting of the League of Iron.

Now, surely, there would be answers.

CHARLIE

The room Rosa showed me into was cold—far cooler than the rest of the house—but to my relief it was decorated in a simple style. The walls were plain white and the curtains a dark, silky red. Matching cushions were strewn across the bed, which was made up with a white duvet and pillowcases. A fitted wardrobe ran the length of one wall, a small table stood in the far corner.

"You can use that as a dressing table, for all your, er, makeup and, er, stuff . . ." Rosa trailed off, presumably having noticed that I wasn't wearing any makeup. I shrugged. I did sometimes put on a little mascara and I used gel to control my curls, but I never applied eyeliner or eye shadow anymore, and I didn't own a single lipstick. Back when Mum was alive, I used to love all that stuff, just as I used to want a tattoo. Now makeup and fashion seemed like toys to me: childish and pointless and belonging to a long-distant past.

"This is a spare room, where the au pair used to live," Rosa went on. "Mum made me leave everything plain so you could choose what paint you wanted, get a new duvet set if you like."

"White's fine," I said. I was starting to feel exhausted.

"Right." Again, Rosa sounded injured.

We stood in awkward silence for a moment, then Rosa walked across the landing and into her own room.

I took off my jacket and sat down on the bed. It was a double—far bigger than any bed I'd ever slept in before. But then the whole room was bigger. The whole house.

I glanced around again. I was grateful that Gail hadn't let Rosa loose on the room. It was bland and bare, ready for me to make it my own. And yet as I sat on the bed, I couldn't help but think back to my old room at Mum's. That had been painted pale green, with an entire wall of shelves groaning under the weight of all the children's books Mum had bought for me. Thinking I was too old for them, I'd left them all with Aunt Karen. Now, suddenly, I felt horribly homesick for the books—and for Mum.

My heart seemed to shrink in my chest, tears bubbling up into my eyes. In Karen's apartment there were pictures of Mum everywhere. Here, it was like she had never existed. I closed my eyes, intending to summon up Mum's smiling face, but all I could see was that look of disappointment from the last time I saw her.

I wandered over to the window and peered out. The sun was low in the sky, an orange disk setting behind the trees of what was presumably the local park. Up here, on the third floor, I could see over the rooftops and backyards of north London, all brick walls and tiled roofs. I touched the red silk of the curtains. The fabric was soft and smooth. Beautiful. It was *all* beautiful: the house, the view . . . everything. But it wasn't me. I didn't belong here any more than I'd belonged with Aunt Karen.

A sense of desolation swamped me. I was used to missing Mum. I carried her absence with me like a deadweight wherever I went, but right now it felt too hard to bear. All I wanted was to go back to my old life, to be with Mum again. And instead I was here, facing the future without her.

Outside, a police siren screeched into the silence. "There you are." Gail bustled into the room, my carryall in her hand. "Oh, I'm sorry it's so cold in here." She set down my bag, then hurried over to the radiator opposite and fiddled with the knob. "I told Mercy, that's our housekeeper, to turn it on but she must have forgotten. Is everything okay?"

I nodded.

"I hope Rosa explained that you're free to do what you like with the room," Gail babbled on. "I can take those curtains down if you like. You can paint it yourself or we can get the decorators in." She stood, anxiously, watching me.

"It's fine," I said.

Gail coughed nervously. "Look, why don't you take a moment up here to settle in, unpack some of your things. You need to let us know if you'd like some money for clothes or a new phone. I was thinking that if you decide to stay you'd probably want a new laptop too, for your schoolwork?"

Wow, my own computer. I knew I should feel excited—and grateful. I forced a smile onto my face. "Thank you," I said awkwardly.

"I'll get Bri to bring up your other bag. We'll have supper in a couple of hours, but come down whenever you like. I could help you unpack. . . ."

"I'll be fine."

"Okay, well we need to talk about school too. I think you'll fit into Rosa's uniform for the first few days, then, if you're happy to stay, we can get you your own."

I nodded again. Part of me wanted to ask about the school, but a painful lump had lodged itself in my throat. Gail waited a second, then backed away, closing the door behind her. As I heard her footsteps on the stairs, I took one of my photos of Mum out of my bag, set it beside the bed, then lay back on the soft white duvet. Sometimes it was still impossible to believe she was gone.

Bitterness crept through my veins. It wasn't fair that she had been taken away from me, that my life had been turned upside down, that I had been left so alone, not belonging anywhere . . . to anyone. . . .

I wished I had someone specific to blame. There was the League of Iron, of course, but that was a faceless organization. I wanted a name. A person. My guts twisted. Tears rose up again: hot, furious tears. I let them trickle down my face. I would stay here. I would go to the new school. I would get on with my life. The League of Iron wouldn't beat me.

And, one day, I'd find a way to get my revenge for Mum's death.

NAT

As I trudged up the stairs to math, I couldn't stop thinking about the League of Iron meeting. When would it happen? Who would be there?

Would they talk about the Canal Street market bomb?

Probably not in an open meeting, but Lucas's contacts were sure to be there. I was hoping that if I made it clear I was his brother, they might speak to me privately about his involvement.

I'd spent the entire time since I received my invitation thinking about what I should do and say at the meeting. I'd been checking the League forum several times an hour, but no new details had appeared among either the general posts or as a private message to me. In the end, I'd been so preoccupied with it all that I was late for homeroom twice, which meant another break-time detention.

I didn't care. All I could think about was the meeting—and what I might find out there.

"Hey, Nat, you missed homeroom."

I turned to see who was speaking. Rosa Stockwell was hurrying up the steps behind me. Considering she was in my house,

I didn't know Rosa that well. If I was honest, I didn't particularly want to. Rosa was okay, but she had an irritating giggle and a coy, teasing manner, like she was always thinking about the effect she was having on you. Some of my friends liked her, but, to me, she came across as a bit of an airhead.

"Yup, I missed it," I said, turning to check my phone again. "I was late."

Rosa giggled. I had no idea why. Still, maybe Rosa didn't need a reason. I much preferred girls who chatted like normal people, instead of getting all weird when they were around boys.

"Nat, you're so funny." Rosa nudged my arm as we walked up the stairs side by side. "Hey d'you want to hear my big news?"

"What is it?" I was barely listening. I'd just spotted a private message from Saxon66. It read:

London MEETING next Tuesday, 7pm. Stand by for details.

Iron Right

Iron Might

Iron Will

". . . and she's in our house too." Rosa finished with a flourish, as we reached the top of the stairs.

I glanced at her blankly. I'd missed most of what she'd said. This was it. I had an actual time. The meeting was next week. It was going to happen.

"Uh-huh," I said, attempting to stride ahead of Rosa.

"Were you listening to me?" Rosa demanded.

"'Course," I lied.

"What did I say then?"

I forced myself away from my phone.

"Sorry, I've got to get to math." I felt a brief stab of guilt as I hurried off, but a moment later I'd forgotten all about Rosa as I bent over my phone again, full of excited anticipation.

CHARLIE

I was relieved Rosa wasn't in my math class. It turned out Newbury Park put people into sets for just about everything and, despite my lack of interest in school over the past few months, I was down to be in the top group.

On the other hand, it did mean I had to deal with everyone's pity all on my own. A couple of girls stopped me in the hallway as I checked my schedule. It was hard to follow, much like the map I'd also been given.

"Hi, Charlie," one said. She smiled at my look of surprise that she knew my name. "Rosa told us about you."

"Sorry about your mum," said the other girl. She peered at me intently. "Were you actually *there* when it happened?"

I was used to this. Back in Leeds there had been a succession of people asking about Mum dying in the bomb. They all started out by saying how sorry they were, but in the end, it was obvious they didn't really care about me at all. They just wanted a load of gossip they could spread around.

"I don't want to talk about my mum," I said.

The two girls exchanged a swift glance.

"Rosa said you were still really, really upset." The girl's voice exuded syrupy sympathy.

Irritation rose inside me.

"I'm fine," I said. "I'm just trying to find my math class. I have Mr. Pritchard."

The girls looked at each other again and then back at me. The second girl curled her lip.

"Oh, sorry," she said sarcastically. "We're not in that class."

"Good." The word was out of my mouth before I could snatch it back.

"Fine." They sniffed, stuck their noses in the air, and stalked off.

I sighed. Why did stuff like that always happen around me? I hurried on, looking for the right room.

NAT

I reached the classroom at the same time as Mr. Pritchard and stood back to let him through the door. As he strode to the front, the class took their seats. I slipped into my usual spot at the back. Callum leaned across from the next desk and asked in a whisper if I wanted to play soccer after school. I nodded. I could easily spare a couple of hours in the park so long as Jas bought some pasta and sauce on her way home. I needed to remind her to get some milk as well. I scanned the room, wondering where she was sitting. We never sat together in class. Jas said it was because we had enough of each other at home but sometimes I wondered if she minded always being seen as "less academic" than me. I'd got a full scholarship to Newbury Park while Jas had gotten in on a music scholarship, because she used to play the piano. She had always struggled to stay in the top math group, though, thanks to her hard work, she was still here.

After a moment or two I saw her. She was sitting right at the front of the class, copying something down in a notebook. As I watched her, struck by how hard she was concentrating, a girl passed my desk. Someone new, with masses of wild, curly hair down her back. The girl hurried over to Mr. Pritchard and a vague memory stirred deep inside me. I stared at the back of her head, wishing she would turn around so I could see her face.

Callum nudged my arm. "Hot, isn't she?" he said under his breath.

I opened my mouth, wanting to ask Callum who the girl was, but Mr. Pritchard was peering around the room, ready to begin. He was ultrastrict about not talking in class and if I got another detention I might have to stay after school next Tuesday. I couldn't risk that. For all I knew the League of Iron meeting would be held on the other side of London. My travel card only covered the bus, which meant it could take hours to get to wherever I needed to be.

"Ah, Charlotte Stockwell, welcome," Mr. Pritchard said, holding out his hand.

The girl hesitated a moment, as if she wasn't used to shaking hands. She was standing at the front of the class with her back to the room. I shivered, a feeling of dread creeping over me. I'd definitely seen this girl before somewhere, but the memory remained just out of reach. Beside me, Callum sniggered.

"Charlie," the girl said, shaking Mr. Pritchard's hand at last.

"Charlie." Mr. Pritchard smiled. "Take a seat, I'll come over when I've assigned some work."

The girl nodded. Then she turned around and headed for the nearest empty desk. She was strikingly pretty, with high cheekbones and a strong chin. My stomach dropped away as I remembered where I'd seen her before: in the market, a few minutes after the bomb had gone off, her mouth open in a scream.

The memory flashed, sharp and cruel, into my mind's eye as the girl, Charlie, sat down next to Jas.

She had lost her mother because of that bomb.

Because of Lucas.

And now she was in our math group at school.

Mr. Pritchard started writing a quadratic equation on the whiteboard, but all I could see was the market after the bomb. The girl and her mother. The blood and the smell of fear in the air.

I closed my eyes, but the images remained.

CHARLIE

The bell rang and the class rose as Mr. Pritchard dismissed everyone. Most people were wandering away, chattering, though the girl next to me was still buried in her notebook. I looked around, wondering what came next. The schedule was really confusing. And, anyway, I was too embarrassed to look at mine when no one else needed to look at theirs.

I was hoping the next class didn't involve Rosa. From the way she'd acted earlier, I had the strong impression that she loved all the attention she was getting thanks to my "sad orphan" history.

The math class had been okay at least. I'd liked the teacher and understood all of what we'd covered. I looked around. Mr. Pritchard and most of the class had gone now. I needed to move. The girl next to me was still writing, her tongue peeking out from her mouth in concentration. She had been working hard all class, looking up only when Mr. Pritchard spoke and chewing on her pen in between taking copious notes. She was very slim, with a long, sloping nose and sleek dark hair.

"Er, excuse me," I said.

The girl turned. She had gentle eyes and an open expression.

Her long hair framed a perfectly oval face. "Hi." She smiled—and there was nothing fake or overdone about the smile. "I'm Jas."

I smiled back, liking her immediately. "Charlie," I said. "Er, I'm new and I wasn't sure . . ." I trailed off.

"It's just break time now," Jas said, standing up and shoving her notebook into her bag. Despite being a little taller than me, she had really skinny legs that stuck out from under her skirt like sticks. "Would you like me to show you the canteen? Or the bathroom? Or your house room? Which house are you in, by the way?"

"Plato," I said. "What about you?"

"Socrates," Jas said. "That's why I didn't see you earlier, but I remember Rosa talking about you yesterday. You're her cousin, aren't you?"

I nodded. Jas led the way to the door and out into the bustling hallway. Students were herding toward a sign marked CANTEEN. I really didn't want to face the crowds so, when Jas looked at me expectantly, I asked if she'd show me outside.

"I've been in three different buildings so far," I said. "And I have no idea how they all connect."

Jas laughed. "I know, it's crazy. It's such a big school. It took me two weeks to find my way around." She pointed in the opposite direction from the students rushing past us. "That's the nearest exit."

We walked along, hugging the wall.

"I got a map earlier," I said, "but I couldn't figure out where I was on it."

Jas grinned. "I know. I couldn't figure out that map at all my first few days. In the end, Nat drew me another one."

"Nat?"

"My brother," she said. "We're twins. He's in your house, actually. They like to split twins up."

"They put me in with Rosa," I said. "Though I think Rosa asked for that before I started."

"What did *you* ask for?"

"I said I didn't mind."

We reached the exit. Jas pushed the door open and we emerged onto a large, asphalt concourse. A few boys at the far end were playing soccer. Two fields stretched away into the distance.

"Is that all part of the school?" I asked.

"Yup, it's massive," Jas said with a sigh. She was peering over at the soccer-playing boys. "I don't know where Nat is. He was in our math class just now and he's usually out here at break."

I nodded, relieved that I wasn't going to have to meet anyone else for the moment.

Jas took me over to the fields, then guided me down some steps to a separate building that turned out to house the gym and a big indoor swimming pool.

"Newbury Park has its own pool?" I asked, incredulous.

"Wait till you see the golf course." Jas rolled her eyes. "It's wrong, isn't it, when so many people these days are starving?"

I nodded. It *was* unfair, of course. I'd thought the same thing myself when I'd seen Brian and Gail's house. Still, I couldn't deny that it was also pretty cool. "It wasn't like this at my old school."

"Right." Jas hesitated. "Look, you'll hear anyway, so I might as well tell you, I know about your mum, in . . . in the bomb. . . ."

"Oh." I looked away, past the swimming pool, toward the trees that marked the Newbury Park school boundary. I'd thought for a moment that Jas might be different from the other girls, able to stop herself from prying into my past, trying to get all the gossip.

But clearly I'd been wrong.

"My brother was in the same explosion," Jas went on.

I looked back at her. I hadn't expected that.

"I thought you said your brother was here, at school?"

"Not Nat. He's my twin. I mean my older brother. Lucas. He was left in a coma." Jas's voice was steady, but I could see the pain behind her eyes as she spoke.

I remembered now the toll from the blast: four dead, including Mum and that security guard, and seventeen injured. I'd vaguely heard that one of the injured still hadn't regained consciousness ,but it was a long time since I'd thought about it.

"It's ironic you and me meeting, really," Jas said.

I shrugged. "I guess it is, though my parents used to live around here before I was born. It's where my dad was from. That's how come his brother lives here now, why I'm here. . . ." I stopped, suddenly aware that I'd told Jas more about myself in the past minute than I'd said to anyone else since Mum died. "I'm sorry about Lucas."

Jas nodded. "It was worse for Nat than me. He was actually there, at the market, when the bomb went off. . . ."

I had no memory of a boy our age at the scene, but then most of my memories of that horrible time were a blur now. Jas looked awkward, like she didn't want to say any more. Well, I could relate to that.

"So I've got history after break," I said, determined to change the subject. "Do you take that? And, if you do, can you help me find the classroom?"

"Sure." The tension ebbed from Jas's face as she led me around the swimming pool building and back to the main school. We chatted on. Jas told me a little bit more about her brother Nat. She said he was a soccer nut, and really smart . . . that he had an academic scholarship to the school while Jas had gotten a free place based on her piano playing. I was almost looking forward to meeting him, but when the bell rang and Jas and I arrived for history, Nat was nowhere to be seen. Jas frowned as she gazed around the room. "I hope he's not cutting again," she said. "He's spent half the semester arriving late and leaving early. Not that he ever gets into real trouble over it. Nat's good at talking his way out of things."

I raised my eyebrows. Smart and rebellious. I was liking the sound of Nat.

History was fun. The teacher was one of those people who like to make everything relevant to today and all chatty and friendly with the class. I was amazed by how disciplined everything was. Of course there was a bit of backtalk and a few students messing around, but the vast majority did their work and everyone paid attention when the teacher insisted on it.

Rosa wandered over at the end. I hadn't even noticed she was in the room, having sat down at the front with Jas before class started.

"Where did you go during break?" Rosa asked, looking miffed. "I waited for you in the canteen, but you didn't show up."

"Oh." I racked my brains. Had I said I'd meet Rosa there? I was pretty sure I hadn't. "I didn't realize."

Rosa made a face. "Really? But *everyone* goes to the canteen at break. You have to eat then because lunch for eleventh grade is so late."

I resisted the temptation to point out that I'd had no way of knowing that.

"I wanted to take a look outside," I said. "Work out how all the buildings fitted together. Jas from my math class showed me."

Rosa wrinkled her nose. "Jas?" she said. "She's a little weird."

I bristled. So far, Jas was the only person I'd met at Newbury Park that I'd really liked. "Why d'you say that?" I asked.

"Well she's totally anorexic for a start. Hardly eats a thing. And she wears odd clothes out of school. *And* she works really hard at everything."

I thought about what Jas had told me earlier.

"I don't think being a little bit skinny, trying to make sure you don't let your parents down by working hard, and having an individual taste in clothes make you weird," I said.

Rosa pursed her lips, her eyes hardening. "Fine," she said. "Just remember I told you she was odd. And her brother's really arrogant."

"You mean her twin brother?"

"Yeah, Nat. He's in our house." As Rosa spoke, a look of hurt flashed across her face. "Acts like he's God's gift to girls. Just because he's good-looking he thinks he can get away with being rude."

"Thanks for the tip," I said, letting an edge of sarcasm creep into my voice.

Rosa looked like she wanted to say something else, but thought better of it. We agreed we'd meet up later, then I shoved my schedule away and headed outside to find my Spanish class. Luckily it was next door.

I settled myself into a desk at the back. I tried to focus, but my thoughts drifted to Jas's twin brother. None of the guys in my Spanish class looked particularly attractive to me, but then Rosa's idea of "good-looking" might well be completely different from mine. Or perhaps Nat didn't take Spanish.

Either way, I was intrigued.

The class itself was hard—far more difficult than I was used to—and I soon forgot about everything else. After Spanish, came PE with the other girls from my year. I didn't have any gym clothes but Gail had given me some spare things of Rosa's. I did okay with the handball and running activities. I've always been well coordinated and love that feeling you get when you run hard and your muscles warm and loosen. I noticed that while Rosa appeared to be enjoying herself too, poor Jas was in agony. Hopelessly uncoordinated, she was the last to be picked by the team leaders and dropped more balls than she caught.

She offered me a rueful smile as we headed off to the science lab. The setting for science subjects followed the math group which meant, again, no Rosa. It was a relief, to be honest. I'd just had to deal with her bringing over another one of her friends to tell me how awful it was about Mum dying, an anguished smile of sympathy on her face.

Jas and I strolled along, chatting about the upcoming physics class. Jas was just warning me that the teacher was a little boring when she looked up and waved at someone across the hallway.

"There's Nat," she said.

I looked up, interested. I couldn't see who Jas meant at first. There were several boys standing around the science lab door. Then one of them pushed another, they both stepped back and I saw him.

He *was* good-looking, just as Rosa had said. He had the same dark, sleek hair as his sister, though his was cut short and messy. He was tall, like Jas, and slim, though not anywhere near as skinny as her.

He turned and I could see that his face was a male version of hers—longer and squarer in the chin—and that his eyes were a bright, intense blue. Wow. He was gorgeous.

He stared back at me. My stomach gave a little skip.

Jas took my hand and dragged me over. My heart beat fast.

Nat didn't take his eyes off me the whole time I was walking toward him.

"This is Charlie," Jas said.

"Hi." His voice was cold and hard.

"Hi." I tried to smile, but my face didn't seem to move properly. Why was he being so unfriendly?

Nat stared at me for a few more seconds. Then, without another word, he turned and strode into the science lab. Jas looked after him, a frown on her face. I could feel myself flushing. Rosa had been right about Nat's rudeness, as well as his good looks.

The physics class was practical and interesting. I worked with Jas and another boy on the experiment we were doing. Every now and then I looked over at Nat. Once I thought I caught him watching me but the rest of the time his face was turned away.

Maybe I was being over sensitive, but it felt like he was deliberately ignoring me. At the end of the lesson he stalked out without looking over, even though Jas called out after him.

That was strange, wasn't it? I mean, he really seemed to have taken a dislike to me. What on earth could I have done to upset him?

NAT

I felt sick to my stomach. It wasn't just the horrible images from the bomb blast that had been flashing through my head ever since that math class earlier this morning. It was also the fact that Charlie was so closely connected to something that, so far, I had thought about only in terms of my own family. Suppose she guessed that Lucas had taken the bomb to the market? No, that was stupid and irrational. There was no way she could know about Lucas's involvement.

Even so, my heart raced whenever I thought about it.

I tried not to look in Charlie's direction during class, but I still made a total mess of my experiment, much to Callum's and Rick's annoyance. They were used to coasting through all their science classes, reliant on the fact that I normally found the work fairly easy. But today I seemed to have forgotten everything I knew.

What was Jas doing making friends with her? Had either of them talked about the bomb? About Lucas? I shuddered. Man, if I had recognized Charlie, perhaps *she* would remember *me*? I looked up at the end of the experiment. Charlie was watching me, an expression of curiosity on her face. What was that about?

I told myself I was overreacting. She was probably just curious because Jas and I were twins. People were often interested in the twin thing. I snuck a final glance at her as she packed her bag, then I grabbed my own and strode out of the room.

Jas came running up behind me. "What's the matter?" she asked.

"Nothing," I said. Then, knowing Jas wouldn't buy that for a second, I lowered my voice. "I recognized that girl . . . from that day in the market, you know . . ."

Jas's gaze softened with sympathy. I looked away, hating myself for not telling her the whole truth. Still, what choice did I have?

"I wondered why you acted like that earlier," she said. "I get it, but Charlie seems nice." She leaned closer. "Nothing like her cousin."

"Yeah, that's not hard." I grinned. "Anyway, I'm sorry for showing you up."

"Timbuktu sorry?" Jas said, raising her eyebrows and smiling.

"And back again," I said.

We laughed, but it made me feel sad. Moments like this were just faint echoes of a time long past, when our home had been full of nonsense in-jokes like that one from *Oliver* . . . stuff that didn't really make sense, but that connected us in a way that outsiders couldn't hope to understand. I'd always been close to Jas—I was older than her by half an hour: "You were fighting to come out," Mum once told me, "unlike poor Jas who didn't want to come out at all"—but I missed the closeness that our whole family once shared.

Charlie was hovering about, waiting for Jas. She was looking vaguely in my direction, though not meeting my eyes. She really was very pretty. I tore my gaze away.

"See ya later," I said to Jas, then headed to the canteen, praying that Charlie wasn't going there too.

She wasn't. In fact, I didn't see her again that day and managed to avoid her for most of the rest of the week. To my relief, Charlie didn't try to speak to me again either.

But I always knew when she was in the room, almost as if I had a sixth sense for her presence. And, as the week drew to a close, I was forced to admit that Jas had been right—Charlie *did* seem nice. She wasn't all giggly and simpering like Rosa and so many of the other girls and she was certainly good with Jas. I hadn't seen my sister smile so much at school in a long time.

I was also increasingly certain that Charlie had no idea Lucas had been involved in the bombing. Which of course made sense. After all, it had been chaos in that market. If the police hadn't realized Lucas was involved with the bomb, why would an innocent bystander like Charlie have?

The weekend came and I did all the usual stuff: a meager food shop with Jas, then several hours helping Dad at the garage. Two of our regular clients announced they were no longer able to pay their bills. It was a blow but, as Dad pointed out, at least we didn't need the Future Party's free food bags just yet. Posters featuring Roman Riley had sprung up all over north London, advertising where the next handouts were going to take place. Since the Canal Street market bomb, the Future Party no longer used any covered or indoor venues, but they were still organizing free food in the poorest areas of almost every town in the country. As a result, they had won the last two special elections—which meant more seats in Parliament. There were ten Future Party MPs now, including, of course, the leader, Roman Riley.

On Sunday, I met Callum and the others in the park for a game of soccer. Mum was in when I got back that afternoon. She was watching the news on TV, a cup of coffee growing cold in her hands. There had been a riot in south London in response to the Government's latest austerity measure: the closing of two local hospitals.

Mum didn't take her eyes from the screen as I came in and sat down at the table.

"Imagine if they closed Lucas's hospital," she breathed, worry etched across her face.

The screen switched to an interview with the mayor of London. He was surrounded by a bunch of reporters.

"There is simply no choice," the mayor said. *"I know it's hard, but everyone has to bear their fair share."*

Mum shook her head.

The shot switched to a studio panel containing three opposition politicians. The Future Party's Roman Riley sat at the end of the row.

"We have just heard Mayor Latimer claim that everyone has to share responsibility for the crisis," Riley said. *"But why? If a man robs a shop,*

we expect him to pay for his crime. Him. Not the shop. And certainly not his neighbors. Yet in closing a hospital, the Government is forcing the poorest and most vulnerable to pay a heavy price for crimes they did not commit."

Mum smiled at the screen. I knew she was remembering how much Lucas had looked up to Roman Riley in the months leading up to the bombing. But all that adulation had been a con. Lucas's real heroes had been the hate-filled bigots in the League of Iron. I got up and grabbed a bag of cookies. For the millionth time, I wondered how on earth Lucas could have turned away from Riley to sign up for the League's ugly violence.

A shiver snaked down my spine as I thought about the meeting I was going to on Tuesday. After all the months of watching and waiting, I would hopefully find out exactly what Lucas had been involved with at last.

CHARLIE

More than once during that first week I felt so overwhelmed that I seriously thought my head might explode. It wasn't just having to get used to a new home, a new school, and lots of new people, it was also having to decide whether or not to stay on with Brian and Gail after my two-week trial period.

I was torn. Sometimes I missed Aunt Karen badly. She had loved Mum as much as me and we'd spent a lot of our time together—before the fights started—sharing our memories of her. Brian and Gail had barely known my mother and, though I was sure Gail would have been all too delighted if I had opened up, there was no way I could imagine chatting about Mum with her.

On the other hand, now that I'd actually made the break and moved away from Karen, there seemed little point in returning to live with her again. It would never bring Mum back. Plus Karen's home was in Leeds while I belonged in London.

And she had no money while Gail and Brian were rich.

I guess that makes me sound materialistic but I was fed up with being poor. Everyday life with Mum had been a struggle, but Gail and Brian had money to burn—and to spare. Right now, for example, I was borrowing Brian's old laptop but I knew that, if I stayed, I'd get a brand-new one of my own. I was also about to upgrade my phone and Gail had made it clear I was free to buy whatever clothes I liked.

The biggest downside to staying was Rosa. We just had nothing in common. For example, she was obsessed with some reality-TV-based boy band that played the kind of music I'd been into when I was ten. She would talk for hours about which of the singers was the best looking—that's when she wasn't poring over her hideously girly clothes or gossiping with her silly friends.

About the only thing Rosa and I agreed on was that Nat was hot, but rude. He'd still made no effort to speak to me, even though it was obvious his twin sister and I were becoming really good friends.

Jas asked me back to her house the following Tuesday.

"Dad gave me some money earlier so I could buy some food on the way home," she said, blushing. "Mum's always out at the hospital till late and Dad said he had a load of paperwork to do at the garage so they won't be in."

"What about Nat? Will he be there?" I asked, trying to keep my tone light.

"I don't know," Jas said, looking at me sideways. "Nat goes out a lot."

"Oh, right." I wanted to ask if he had a girlfriend, but the words stuck in my throat. I hadn't seen Nat spend time with any girls, but that didn't prove anything.

I sent Gail a text telling her I'd be back late. I avoided speaking to Rosa, slipping away to meet Jas as soon as the bell rang instead of going back to Plato House.

Jas and Nat's home wasn't what I expected. Even though I knew they were both on scholarships, I'd assumed that anyone going to private school must live in a big place, like Brian and Gail did, but Jas and Nat's house was tiny. Jas showed me around, constantly apologizing for the mess.

"Mum and Dad are out a lot, so it's hard . . . ," she kept saying as we wandered into the living room.

I told her it was fine as I stared at the piano in the corner. The lid was down and covered with dust.

Jas wrinkled her nose. "I used to play all the time, but since what happened to Lucas I only really do stuff at school. . . ." She trailed off with a sigh.

We went upstairs to Jas's bedroom. It was small—barely bigger than the room I'd had at Karen's—but beautiful, with different fabrics draped across the walls and soft lights. Somehow Jas seemed to have the knack for putting all sorts of different colors and textures alongside each other and making the overall effect look effortlessly stylish.

"You should be a designer," I said.

Jas shrugged, but she looked pleased.

I wandered over to the bed where pieces of fabric had been laid out in a series of broad, dramatic swaths. A length of soft, black and cream check wool caught my eye.

"That's lovely," I said.

"I was going to make a coat with it," Jas said, "but I've gotten stuck on the darts. I can't make them even."

"Wow." I turned to her, impressed. I'd never met anyone who could make their own clothes before. "How did you learn to do that?"

"Mum taught me, before . . ." Jas trailed off and I knew she was referring to the bomb and to her older brother being in a coma.

I quickly steered the conversation back toward the fabrics on the bed. Nat must have come in quietly because I hadn't heard the front door, but after we'd been upstairs for an hour or so, he poked his head around the door. A strand of hair fell over his face.

"Hey, Jas, I'm off, so—" He stopped as he saw me, his blue eyes widening in horror.

I opened my mouth to say hello, but before I could speak, Nat had mumbled something and ducked out of sight. A few moments later, the front door banged shut. He was gone.

There was an awkward silence. My face was burning. I didn't want Jas to see, but there wasn't much chance of that as she was sitting right opposite. In the end I looked up to see her watching me, concern in her eyes.

"Did I do something to upset him?" I asked, the words slipping out before I could stop them.

Jas shook her head slowly. "I don't know what it is . . . he's not usually like that with my friends." She cleared her throat. "He said he remembered you from that day . . . at the market. . . ."

"Oh." I looked away. I could see that might bring back

horrible memories for Nat, but I still didn't understand why he had looked so disgusted at finding me in his house.

Jas made some sandwiches for us to eat, though I noticed she only picked at hers. We chatted for a bit, then her dad called to ask her to check some invoices he'd left at home. Apologizing again, Jas went downstairs. I popped into the bathroom, wondering how late her dad worked. It was already almost seven. Brian was usually home by six thirty. As I came out, the open door across the landing caught my eye. It was covered in ancient soccer stickers. Was this Nat's room? I hesitated for a second. He was out and I could hear Jas downstairs. No one else was around. Why shouldn't I take a sneak peek?

I peered around the door. The room was slightly larger and much emptier than Jas's with a bed on either side of the window. Did that mean Nat had once shared the room with Lucas? Nat's school uniform was hung neatly in front of the wardrobe though most of his other clothes were in piles on the floor. The paint on the furniture was peeling away while the walls were covered with Blu-Tack marks, where Nat had presumably taken down old posters. Only two remained—one of some soccer player I'd never heard of, another of a girl in a bikini. She was posing with her hands on her hips—some model or singer, I guessed. I didn't recognize her.

I turned away, feeling a twinge of jealousy. Well, that was stupid. Nat was perfectly entitled to like anyone he wanted. Just because he clearly couldn't stand me . . .

Shaking off these thoughts, I wandered over to Nat's

computer. It was an old model—secondhand by the look of it—
and still open, though the screen was dark. I touched the keys,
thinking idly that if I stayed with Gail and Brian, I would be able
to get something much sleeker and faster.

The screen lit up. I hesitated, intrigued, then I bent down to
take a closer look. It was wrong to snoop, of course, but I could
still hear Jas talking on the phone downstairs—and there was no
harm in just taking a peek.

Nat's desktop was covered with folders and files. Some of
them looked like they contained soccer stuff, others were clearly
labeled with the names of school subjects. There was nothing
that looked particularly interesting.

As I turned away from the computer, it beeped.

I glanced back. The browser icon was flashing at the bottom
of the screen. One of the programs must still be open, presumably
something from the Internet that Nat had minimized before he
left. Downstairs, Jas was still chattering away. Without thinking
about what I was doing, I clicked on the file.

It opened in front of me. A second later I gasped, unable to
believe what I was looking at.

NAT

I stood outside Deakin's Electrics and took a deep breath. Man, my hands were actually trembling. I shoved them into my jacket pockets. It was just the cold.

I glanced up at the shop entrance. If I'd worked out Saxon66's coded message correctly, I was about to meet people from the League of Iron, probably including those responsible for the Canal Street market bomb. They must know Lucas—and exactly how and why he had been involved in the bombing.

I blew out my breath. I needed to appear strong. And calm. An image of Charlie in Jas's room flashed into my mind. I'd been shocked to see her there. In fact, if I was honest, I hadn't handled it well at all. It was just because of the connection with Lucas. Definitely nothing to do with her looks—or the way she'd stared at me in that haughty way of hers, her dark eyes slightly slanted like a cat's.

Enough stalling. I rang the doorbell. The shop behind was wreathed in shadows from the secondhand stoves and fridges that filled the small showroom. No one came. I waited a moment, then rang the bell again, harder this time.

A slim man in a black shirt and glasses hurried toward me, past a line of freezers. He shot back a bolt and pulled open the door.

"Yes?"

"AngelOfFire." I gave my user name, as the coded message had instructed.

The man, who looked in his early twenties, let me in, rebolted the door, then checked the tablet in his hand. I waited, feeling anxious. After what felt like an age he nodded.

"You're on the list. Follow me." The man led me through to a storeroom at the back of the shop. About thirty people were gathered, mostly guys in their late teens or twenties, though there were a few women too. I straightened up, grateful for my height. If anyone asked, I was planning on saying I was eighteen. But, as I gazed around the room, I realized nobody was actually paying me any attention. I slunk over to the far wall, trying to lose myself among the stacks of cardboard boxes. Most people were staring toward the front of the room. A second later a man in a black shirt got up onto a packing crate.

Everyone looked at him expectantly.

I glanced around again. Most of the men wore black T-shirts and had shaved heads or crew cuts. I smoothed my own hair off my face and slid farther into the shadows cast by the boxes.

The chatter in the room died down.

"Welcome," the man on the crate said. He was thickset, with stubble on his chin and a deep groove etched into the center of his forehead. "Some of you know me as Saxon66. I called this meeting. We are the London branch of the League of Iron and we are ready to fight." His voice rose as he spoke. The room erupted in a cheer.

I gulped.

"Tonight's meeting is an opportunity to confirm our intentions," Saxon66 said, looking around the room. "To prepare for action."

Really? On his forum post Saxon66 had specifically said the meeting was for those "seeking answers." I had assumed he'd meant answers to questions about the League of Iron's terrorist activities. Had I misunderstood? It looked like it, as most of the other people in the room were nodding approvingly at Saxon66's words.

Saxon66 pointed to a young man in the front row with a shaved head and a clenched fist. "Why don't you start, Inquisitor?"

The young man nodded. "We should get the Government and everyone in a religion. We should have village squares and public executions like they used to. I'd do it myself. Cut their freakin' heads off."

The two women opposite me nodded.

"The real problem's all the immigration," one of the woman called out, her sallow-skinned forehead screwed into an angry frown.

"Yeah, we should gas them, all of them," added the other. She was wearing a black dress, with heavy Goth makeup and a white streak in her long dark hair.

I wriggled farther back against the boxes that lined the wall.

"One at a time," Saxon66 said. "Go on, Inquisitor."

Inquisitor stared around the room. "They're taking our jobs: blacks, Pakis, that lot from Poland, too."

"And the Government let it happen," shouted another voice. "We should bomb Parliament."

"*And* gas the foreigners," Inquisitor insisted.

"*And* put all the freakin' bankers in with them," snarled the Goth woman.

Everyone cheered.

I looked down at the floor, my head spinning. After spending so much time on the League of Iron forum I'd been expecting some extreme views, but not all this incoherent hatred. These people weren't interested in organized attacks, they just wanted a place to vent their anger and resentment. Clearly I'd been totally naive thinking it would be easy to bring up either Lucas or the bombing.

"Another view?" Saxon66 roared. "What about you?"

A girl near me with mousy blond hair shuffled nervously from foot to foot.

"I'd like us to make the politicians do more," she said, her voice barely above a whisper. "They say a bunch of stuff, make everyone think they care, but nothing ever happens."

A murmur of agreement ran around the room.

"Sometimes I think all Roman Riley does is talk," the girl went on.

"Yeah." Saxon66 snorted with contempt. "Riley's good at *talking*."

Everyone apart from me grunted in agreement.

I frowned, trying to make sense of what I was hearing. These were Lucas's contacts, responsible for organizing the market bombing. Their blind rage fit with the ugly violence of the explosion, though I still didn't understand why they thought bombing people lining up for food would get rid of the government or black people or any of the other groups they hated.

"What about you?" Saxon66 was pointing into the audience again.

Oh, *no*. He was pointing at me. Everyone looked in my direction. What the hell did I say now?

CHARLIE

If I'd stopped to think about it, I don't know what I would have expected to find on Nat's laptop: maybe a soccer website or one showing pictures of girls or perhaps something relevant to his homework. Instead, I found myself on a forum thread with the title: *Who should we bomb?*

Forgetting Jas downstairs, I scanned the posts. The top few consisted of an argument between two users debating whether black people generally or just Muslims should be blown up.

What was Nat doing looking at this horrible conversation? The language—and the hate behind it—made me feel sick.

Beneath this were similarly ugly comments about death camps and how immigrants were stealing English people's jobs. And then I saw an entry from another forum member with the user name AngelOfFire. . . . It had been made just twenty minutes ago:

People need to see how POWERFUL we are. Bombing ordinary people causes PANIC and makes them realize they need strong leadership. Like in the Canal St market bomb. Iron Will FOREVER.

I froze. The lettering on the AngelOfFire user name was in bold, which surely meant that it had been made on *this computer.* I clicked to start a new post.

AngelOfFire make your comment here . . .

I stared at the words. Twenty minutes ago Nat had been in here while Jas and I had been in her bedroom across the landing.

He was AngelOfFire.

I scrolled back, looking for other entries under the same name. There were several, all filled with ugly, mindless, hate-filled rants. A couple mentioned the Canal Street market bomb specifically, while one from a week or so ago actually said the country needed "bombs not talk."

Footsteps sounded on the landing. Jas must have come upstairs without me hearing. Palms sweating, I quickly closed the page and turned away. As I crossed the room, Jas called out my name.

"I'm here," I said, stepping out of Nat's room and onto the landing. No way could I tell poor Jas what I'd found. I needed time to think about it. "Just being nosy."

"It's fine." Jas smiled. "Nat won't mind."

Right.

"I just wanted to see what his room looked like," I went on, following Jas back into her room.

I left soon after, saying that I had to get home or Gail and Brian would worry. Jas frowned when I said this. It flashed through my head for a second that no one was worrying about her, then I set off on the ten-minute walk home. My head spun as I tried to make sense of what I'd seen on Nat's computer.

There was no escape from what it meant: Nat was secretly a racist thug who believed in violence, in *hurting* people.

And then it hit me.

Nat had been there when the Canal Street market bomb went off. His brother had been caught in the blast but Nat hadn't. He'd been safely out of the way in another part of the market, arriving immediately *after* the explosion.

Surely that was all too big a coincidence?

I stopped in the middle of the pavement, the chill October wind whipping at my face.

Why had Nat been in the market at all?

Had he *planted* the bomb?

That would certainly explain why he acted so weirdly around me. But what about his brother? I thought it through. Maybe Nat hadn't realized his brother was there until it was too late.

Maybe he didn't care.

The world spun inside my head. What had he written on the forum? Something about bombing ordinary people to create panic "like in the Canal Street market bomb."

I didn't understand how but I was sure that aloof, good-looking Nat, my new best friend's brother, had been involved with the bomb that killed my mother.

As confusion settled into certainty, all I could think about was how I could prove it—and how I could make Nat pay.

NAT

I gazed around the storeroom. The light was dim, flickering across the crowd, highlighting the sheen of their black T-shirts and the glint in their angry eyes.

This was my chance to find out how Lucas had gotten involved with the League of Iron. I looked straight at Saxon66.

"I support everything you say," I said, my heart beating fast at the lie. "But you promised tonight you'd talk to anyone seeking answers. And . . . and I want to know about the Canal Street market bombing."

A series of shocked gasps rippled around the room.

Saxon66 let a thin smile play across his lips. "We're not here to talk about the past. We're here for the future."

"Yeah." The guy from the front row, Inquisitor, pushed his way closer toward me. He was thin, but wiry-looking. There was a terrifying tension about his whole body, as if he were coiled, ready to spring. "We're talking about the future. We're making plans." He turned to the crowd and punched the air. "Iron Will!"

The crowd roared approval.

"I can do that too," I said desperately. "But first I want to know—"

"You've got a plan?" Saxon66 interrupted.

"Come off it, he looks about twelve," Inquisitor said.

Everyone laughed.

"Go on then, *boy*," the Goth woman sneered. "What's your *plan?*"

Blood thundered in my ears. My hands were still shaking so I shoved them back into my pockets. An image from years back of Lucas laughing at me as I played soccer flashed into my mind. Back then, I would have given anything for his approval: Lucas the brave, who had point-blank refused to take entrance exams to private school and so had ended up at the local high school. I had badly wanted to follow him there, but Mum and Dad had overruled me, insisting I took up my free place at Newbury Park.

"Okay," I said, trying to steady my voice. "Firstly I don't get why all your bombs and death camps, whatever, have to be aimed at immigrants—or at poor people in food lines. Bombing people just makes everyone hate you. It's pointless."

Inquisitor narrowed his eyes. "What?"

"Killing blacks is *pointless?*" The Goth woman raised her eyebrows.

"Listen." I took a deep breath. "There has to be a system— specific goals for specific reasons."

"You mean like gas chambers?" Inquisitor's eyes lit up. "Gassing the freaks until their eyes pop?"

I shook my head, trying not to show how sick his words made

me feel. "No," I said. "There has to be a big picture. A real plan to put the country back on its feet."

"He sounds like a politician," Inquisitor jeered.

"No, it's . . . I . . ." I trailed off.

"Go on." Saxon66 folded his arms. "Explain."

I held his gaze and thought fast. Saxon66 seemed to be the leader here. Surely he must have known my brother. If I could impress him, maybe he would open up and talk about Lucas.

I tried to gather my thoughts. "Okay," I went on. "You need a vision, a clear, strong vision of how you want the country to be. Then all you have to do is make people believe in that vision."

"That sounds a lot more vague than a freaking bomb," Inquisitor snapped.

The crowd laughed.

"Bombs aren't the answer," I persisted. "And massacres and death camps aren't either. There doesn't always need to be a big show of violence. It's about being focused—prepared to do any-thing and risk everything to get what you believe in. Like a family would."

It struck me that our entire family life had revolved around Lucas: Mum and Dad had indulged him; Jas and I had adored him. And yet somehow Jas had also found her own way with her music and, later, by making clothes. Whereas I, though I'd gotten better marks at school than either of them, had always lived in Lucas's shadow.

A silence fell across the room.

"Nothing else to say, *boy?*" Goth woman said nastily.

"Bombs just make people hate you," I said. "And you need people on your side. You have to do what it takes. You might think that a big explosion makes a powerful point but it creates so many enemies that—"

"You mean like with 9/11 and the Twin Towers?" Someone across the room I couldn't see interrupted.

"Yes," I said. "Al Qaeda must have—"

"How *dare* you talk about Al Qaeda in here," Inquisitor snarled. "We're not going to take any lessons from a bunch of Muslims."

I frowned. "No, I'm saying that—"

"Enough." Saxon66 motioned me to be quiet. "Who put all these ideas in your head, lad?" he asked.

I drew myself up. This might be my only chance. "My brother," I said. "His name is Lucas Holloway. He—"

"Never heard of him." Saxon66's voice cut over mine. Our eyes met. Despite his flat denial, I was sure he had recognized Lucas's name. He cleared his throat and looked away. "Let's move on."

My heart sank. Clearly Saxon66 wasn't going to admit he knew Lucas, though I was sure that he did. It hit me suddenly that coming here had been a total waste of time. Lucas, carrying a bomb into a market, had been a mindless idiot, lashing out to make some point I still didn't even really understand.

And I wasn't going to understand it any better by staying here a minute longer.

I stood up and walked to the door. Inquisitor and another

man blocked my way. For a second I thought they were going to hit me but then Saxon66 called out:

"Let him go, he's just a kid."

Sarcastic shouts rose up behind me as I stumbled out of the storeroom. I bolted for the shop exit, abuse echoing after me. Out on the pavement I raced along the dimly lit street, desperate to get away.

Bound up in my own, dark thoughts, I was so intent on getting home that I barely noticed the rain that had just begun to fall. Once or twice I thought I glimpsed someone following me—just the merest hint of a shadow moving in the corner of my eye. But when I turned around, no one was there.

CHARLIE

The next few days were hell. I didn't know what to do. Nat was obviously involved with the League of Iron and, though his angry post stopped short of actually saying so, it was clear to me that he'd helped set off the Canal Street market bomb: As AngelOfFire he supported the League's views and the League had claimed responsibility for the bombing. On top of which, he had actually been there during the explosion.

It was sickening, especially considering what happened to his own brother. But, before I could go to the police, I needed proof that Nat was AngelOfFire. Simply explaining what I'd seen on his computer wasn't good enough.

I would have liked to talk to Jas, but telling her I was sure that one of her brothers was a murderer who had left the other in a coma was impossible. So I kept my mouth shut, though finding some way to expose Nat was all I could think about.

I woke early on Saturday morning. Gail and Brian were talking in low, serious tones as I walked into the kitchen.

"Hi," I said, drifting over to the kettle, my angry thoughts still all on Nat.

"Morning, Charlie," Brian said.

Gail gave a nervous cough. "I'm glad you're up," she said. "We want to talk to you."

I turned, focusing on them at last. "What is it?"

Gail wouldn't meet my eyes. Suddenly filled with foreboding, I looked at Brian.

"We need to talk about the future," he said. "It's almost two weeks since you came here and we'd like to know how you feel . . . how you're thinking . . . about moving in permanently."

"Oh." I looked at them both. I'd been so caught up thinking about Nat and what to do that I had forgotten our two-week deadline.

"Do you like being here, Charlie?" Gail asked nervously.

"Er, yes," I said.

"It's just we've noticed you spend a lot of time on your own in your room," she went on. "I mean Rosa does too, it's the age you're both at, but . . ." she trailed off.

"Do you need more time to work things through?" Brian asked. "We don't want to put you under any pressure. The school says you've settled in well, no problems with any of the classes or staff."

I nodded. The three of us stood in an awkward silence.

"It's just we were wondering if you wanted to do anything to your room?" Gail went on. "It's a bit bleak at the moment because we've had it as a spare, but it might help you feel more at home if you decorated."

"I like it bare," I said truthfully.

"Is there anything you'd like from your Aunt Karen's?" Brian asked. "Or anything from your mum's old apartment? We've got the space here for furniture or whatever."

I thought it over. The only possessions I had that were truly important to me, apart from a few photos, were all those kids' books that Mum had bought me.

"I'd like to put up some bookshelves," I said. "Get my old books from my aunt's."

Gail nodded eagerly. "Sure, we'll send Karen the money so she can pack them up and send them to us."

"Thanks." Gail and Brian were being so nice. This place would never be home, but I appreciated them trying so hard to make me feel welcome.

"There's just one thing, Charlie," Gail said, twisting her fingers together.

I stared at her. "What's that?"

"It's Rosa." Brian and Gail exchanged a swift glance. "Don't take this the wrong way, but we're not sure you and Rosa have really hit it off like we'd hoped."

I shrugged, feeling embarrassed.

"If you do want to stay," Gail ventured, "we'd like you to make a bit more effort with her. You know, talk to her about school. Just . . . just . . ."

"Try and get to know her a bit," Brian continued. "She's a lovely girl and she says she's always trying to involve you in things with her friends, chat about school . . . like girls do."

I stared at the kitchen floor, a dull ache in my chest. So it was all about Rosa. For a moment I'd thought that Brian and Gail were offering me a real home. But a real home exists only when the people inside it truly love one another more than anyone else in the world. And Brian and Gail didn't . . . couldn't . . . love me like they did their own daughter. I couldn't blame them. I loved Mum more than them. That's how it's *supposed* to be: parents and children on the inside together, with the rest of the world on the outside.

"We don't want you to hear this as criticism," Gail said softly. "We know this adjustment period is hard for you, but it's a challenge for all of us, especially Rosa. You're the same age, though I know she's not quite sixteen yet and . . . Look, all we're asking is that you give her a chance, maybe open up a bit."

"I understand," I said, looking up. "I'll try."

Well, what else could I say?

"Thank you, my love." Gail crossed the kitchen and gave me a hug.

"Does this mean you want to make this your permanent home?" Brian asked.

I nodded. I knew now that I was staying for just one reason. I went over it in my head as Brian talked about dealing with Social Services. Thanks to the cuts he was sure it wouldn't be hard to get the paperwork done, even if it meant slipping a social worker some extra money to move things along. He and Gail were smiling. So was I. But my smile was only for my lips.

In my heart was ice and fire.

Living here with Brian and Gail would never feel like my real home. I would never *have* a real home because I didn't have Mum. And I didn't have Mum because of the League of Iron.

And because of Nat.

NAT

I had to drag myself out of bed on Sunday morning. I had spent so much of the past six months trying to find out how on earth Lucas could have set off a bomb for the League and it all, now, felt like a gigantic waste of time. Even if Saxon66 had admitted Lucas's involvement, I would still never understand it.

Everything was garbage, basically. Dad was exhausted from trying to hold things together at the garage, while Mum remained anxious and obsessed with Lucas in the hospital. Even in the wider world, the latest coalition Government was on the brink of collapse as the political parties failed, yet again, to agree on another round of austerity measures.

I'd caught Charlie staring at me a couple of times at school—a fierce look in her dark eyes I was certain hadn't been there before—but we never spoke. I assumed she was annoyed because I'd made so little effort to get to know her. Well, I wasn't going to let that bother me. I had enough to deal with.

The only person who noticed how bad I was feeling was Jas. She'd asked me what was wrong yesterday. I'd lied, telling her I had a stomachache from food poisoning. Jas had made me a hot-water bottle, just like Mum used to.

I felt guilty for lying, but there was no way I could have told her the truth about how I was feeling. To be honest, I didn't really understand it myself.

It was almost noon by the time I got up and poured myself a bowl of cereal, then realized no one had remembered to buy any milk. Cursing my entire family, I scraped together some loose change and popped to the corner store. As I walked home again, a jogger barged past me, almost pushing me into the road. I swore at him, but he just ran off along the street. I got back home just as Dad—gray-faced and pink-eyed—was leaving.

"Gotta get to the garage," he muttered, hurrying outside.

Feeling more disgruntled than ever, I retrieved my bowl of cereal, added milk, then trudged up the stairs back to my room. Mum always used to insist that we sat down together for a roast lunch on Sunday. She would have the radio on in the kitchen as she chopped vegetables or made gravy with me and Jas. Sometimes Dad would wander in when a dance tune was playing and sweep her round the floor. Mum would laugh and scold him that we "wouldn't be eating till five at this rate." Jas and I would watch, rolling our eyes and giggling, before arguing over whose turn it was to peel the potatoes or set the table. Lucas—who inevitably stayed out on Saturday nights—would turn up just in time to eat, sometimes with a pretty girl on his arm and always with a little bunch of flowers for Mum.

It was obvious to me that Lucas had picked the flowers from

passing gardens and window boxes and I was pretty sure Mum realized this too. But she was still delighted every time, her eyes shining as Lucas hugged her and told her she was the best mother in the world. On days like those, the house had been full of chatter and laughter: lots of happy noise. Now it was so quiet you could hear yourself breathe.

I chucked my jacket on the floor and took a big spoonful of cereal. As I sat down on my bed my phone rang. I registered the sound dully, not sure I could be bothered to answer. Except . . . wait. The sound wasn't coming from *my* cell. The ringtone was slightly different.

I set down my cereal bowl and fished my handset out of my jeans. It definitely wasn't ringing, yet the trill of a phone still filled the air. I looked across the room. The sound was coming from my jacket on the floor. I sped over and put my hand in the pocket. My fingers closed on another phone. Heart thumping, I pulled it out. It was a basic model, with "number withheld" flashing up on the screen.

The phone rang a third time. Where had it come from? It definitely hadn't been in my pocket when I left to buy milk earlier. The only person I'd passed had been that jogger.

The cell rang again. There was nothing else to do but answer it.

"Hello?" I said.

"Hello, Nat." It was a man's voice: smooth and slightly amused.

I started. "How do you know my name?"

"I'm a friend of Lucas's. We were in the same organization together."

There was a long pause. I sucked in my breath. "What do you mean?"

Silence.

"Are you . . . are you talking about the League?" I stammered.

"No."

I waited, but the man didn't elaborate.

Was this some kind of trick? I had seen Lucas's texts about the bomb. The League of Iron had claimed responsibility for the explosion. How could Lucas not be part of their group?

"Who are you?"

"I will explain when we meet," the man went on.

"Meet?"

"Yes. Now. Come to the bandstand in the park where you played soccer last weekend."

"How did you know I—? Who are you? Why are you—?"

"I'll answer your questions later," the man said firmly. "Now get your laptop and bring it to the bandstand. One p.m. Don't be late."

"Wait, tell me—"

But the man had hung up.

CHARLIE

The drizzling rain matched my mood as I hurried along the pavement toward Jas's house. It was Sunday and I'd just had to sit through a family breakfast with Gail, Brian, and Rosa. The conversation had revolved around their vacation last year, which of course I hadn't been a part of. Gail tried to draw me in by talking about the upcoming memorial service for Mum and the other bomb victims. She seemed to think it would be a great way for everyone to pay their respects, but I could just imagine how fake it would be: full of smiling strangers pretending to grieve for people they barely knew. I'd had enough of that in the days immediately after the explosion. I'd met a lot of people who'd said how sorry they were that Mum had died, but where had they all been in the months before it happened, after Mum lost her teaching job and started having to line up for Roman Riley's food bags?

As I reached Jas's house, my thoughts inevitably turned to Nat and my need for proof about his involvement with the League of Iron. Jas let me in, chattering excitedly about some material she'd bought.

"I was going to use it for me, but the color will be better on you. I can do it after I finish my coat if you like?"

"Sure," I said, only half-listening. The house seemed empty and quiet. But then Jas's house always did. "Hey, is Nat around?"

Jas shook her head. "He just went out."

"Oh?" I tried to sound casual. "Where was he going?"

Jas shrugged. "No idea." She rolled her eyes. "He's gotten so secretive recently. I've been wondering if he's seeing some girl . . . Anyway, come and see this material. It's blue and, like, a jersey but with a silky finish . . . *soo* pretty . . ."

I followed her into her room, my mind racing over this new bit of information. So Nat had become secretive. Surely that was yet another indication that he was involved with a new attack the League of Iron was planning?

Jas showed me the blue material. It was, as she'd promised, very pretty. I feigned an interest in the dress she wanted to make and Jas skipped off downstairs, delighted, to make us tea.

I sat in the silence of her room for a few moments. Through Jas's open door I could see the door to Nat's bedroom across the landing. It was shut. Which was when it struck me. The only way to prove that Nat was AngelOfFire was to take his actual computer to the police. I grabbed my bag—just about big enough to conceal a laptop—and headed for Nat's room. I could hear the kettle boiling downstairs, Jas padding about in the kitchen. I opened Nat's bedroom door slowly and peered inside.

The laptop was not on the table where it had been last week. I looked, quickly, around the room. There was no sign of it in the wardrobe, on the bed, or under any of the piles of clothes that littered the floor.

It was gone. Or hidden. And I didn't have time to go looking for it, not with Jas about to come back upstairs.

I retreated to Jas's room, furious with myself. I should have taken the computer as soon as I saw what Nat had written on that forum. Now I was going to have to find another way of getting the proof I needed.

NAT

It was raining as I left the house. I made sure my laptop was covered with a plastic bag, then tucked it under my arm and hurried to the park. Questions swirled in my head: Who had called me? Why did they want to meet me? What did they want with my computer? The rain grew heavier as I sped along, soaking through my jacket and leaving my clothes damp against my skin. I paid no attention. More questions ran through my mind: How had someone slipped that phone into my pocket? What did any of this have to do with Lucas? Was it all some kind of trap?

I checked the time as I jogged through the park entrance and across the grass. It was almost 1 p.m. My heart thudded. I must be crazy to be going to meet a complete stranger like this. No one else even knew where I was.

The iron bandstand was in the middle of the park. I waited at the bottom of the stairs where weeds grew up through the rusting metal. The place was deserted. I had only ever seen it used a few times, for summer concerts and local fairs. We used to come here years ago. I could remember eating ice cream with Jas and Lucas,

Mum fussing over us with a hanky, then Lucas and me wriggling away to play soccer.

I paced around the bandstand. There were trees over to the right, then the main grassy area of the park to the left. A few solitary walkers were wandering about, but no one was heading in my direction. It stopped raining as I checked the time again. One p.m. exactly.

"Hello, Nat."

I spun around. A man stood in front of me. He was tall—easily over six foot—with a narrow, foxlike face and green eyes.

My mouth fell open. How had the man gotten so close without me hearing him?

"How are you?" the man asked. From the sound of his voice, this was definitely the same person I'd just spoken to on the phone.

"What's this about?"

The man smiled. He wore a black beanie pulled low over his forehead and a dark, wool overcoat. I knew nothing about clothes, but I could still see that the coat was very expensive.

"Thank you for trusting me," the man said. "May I have that?" He held out his hand for my computer.

I tightened my grip. No way was I giving up my laptop to a complete stranger. "Who are you? How do you know Lucas?"

"You can call me Taylor. I just want to check that it's your computer in that bag and that it's turned off. Perhaps you'd take it out for me, then we can talk."

I shucked the plastic bag off the laptop and opened it up to show the man it was switched off. What did he think was inside here?

Taylor nodded, apparently satisfied. "Thank you," he said politely. "Let's take a walk."

He led the way toward the trees. His movements were quick and powerful, like a tiger's. Was this all some elaborate trap to trick me into saying what I knew about Lucas? No, that didn't make sense. For a start, Taylor was unlike any police officer I'd ever seen. He wasn't like *anyone* I'd ever seen. His eyes darted around, all wary, and though his walk was calm and relaxed, he moved so fast that I almost had to run to keep up. As we reached the trees, Taylor stopped.

"We were impressed with you at the League of Iron meeting, Nat," he said.

"You were there? I thought you said—"

"Not me personally," Taylor interrupted. "Our undercover agent."

"You have an undercover agent in the League of Iron?" My mouth fell open.

Taylor nodded. "He kept an eye on you. Made sure you got home okay afterward. He recorded the meeting too, so we have what you said on tape."

I remembered the shadowy figure I'd fleetingly thought might be following me after the meeting. "Kept an eye on *me*? Why?"

"Because the Commander ordered him to."

"Who's the Commander? I don't understand."

"The Commander is our leader. He was very impressed by

your passion and your courage in speaking out at the meeting. You got right to the heart of what matters: 'Be prepared to do anything and risk everything for what you believe in. Like a family.'" Taylor paused. "The Commander said, and these were his exact words: 'I couldn't have put it better myself.' That is high praise, I'm telling you."

"I still don't understand. You're talking about this Commander and an undercover agent, but you said on the phone that you weren't part of the League of Iron, so . . . so what *do* you belong to?"

"The English Freedom Army," Taylor said. "We are soldiers, fighting to reclaim England from corruption and extremist violence."

"An *army*?" Somehow the word fit Taylor. He certainly seemed like a soldier, all power and focus.

"Yes, the Commander set us up less than a year ago. Lucas was one of our first recruits. We spotted his potential at an anti-cuts rally."

"Lucas was at a *rally*?" I said, surprised.

"Yes," Taylor said. "He had come along with some friends. . . . I think he was more interested in one of the girls he was with than any actual protesting. But his leadership qualities were obvious right from the start and he really blossomed under our training. I was his cell captain. I saw him go from boy to man. You must have noticed a change in him yourself?"

I nodded. Lucas *had* changed in the last few months before the bomb. He had become more serious, more purposeful, more grown-up.

Taylor sighed. "What happened to him at the Canal Street market was a tragedy."

"So what does this army do? What did Lucas do?"

"The English Freedom Army's aim is to protect the public from the ignorance and violence of the extremist groups that are inciting riots and taking their anger out on some of the country's most defenseless people."

"But isn't that the police's job?"

Taylor raised an eyebrow. "Of course it is, but I'm sure you've noticed that the police force are struggling just like everyone else: their numbers have been cut, they're demoralized and stretched thin, with riots every week. And that's before all the bombs—the Canal Street market explosion wasn't the only one in the past year. Simply put, the police can't cope. Anyway"—he paused—"a lot of police are sympathetic to some of the extremist groups, especially the ones on the far right."

"Like the League of Iron?"

"Exactly. You must have wondered why, despite the League claiming responsibility for that bomb, not one single person has been arrested."

"So you're saying that this . . . English Freedom Army . . . that you try to stop the violence?"

"When we can," Taylor said. "We make it our business to find out what's going on . . . who's planning what. Then we do our best to protect the innocent, doing whatever we have to, like a family . . . like you said."

I stared at him. "And Lucas was part of this . . . this army?" My breath caught in my throat as I remembered Lucas's second cell phone, the one with the text about the bomb. "You gave Lucas a phone too, didn't you?"

"Yes."

"But I saw the text on the day of the bomb. It told him to 'take the package to the market.' It—"

"No," Taylor said. "The text just said 'take package' then gave the place and time. I know because I sent it myself. It was an order to take the bomb *from* the market, not *to* it."

Whoa. Finally, an explanation that made sense. And it meant my brother *wasn't* a terrorist. Far from it. Lucas was one of the good guys. He was trying to *stop* the bombing. Relief flooded through me.

"Lucas was one of our most promising soldiers," Taylor said. "I tasked him to go into the market and take the bomb from where one of our agents was sure it was being stored. Unfortunately, our information was only partial. We knew the bomb would be in the market at 3 p.m. We didn't know that was when it was primed to go off." He sighed. "The damn thing exploded before Lucas got there, but while he was close enough to be caught up in the blast."

A shadow crossed Taylor's face. He rubbed his forehead and I caught sight of a tiny open-hand tattoo on the inside of his wrist. It was identical to the one Lucas had, which none of the family had known about.

"Is that something to do with the English Freedom Army?" I pointed to the tattoo.

"It is," Taylor said. "It's our insignia."

This, as much as anything, finally convinced me that he was speaking the truth about Lucas.

"Your brother was *not* a thug or a terrorist," Taylor went on. "He was a solider, a hero, trying to protect and defend his country."

As he spoke, I felt a weight lifting from my back. Taylor watched me, a mix of curiosity and compassion in his eyes.

"Why are you telling me this?" I asked.

"Because the Commander and I both felt you were owed an explanation." Taylor smiled. "Believe me, it's a big deal for us to speak out. I wouldn't normally meet anyone like this, but you're worth making an exception for."

I could feel my face flushing. Why would anyone think that?

Taylor tilted his head to the side. "Maybe you don't realize how exceptional you are, Nat. I'm not talking about your academic record, though I know from everything Lucas said about you how impressive that is."

"Lucas talked about me?"

"He was incredibly proud of you." Taylor smiled.

My throat tightened.

"I know that Lucas's sacrifice has had a terrible impact on your family," Taylor went on. "Your parents barely speak, your mother lives in the hospital, your father is working himself into an early grave even as his business is on the verge of collapse, your sister—"

"How do you know all this?" Bile rose in my guts. It was too much, hearing this man reel off such private bits of information.

"Lucas was a soldier who paid the ultimate price," Taylor said smoothly. "The Commander makes it his business to keep an eye on the people our soldiers leave behind, to help them if he can."

"This . . . Commander . . . wants to help my family?" I stared through the trees, feeling angry and confused. The air was heavy with the smell of damp earth.

"Yes, as do I. That is, we want to help *you*, if you'll let us. That's the other reason I'm here." Taylor turned up the collar of his expensive coat. "The Commander wants to give you a chance to serve your country, just as Lucas served it. The English Freedom Army is the real deal, Nat, and we want . . . The *Commander* wants . . . you to join us."

I stared at him.

"It will be dangerous, but rewarding," Taylor went on. "We will train you just like we trained Lucas."

"You mean I'd be able to help stop the League of Iron?" My mind sped ahead into a future where I could find out who set off the marketplace bomb, then take revenge for Lucas's injury.

"The League of Iron is one of the groups we are monitoring," Taylor said, giving me a shrewd look. "There are others too, but the Commander will understand if you have a particular motivation to work in a specific direction. It's good timing, in fact. Our goal this year is to recruit young, intelligent, enthusiastic cadets. You're a perfect choice."

I looked away, feeling embarrassed. And pleased.

"Just one more thing. I'm afraid I have to take your laptop,"

Taylor said. "You'll get it back when we've replaced the hard drive."

"What?" I tightened my grip on my computer. "Why?"

"To erase all trace of your user name; AngelOfFire can no longer exist." Taylor's green eyes bored into me. "I know you don't understand yet how we work but, when you do, you'll see just what a massive risk I've taken coming here. Even slipping that phone in your pocket was—"

"How did you do that?"

"The jogger did it." Taylor waved his hand to suggest that planting the mobile in my pocket had been a minor matter. "I've got a memory stick with me so you can back up any important files."

"I don't need that," I said slowly. "It's all backed up."

"Good." Taylor fished in his coat pocket and pulled out a bundle of notes. He counted out eight fifty-pound notes and offered them to me. "Look, if you don't trust me, let me buy the laptop. You can get a decent replacement with this."

I stared at the money.

A couple wandered through the trees nearby, deep in conversation. Taylor turned his back and shrank deeper into the upturned collar of his overcoat. He tried to palm me the money, but I backed away.

"Here, take it." I held out the laptop. "I don't want your cash."

A smile flitted across Taylor's face. He repocketed his money and took the plastic bag with the computer inside. "Hang on to that phone," he said. "Keep it secret, keep it safe. You won't be able to make calls on it yet, but someone will contact you." He took a step away.

"When?"

"Soon." Taylor strode off, through the trees. He was quickly out of sight.

I stood for a moment, reeling at everything I'd just heard, then I hurried after Taylor, determined to see where he went. But by the time I reached the edge of the trees, he had already disappeared.

CHARLIE

I stared out of the window at the clear blue sky. It was a beautiful day—cold and crisp—and the first Saturday of midterm. It was also the morning of the memorial service for Mum and the other bomb victims.

Brian squeezed my hand as we walked to the car.

"You're a brave girl, Charlie," he said. "I'm sure your dad would have been proud of you."

I nodded, a lump in my throat. Brian was the only person who ever mentioned my dad. Aunt Karen hadn't really known him—he'd been stationed in Afghanistan for most of the two years he and Mum had been together before he died.

"I was wondering . . . ," I stammered. I'd been thinking about asking this question for a while, but had never quite been able to summon up the courage before. "How come you and my dad fell out?"

Brian opened the car door. He looked at me. "It was a long time ago," he said. "When your dad joined the army. I thought he was running away."

"From what?"

Brian shrugged. "Responsibility. Like I said, it was a long time ago."

Gail joined us and we drove off. I stared out of the window, turning what Brian had said over in my mind. I didn't understand—how was fighting for your country running away from your responsibilities?

It took just ten minutes to drive to the hall where the memorial service was being held, then another ten to find a parking place. I looked out for Aunt Karen and for Jas and Nat as we approached the hall, but the crowd on the pavement was too thick. Were all these people here for Mum and the other victims? As if to answer my question, a black car pulled up. Brian and I were slightly ahead of Gail and Rosa and we had to stop as the crowd surged forward. I peered past the heads to see who was getting out of the car. It was a singer from a TV talent show. Some relative of hers had been left in a wheelchair after the blast and I knew she had been widely interviewed immediately afterward. She was followed out of the car by the mayor of London and his wife and son.

Brian tutted beside me. "I don't know why they get special treatment," he muttered.

I shrugged and pushed my way through the crowds. I was sure Nat would be here and I wanted a chance to see how he behaved when he had to come face to face with so many people who, I was still certain, were related to those he had helped kill and maim.

"Charlie, wait!" Brian's voice behind me sounded faint among the hubbub. He was probably hanging back, waiting for Gail and Rosa to push their way through the crowd.

I kept going. I'd rather be alone.

I reached the external doors. Two men in suits were standing guard, checking people's official invitations. I drew mine out of my pocket and showed it to one of the guards. He waved me through a small anteroom. Glass doors led into the hall. I took a deep breath and went inside.

The hushed atmosphere inside the hall couldn't have been more different from the chaos outside. People were still milling about, talking, but their voices were low and their heads bowed. The whole place felt subdued yet expectant.

I walked to the front of the room, wondering if Aunt Karen was here yet. A row of photos had been set out on the stage, just in front of the lectern. Mum's picture was at the end on the right. I knew it would be here, yet the sight of it still hurt. The photo was one of my favorites—Mum was looking into the distance, a proud smile on her face. You couldn't tell just by looking at it, of course, but I knew that this picture had been taken as she watched me winning a gym competition when I was at elementary school years and years ago. For a moment, the pain of losing her was as raw as it had ever been. My throat felt swollen and tears pricked at my eyes. Not here. Not in front of all these people. I turned around, intending to look for Aunt Karen again.

And walked straight into Nat.

He was standing right behind me. Had he been *watching* me?

I looked up and, for a split second, I saw the same pain that I felt reflected in his eyes.

"Charlie . . . ," Nat started.

My heart lurched into my throat. But before Nat could say any more, Jas was there, looking thinner than ever in a long, floaty black dress.

"Hi Charlie," she said.

"Catch you later," Nat grunted, and walked away. I watched his back disappear into the crowd. What had he been going to say?

"This is weird, isn't it?" Jas's forehead creased in an anxious frown. "Will you come and meet my parents? They're waiting by Lucas's photo."

"Sure." I let Jas lead me along the edge of the stage to where a middle-aged couple was peering down at a picture of a boy with twinkling dark eyes. It was hard to imagine the same boy lying unconscious in a hospital for the past six months.

"Charlie, this is my mum and dad," Jas said.

"Hello, Charlie, it's a pleasure to meet you at last." Jas's mum gave me a warm smile. She looked exhausted, her eyes sore and lined.

Jas's dad reached out to shake my hand. He was tall, with the same shaped mouth as Jas—and looked as tired as his wife.

We talked for a moment more. Jas's parents commented on the hall and how attractive it was with all the soft lights on the walls. The conversation felt surreal with none of us talking about why we were actually here. I was glad when the ushers appeared and asked us politely to find our seats.

I spotted Aunt Karen in the second row from the front, talking with Brian and Gail. As I hurried over, I passed the mayor and his family. The mayor's son caught my eye and smiled. Despite his formal clothes—a stiff blue blazer and gray trousers—we were about the same age. He was maybe a tad taller than me, with rosy cheeks and a shock of thick, fair hair.

I sat down next to Aunt Karen. It flashed through my mind that she might still be angry with me for all the fights we'd had when we'd lived together. But then we hugged and she whispered that she loved me and I could almost feel all the bad stuff between us melting away into the past. The hall was full now, the noise of hushed chatter filling the air. Nat was across the aisle with his parents and Jas. I stared at him, but he didn't look up. Jas and her mum put their arms around each other. Another wave of longing washed over me. It was good to see Aunt Karen again, but I would have given anything to have been able to hug Mum like that.

The service began as a man I didn't recognize read the names of the four people who died in the bomb, then went on to list those severely injured—a roll call that included Lucas. Aunt Karen held my hand, weeping quietly. She was sitting next to Gail. On Gail's other side, Rosa was crying too—with plenty of ostentatious sniffing and eye-wiping. It was drawing a lot of attention. People probably thought *she* was the bereaved daughter, not me. For a second I felt angry with her. She hadn't even known Mum. What was she so upset for?

The service moved on to short talks on each of the people

killed. Aunt Karen went up to the front to speak about Mum, how dedicated she'd been as an elementary school teacher before she'd lost her job in the cuts, how much she had loved life and her friends and her family, especially me.

After feeling so raw earlier, I was numb now. I watched as Mayor Latimer stood up to speak. He was trying to sound concerned, but the hushed and humble tone he used came over as phony to me. He talked for ages: firstly about the process of grieving, then how we mustn't let it stop us loving, or else we let the terrorists win.

At last the mayor finished speaking and the music part of the program began. Rosa was still crying noisily. The service went on for another fifteen minutes or so, then we all filed into the back room for wine and chips and fancy canapés. I vaguely wondered who was paying for everything. The TV news this morning had announced another pay cut for all public sector workers and said that the mayor's budget was to be severely reduced too.

I stood in the corner. The mayor and his wife were in the middle of the room, talking with Jas and her parents. I watched Jas take a bite of a cracker then put the remainder on her mum's plate. No wonder she was so skinny. It struck me that though we'd shared snacks together many times I'd never actually seen her eat a full meal.

I sighed. The service had just turned into a drinks party and Nat was nowhere to be seen. The least I could get out of the whole stupid experience was a bit of information, something I could properly use against him.

I headed to the drinks table wondering if he was somewhere in the crush. The mayor's son was standing on the edge of the crowd. As I walked over, he smiled.

"Hello," he said.

"Hi." I looked around. No sign of Nat here.

"Are they your parents?" the boy asked, indicating Nat and Jas's mum and dad.

"No," I said.

"Are you a friend of the family?"

Irritation flickered through me at his persistence. "I'm their daughter's friend," I said. "We go to the same school. Why are you asking?"

The boy shrugged. "It's just nice to see people my age. Girls especially." He grinned and a dimple appeared in his left cheek. "I'm Aaron by the way." He held out his hand.

I shook it, feeling even more annoyed. Aaron seemed to be treating the whole event as some kind of flirting opportunity. "Charlie," I said.

I turned away, determined to find Nat.

"Nice to meet you, Charlie," Aaron said.

"Whatever." As I stomped off, it occurred to me that I'd probably been a bit harsh. After all, it couldn't be much fun for Aaron to spend his Saturday morning at a ceremony with a bunch of unhappy people just because his parents had to. And there was no way he could have known that I was the daughter of one of the blast victims.

I walked on, still looking for Nat. I might have failed to steal his laptop, but if I could just get him talking, I was sure I could force him to let something slip about his involvement with the League of Iron, some detail I could use to start building evidence against him.

There he was, hunched over his phone, crossing the room. He was heading for the fire door in the corner. My jaw dropped as he looked around—a quick furtive glance—then pressed down on the bar. Was he leaving the memorial service? A moment later he slipped outside and out of sight.

Where on earth was he going?

I hesitated for just a second, then I sped across the room and followed him outside. He was still studying his cell phone, walking purposefully up the road. Before I knew what I was doing, I was hurrying after him. My pulse raced. Rationally this was crazy: Nat was probably going somewhere completely unconnected with the League of Iron. On the other hand, why would he walk out on the memorial service like this if it was for some innocent reason? In my bones I was sure that whatever he was doing was linked to the bomb and to his brother and to that disgusting League forum he had written on as AngelOfFire.

The wind pinched at my face, despite the bright sunshine. I hurried along, tugging my scarf around me. Nat turned right at the end of the road. He was walking fast. I sped up, almost having to run in order to keep him in view. He took a left, then two rights in quick succession. He stopped for a moment, as if deciding which way to turn next, then headed toward the canal. I followed him past a pair of homeless women arguing over the contents of a bin. A moment later, Nat reached the water and the first of the three low-rise public housing buildings that ran along its banks. I lost sight of him as he walked through the entry arch.

I sped up again, racing under the arch myself, out to the other side. Two men in the distance were shouting.

Without warning, a hand grabbed my arm. Nat swung me round, his eyes blazing in the bright sunlight. "Why are you following me?" he snapped.

My breath caught in my throat. I tried to pull away, to run, but Nat held me fast.

NAT

I gripped Charlie's arm. There was shock—but no fear—in her eyes. As she stared up at me, I had the weird sensation of falling through air. The dirty public housing around us vanished, the shouts of the men in the distance faded to background noise. It was like I was seeing her for the first time, really *seeing* her, from the stubborn tilt of her jaw to those dark, fierce eyes that seemed to penetrate right inside me.

It struck me that Charlie wasn't just pretty, as I'd first thought. She was beautiful.

I dropped her arm. "I asked you why you're following me."

Charlie stuck out her chin. "Who says I'm following you?"

I smiled. Her expression was just so ridiculously haughty. "Yeah, right. You've been behind me since the memorial. What are you, some kind of stalker?"

"Of course I'm not." She was still sticking out her chin, but the shadow of embarrassment flickered across her face, presumably at the fact I had spotted her so easily.

"It's your hair," I said. "It's kind of hard to miss."

Charlie shook her curls away from her face—a gesture of

defiance. My pulse raced. What the hell was happening to me? I'd liked plenty of girls before, but this . . . this was completely different.

"So are you going to tell me what you're doing?" I demanded, trying to make my voice sound hard and angry.

"I wanted to see who you were meeting," Charlie said.

"What makes you think I'm meeting anyone?" I asked, genuinely astonished.

Charlie put her hands on her hips. She was dressed in a black skirt and sweater, a red scarf around her neck and a red hat over her wild curls. No makeup. No jewelry. Unlike Jas, I didn't normally take much notice of how people put together what they wore, but it struck me that Charlie looked cooler than anyone I'd ever met.

"You're going to meet people from the League of Iron, aren't you?" she said.

"*What?*" I stared at her. How on earth had she connected me with the League?

"You're a member of the League. You were there when the market bomb that killed my mum went off," Charlie said. "You were *part* of it."

"How can you think—?"

"I know you belong to the League of Iron and they already said that they set off the bomb. Don't deny it, I've seen what you write on their forums as AngelOfFire. It's *disgusting.*"

How the hell had she identified me from the forums? "What are you talking about?" I said.

"Don't lie to me. I saw on your laptop. All that stuff about who to bomb and hating black people and—"

"Shh." I looked around, but no one was near us, nobody was listening. "You sneaked into my room and looked on my computer?"

Charlie nodded.

A shiver ran down my spine. Up until now I'd thought Taylor's request to replace my hard drive had been a bit over the top. But if Charlie had stolen a look at my laptop, then other people might have too.

Charlie looked up. "I'll give you one final chance to tell me the truth," she said. Her mouth trembled slightly. "Did you set off the bomb that killed my mum?"

"No."

"I don't believe you."

We stared at each other. I felt torn. I had promised Taylor that I wouldn't talk about our meeting, but if anyone deserved to know the truth, it was, surely, Charlie. I had seen the hurt in her eyes at the memorial service. She ought to know that someone, somewhere, was trying to stop the League of Iron.

"It's complicated," I said.

"What is? Being a Nazi thug who thinks bombing random people in markets is a great thing?"

"I don't think that."

"So how do you explain being AngelOfFire?"

I hesitated.

"The League left your brother in a coma. Your *own* brother. And my . . . my mum . . ." Charlie's voice cracked.

I racked my brains, frantic for a way to explain at least part of the truth. "I . . . I was just doing the forums because I need . . . I want . . . to understand why the League of Iron did the bombing," I said.

"You want to *understand* them?" Charlie folded her arms. She sounded incredulous. "*I* want to *kill* them."

"Yeah, I know." I bit my lip. "Like I said, it's complicated."

"You're lying." Charlie scowled. "It's written all over your face, like the way you snuck out of the memorial service so no one saw you. You're going to meet League of Iron people, aren't you? You're planning who to bomb next."

I thought of the text on the phone in my pocket.

"You're wrong," I said truthfully. "I was actually going to visit my brother in the hospital. You can come with me if you don't believe me."

"Fine," Charlie said. "Let's go."

CHARLIE

I was sure Nat was lying. At the very least, he was holding
something back. I mean he said the text he'd gotten was
irrelevant and that he was really just going to see his brother,
but how did I know either of those things were true? As we
walked to the hospital, I was still sure he had been behind the
marketplace bomb.

It didn't occur to me to be scared. All I could think about was
how on earth I was going to get Nat to admit to what he'd done.
And, as we reached the hospital and crossed the parking lot, I
made my plan.

Harassed-looking people were bustling in and out of the hospital's glass doors. The NHS had been strained to the breaking
point this year because of all the cuts. Even though I didn't follow
politics, I'd still heard the summer heat wave horror story about
the three elderly women who died on the same day—in different
hospitals—because they had been left, untreated and forgotten,
by busy nurses in crowded hallways.

The elevator stopped at the third floor. We got out and I followed Nat along the hallway. A couple of the nurses glanced over

as we passed. They seemed to recognize Nat. He led me into a room on the left. The boy from the picture at the memorial service lay on the bed. This was Jas and Nat's brother, Lucas.

I gasped, shocked by the sight of all the tubes and wires running out of his body. It was hot in the room. Nat took off his jacket and laid it on the end of the bed, then he walked around the bed and sat down in the chair. He looked at me.

"This is why I left the memorial service: to see my brother, okay?"

I stared at Lucas, distracted momentarily from my plan. I was still sure Nat had been lying about coming here, but even so it must be awful to have someone you loved strapped to machines like this. What if it were Mum lying in a coma for six months, in this limbo hell between living and dying? No wonder Nat's mum was always in the hospital and his dad kept himself busy with work; no wonder Jas had stopped playing the piano and only picked at her food. For a whole year I'd envied everyone who'd survived the blast—whatever their circumstances—but now, for the first time, it occurred to me that losing Mum as I did might have been better, after all, than losing her like this.

Nat leaned forward in his chair, his eyes intent on his brother's face. I glanced at his jacket, still lying at the end of the bed, and remembered my plan. I edged closer until I was perching on the end of the bed. Nat didn't look around. Pulse racing, I reached for the jacket. Slowly, carefully, my trembling fingers felt for the outline of Nat's cell. *There.* Silently, I drew the phone out of the jacket pocket. I stood up, hiding the cell behind my back.

"I need the bathroom," I said.

"Sure." Nat didn't look up. "It's just down the hallway on the left."

I scuttled out of the room, keeping the phone out of sight. It felt hot against my clammy palms as I ducked into the bathroom and locked the door. I looked at the phone. It was a basic model. I scrolled to messages; there was only one text here, received fifteen minutes or so ago. This was the message Nat had gotten at the memorial service.

I opened it up and read.

NAT

I barely noticed Charlie leave the room. I was staring at Lucas, so still and pale on the hospital bed. I had been thinking about him all through the memorial service, imagining how he would have laughed at all the solemn faces and at the mayor's pompous speech.

Taylor's text had been the final prompt to come here. And yet, now that I was actually at Lucas's bedside, all I could think was how impossible it was that my brother, who had always been so strong and full of life, could be this shell of a person lying in front of me.

I turned around and saw Charlie standing in the doorway. Her forehead was creased with a frown. Slowly, she held up her hand and, to my horror, I recognized the phone Taylor had given me resting on her palm. She had seen the text.

Charlie walked around the hospital bed, then thrust the phone under my nose. The text Taylor had sent me at the service was on the screen:

We salute a soldier.

"The League of Iron sent this, didn't they?" Charlie asked, her voice little more than a whisper. "Are you the soldier they mean?"

"No."

"Then *what? Who?*"

I didn't know what to say. I turned to Lucas, then looked back at Charlie, watching as the realization dawned in her eyes.

"*Him?*" she said.

I nodded.

"Your *brother* is the soldier?" Charlie gasped. "*He* did the bomb for the League of Iron?"

I kept my gaze on Lucas, as everything I had held on to for the past six months seemed to collapse inside me. "No," I said at last. "Lucas was trying to stop the bomb. He wasn't in the League of Iron any more than I am."

"You're not making sense," Charlie said. "If you aren't in the League, why were you on their forum the other day?"

"I can't tell you," I said.

"Then I'm going to the police." Charlie turned away. "I'll show them this text, see what *they* think."

I caught her hand. "No."

We stared at each other and I knew that I couldn't stay silent any longer. The desire to confess what I knew was overwhelming. Charlie had half-guessed anyway.

"Listen," I said, "and I'll tell you everything."

CHARLIE

Nat's voice was low and even as he told me about the text he saw on Lucas's phone and how he had believed his brother was the League of Iron bomber for six months. I listened, too shocked to feel anything.

At last Nat came to his meeting with Taylor the previous week. He explained how he had given up his laptop, how Taylor wanted to recruit him to a secret group that called themselves the English Freedom Army, how their aim was to stop the random violence of extremist groups like the League of Iron. How Lucas had been part of that group.

His words settled like shards of ice in my brain. Nat seemed totally sincere, but could I really trust him?

"And no one else knows?" I asked.

"No one. I haven't told *anyone* else."

"But . . ." I still wasn't fully convinced. "When you knew there was going to be an explosion back in the market six months ago, why didn't you just dial 999?"

"I wish I had," Nat said with a groan. "Everything was happening so fast. . . . I did tell one of the security guards, but it was too late. He died in the blast before he could say anything to any-one. . . . I guess I thought I could find Lucas before it happened. I can't tell you how much I wish I'd done everything differently, but . . . "

"What about afterward?" I said. "Why didn't you tell anyone then?"

Nat sagged against his chair. "Because my family was fall-ing apart and I thought that if Mum and Dad and Jas knew Lucas had been responsible for the bomb *as well*, it would destroy them. You've seen my parents. . . . Dad's barely coping as it is and Mum . . ." Nat's voice cracked. He put his head in his hands.

I stared down at him, a million emotions careering around my head.

"What about this English Freedom Army?" I said. "How do you know that's any better than the League of Iron? You should tell someone about them, the police, your parents."

"Weren't you listening?" Nat said. "The guy I met, Taylor, from the EFA. He wants to stop the extremists from hurting inno-cent people. The police are useless, so someone needs to act. The English Freedom Army are heroes."

I shook my head. Everything Nat said might be true, but the way he described this army sounded like something out of a superhero comic. How could he be so sure they were the good guys?

"There's something else," Nat went on, his voice barely above a whisper. He glanced at his brother again, lying motionless on the bed. "If I join the EFA I will get a chance to do something about the League of Iron."

"You mean get them back for Lucas? For my mum?" My heart leaped. Now, that sounded like an ambition I could totally go along with.

Nat nodded. "But we have to keep it secret. Promise me you won't tell, please?"

NAT

Charlie stared up at me. She was standing so close that I could have counted the eyelashes that framed her slanting eyes. Her expression was fierce. Fearless.

At last she nodded.

"So you definitely promise me you won't say anything to anyone, not even Jas?" I said. "Because if Jas knows I'm joining some crime-fighting group or whatever, she'll worry about me—in fact, she'll probably end up telling our parents, so . . ." I glanced at the bed. If Mum was right, then it was possible that Lucas had just heard everything the two of us had said. But then Mum lived in a fantasyland where she talked to Lucas for hours on end in the firm belief he would soon wake up.

"No, I won't say anything."

I looked at Charlie. Did she mean that?

"But there's one condition."

"What's that?" I asked.

"I want to join the English Freedom Army too," she said. "If you're going to get revenge on the League of Iron, then so am I."

PART TWO

INITIATION

(n. formal admission or acceptance into an organization)

CHARLIE

Two weeks passed before Nat's English Freedom Army contact called him again. Just as well, since it took me almost all that time—days of snatched, hushed conversations—to argue away Nat's objections to me meeting him. Nat was adamant that the man, Taylor, had insisted on secrecy and that Nat himself had only been approached only because of his brother's involvement with the EFA.

"It was a one-off," he said. "A special case. They won't appreciate me involving someone else."

"I'm not 'someone else,'" I argued back. "I'm a special case just like you are."

Nat was already at the park gates when I arrived. I was determined not to show it, but I couldn't help feeling self-conscious as I walked over. Nat had this way of looking at me with those intense blue eyes of his, like I was the only thing he could see.

"This is what they sent," he said, shoving his phone at me. "I'm assuming it's from Taylor, but the number's withheld."

I peered down at the screen, shielding it from the bright sunlight with my hand.

Building site. Featherstone Rd. Wait.

"Do you know where that is?" I asked.

Nat nodded. "Not exactly flowery language, is it?" he said
with a sudden grin that transformed his face, making his eyes
sparkle like chips of ice in the sunshine.

"Let's go," I said, turning away.

We walked in silence. I was going over what I needed to say
to Taylor to get him to accept me into the EFA. I knew I was going
to have to tell him that I wanted to keep the streets safe. Trouble
was, and I know it makes me sound like a really mean person, I
didn't much care about the streets. Not compared to how much I
cared about getting revenge for Mum.

Featherstone Road was dirty and rundown, with a large, high-
walled estate running all the way down one side. The building
site was opposite one end of the estate, a deserted, stone shell of a
house surrounded by wasteland. The ground-floor windows were
boarded up. The roof was mostly missing. Danger signs were dotted across the front, warning people not to trespass.

Nat gave me a quick glance as we headed around the side
of the house, where the brickwork was low and crumbling. We
clambered over the wall then crept along the side passage, looking for a way in. The side door swung off its hinges. Nat pulled it
open. It was dark in the house. Spooky. Pulse racing, I followed
him inside.

Before my eyes could adjust to the gloom, a gloved hand was

slapped over my nose and mouth, and a damp cloth was shoved between my lips. I gasped in shock, taking in a breath of something sour and smelling of chemicals. And then everything went black, my legs buckled, and I fell to the floor.

NAT

I watched, horrified, as Taylor lay Charlie on the concrete floor then turned and stormed toward me. He gripped my neck with one strong hand, forcing me back against the wall. Before I could even register the coldness of the brick at my back, Taylor whipped a gun from inside his coat and pressed the barrel against my temple. The metal felt like ice against my skin.

"What the hell is this?" He swore. "Who is she? Why did you bring her?"

My heart drummed furiously in my chest. Why hadn't I thought Taylor might carry a gun? He'd said he was part of an army, for goodness' sake.

"She's a friend," I stammered. She believes in the same—"

"Do you think this is a *game*?" Taylor swore again. "Don't lie to me, Nat."

"She *is* . . . She's a friend of mine. She wants to help."

"This is not cool." Taylor let out a grunt of frustration. In a single move, he twisted my arms behind my back and tied them with rope. Then he shoved me to the floor. I landed with a thud on my side. The rope bit into my wrists. Taylor was now binding my ankles. Everything was happening so fast. A moment later and my mouth was covered with tape.

Taylor moved over to Charlie. I tried to speak as he bound her wrists and ankles, but the tape over my mouth was so tight that all that came out was a series of muffled grunts. Once Charlie was securely tied up, Taylor took out a flashlight and shone it long and hard in her face and then strode back to me. He ripped the tape off my mouth.

"Who is she?" he demanded.

"She's a friend. Her mum was killed in that League of Iron bomb. We're at the same school. She wants—"

Taylor shoved the gun against my throat. I gasped. "Do you not remember what I told you about keeping your meeting with me secret?"

"Yes," I stammered. "I just . . ."

"Yes, *sir*," Taylor spat.

"Yes, sir," I repeated. "She followed me. She saw . . . saw stuff on my laptop before I gave it to you. She's smart, she put it all together. She was going to the police if I didn't bring her along today. But she's cool. She wants to help. Especially if it's a chance to get back at the League of Iron. They killed her mother and her dad's already dead. She . . . she's a friend . . ." I ran out of words.

Taylor stared at me for several long, slow seconds, then he holstered his gun under his coat and tugged at the knot around my wrists. To my surprise, the rope released instantly.

I gave my wrists a rub, then reached down and untied my ankles.

Taylor cleared his throat. "I'm sorry, Nat, I overreacted. I didn't mean to scare you, but secrecy is vital. You should have asked me before you brought her." He stood up. "I need to speak to the Commander. Please stay here."

I indicated Charlie, still slumped on the floor. "What about her? Is she okay?"

"She's fine." Taylor reached down and slid the ropes off Charlie's wrists and ankles. "She'll come around in a few minutes." He stalked out of the room.

The side door of the house banged shut. I crept closer to Charlie. Her eyes were closed. Had Taylor been telling the truth about her being okay? I bent down so my cheek rested just over her nose and mouth. Her breath warmed my face, slow, steady, and shallow. Relief flooded through me.

I leaned back against the cold wall. As the shock of Taylor's aggression wore off, I had to admit to myself that he had been impressive. I'd never seen anyone move with such speed and precision—or with such ruthlessness.

No wonder Lucas had become more focused and serious after the EFA had trained him.

I took a deep breath. Despite Taylor's terrifying behavior before, I wanted to join the English Freedom Army more than ever. But what would the Commander decide? Suppose Charlie wasn't allowed to join the EFA? Suppose, after bringing her here, that I wasn't?

A few moments later, Charlie's eyes flickered open.

"Are you all right?" I whispered.

Charlie nodded. She blinked, rubbing her head.

"What happened?" she said. Her eyes widened. "Was I *drugged?*"

I was about to explain when Taylor marched back into the room. He squatted in front of Charlie, a serious expression on his face.

"What's your name?" he asked.

"Charlie Stockwell," she said, jutting out her chin. "How dare you drug me? Who do you think you are?"

I glared at her. I understood that she'd just had a shock, but couldn't she see how angry Taylor was that I'd brought her? For goodness' sake, I'd *told* her it was a risk, that Taylor had emphasized the need for secrecy within the EFA.

"Well?" Charlie demanded.

I closed my eyes. This was it. Taylor was never going to recruit us now. We'd be lucky to get out of here in one piece.

CHARLIE

My head felt sore, but my mind was clear as I stared at Taylor. His gun was poking out from the inside of his jacket. I gritted my teeth. He might make out he was one of the good guys, but genuinely well-meaning people aren't ready with guns and drugs to attack innocent teenagers just because they've walked into a meeting where they weren't expected..

I stared up into his eyes. For a moment he looked surprised, then his expression grew carefully blank.

"*You're* angry with *me?*" he said slowly. Then he sat back on his heels and laughed.

"It's not a joke," I said, furious that Taylor was making fun of me. "How dare you attack me?"

The smile fell from Taylor's face. "You weren't supposed to be here," he said coldly. "Now tell me what Nat has told you about the English Freedom Army."

The last thing I wanted to do was obey, but I didn't really have a choice. I explained, as quickly as I could, what Nat had said. "I came along because I thought joining you might be a way to get back at the League of Iron," I finished. "If Nat's going to get a chance to take revenge on those pigs who killed my mother, then I want a chance too."

Taylor hesitated a moment, then he stood up. "Wait."

"Hey, did you speak to the Commander? What did he say?" Nat asked.

But Taylor was already out of the room. Nat turned on me. Even in the dim light I could see his face was pale and his eyes strained.

"What are you *doing?*" he hissed. "He wasn't expecting you and he is a soldier with a *gun*. This is *not* the way to get him to recruit us."

"Don't tell me what to do." I looked away, anger rising inside me again.

Nat fell silent. A full minute ticked by. Neither of us said anything. At last Taylor came back, making no sound as he crossed the floor. He folded his arms, as Nat and I scrambled to our feet.

"So you want to join us, Charlie?" Taylor asked.

I hesitated. After being attacked just now, I actually had severe reservations about joining the EFA, but there was no point saying that to Taylor. "I want to get revenge on the League of Iron," I said. "If you can help me do that then I want to join."

"Right." Taylor studied me carefully.

"Nat says that the EFA tries to protect people from extremist groups," I said. "To *stop* those groups."

Taylor shook his head. "Nat shouldn't have told you anything about us."

"I—" Nat started.

"Don't blame him," I cut in. "I followed him one day. Snooped on his computer. I didn't give him a choice."

Taylor considered this, then he reached for his backpack and pulled out a laptop. I recognized it from Nat's bedroom.

"Here," he said, handing Nat the laptop. "We've replaced the hard drive. No more forums, okay?"

Nat nodded.

I watched Taylor intently. Did this mean he was going to accept what I'd said? Let me into the EFA?

Taylor turned to me. "Charlie?"

I kept my gaze fixed on him.

Taylor looked for a second as if he were suppressing a smile. "Why aren't you scared?" he said.

I shrugged.

Taylor tilted his head to one side. Then he took a gun from inside his coat and pointed it across at Nat. "I could kill him," he said. "Would that scare you?"

Nat's mouth fell open.

My stomach gave a sick lurch. "No," I said, careful not to let my horror at his words show. "But it should scare *you*."

Taylor lowered his gun.

"Explain," he barked.

"Firstly it's broad daylight and you'd have a body to deal with, which would be messy—and an army's supposed to be efficient. Secondly, I'd be a witness so you'd have to kill me too, which would be *two* bodies. Doubly messy. And thirdly, Nat and I want to join you, to learn more, to help protect people. Sure I want to get back at the League of Iron, but it's not just that." I took a deep breath. "I'm . . . we want to end all the violence that's going on in London and other places all the time. If you kill us, you prove that you are as stupid and as cruel as all those extreme groups you told Nat that you want to protect the public from."

Taylor studied me for a long moment. I stared back, my throat dry and tight. Then, without speaking, he put his gun away. My eyes had adjusted to the light now. The bare room we were in had peeling paint on the walls and piles of rubble dotted across the concrete. Nat's clothes were filthy and there was a grimy smear across his face. I took a good look at Taylor. Stubble darkened the chin of his narrow face, he wore an expensive cashmere overcoat, and those fierce eyes of his were green.

"You want to be a soldier, Charlie?" he asked.

"Yes."

He glared at me, eyebrows raised. "Yes, *sir*—"

I resisted the temptation to roll my eyes.

"Yes, *sir*," I said.

Taylor nodded. He turned to Nat. "This was your final warning. Spring one more surprise on me and you're out. Have you talked to anyone else apart from her about the EFA? Or meeting me?"

"No, sir." Nat sounded as if he were speaking through gritted teeth.

Taylor paused. "The Commander says you're both to be tested before we go any further," he said.

"Tested how?" I asked.

"Well, you obviously trust each other enough to have come here together and strong ties within a cell are very important," Taylor said. "But we need to trust you too." He paused. "You are young and determined and motivated and those are important qualities for us, but if we're going to really use you, we need to know more about your individual skills. And your loyalty. Most importantly at this stage, we need to know that you will follow my orders without question."

"So what do you want us to do?" Nat asked.

"You both have a reason, a good reason, for hating the League of Iron. We understand they're planning another attack but we don't have any details. We want you to break into a senior League member's home."

"What's his name?" Nat growled.

"For your own safety I'm not going to tell you." Taylor cleared his throat. "Now, the house is heavily alarmed, but we need you to get in, steal top-secret information about the plans from a password-protected computer, and get out without anyone seeing you. How does that sound?"

I looked at Nat. He was staring at Taylor, frowning. "It sounds like you want to use us," he said.

"That's right," Taylor admitted. "We do. But if you perform well, we will train you and give you the chance you've been looking for to take revenge on the League of Iron."

I thought it through. It made sense that the EFA would want to test us out before they truly confided in us—and this burglary job would take me into an actual League member's house.

"I'll do it," I said. "Bring it on."

"Nat?" Taylor asked.

Nat hesitated for a moment, then nodded. "Okay," he said. "I'm in."

NAT

I glanced at Charlie as we walked through the park after our meeting with Taylor. The reckless way she had talked to him had shocked me to my core. Yet I couldn't help but admire her guts. I kicked at a can on the grass. I really needed time to myself to think through everything that had happened. Taylor had said from the start that the English Freedom Army was a serious operation. I was just starting to realize how serious. I'd never even seen a gun before and in the last hour I'd had one pointed at me twice.

Charlie, however, didn't seem to understand how shaken I felt.

"What's the matter?" she asked as we walked across the grass. "What's wrong?"

The light was dying from the day and the wind was cold. I shoved my hands in my pockets. What exactly *was* wrong? I wasn't sure. I just kept seeing Taylor in my mind's eye—the intensity on his face when he'd pinned me against the wall. It struck me that not only was Taylor capable of shooting someone but that it was highly probable he had already done so. All of which totally freaked me out. I had been too scared to think, while Charlie had argued defiantly with Taylor. Did that make me a coward? I couldn't decide. And I wasn't going to as long as Charlie kept pestering me to talk to her about it.

"Nothing's wrong," I muttered, stomping along the path toward the trees.

"Then why won't you look at me?" Charlie asked.

Reluctantly, I stopped walking and turned to face her. Her cheeks were flushed from the cold air, her dark eyes glittering in the afternoon light. On top of everything else, she was distractingly beautiful. I tried—and failed—to push this thought out of my head.

"There isn't a problem," I said at last. "I just need a bit of time to get my head around what we're doing. This is real, this test, it means breaking into a house, breaking the law and—"

"And getting back at the League of Iron," Charlie added. "Or at least starting to."

"I know." I checked the time. I couldn't stay here any longer. "So I'll meet you outside the park again tomorrow night after school, like Taylor said?"

"Okay." Charlie's expression darkened. Had I offended her somehow? I didn't want to upset her, but my head was too full of confused thoughts to see anything clearly. I hesitated for a moment then, unable to think of what to say to make things okay between us, I said good-bye.

Charlie said good-bye too, then headed off along the path. As soon as I was alone, I checked my laptop. Most of my schoolwork and soccer content had been transferred to the new hard drive, but all my old Internet downloads were gone. At least the computer still worked. I shoved it in my bag and hurried home.

The house was deserted. Dad must still be at work and Mum, presumably, was at the hospital. Jas, I knew, had gone to the Canal Street market to buy some cheap material to make clothes with. I had no idea how she could bear to go there, after what happened to Lucas, but Jas often didn't seem bothered by the same things that got to me. She had promised to get some food on the way home. Hopefully, she wouldn't be long. I was starving and the kitchen cupboards were virtually bare. I found some rice and set a saucepan of water on to boil. I sat down at the kitchen table, determined to put all thoughts of Taylor, the EFA, and Charlie out of my head. At least I had my computer back. For the past few weeks I'd had to borrow Dad's laptop whenever he could spare it and I was behind on almost every subject. I decided to make a start on my history essay right now but, as I opened the relevant files, I found I couldn't stop thinking about Charlie. I had never met anyone like her before.

You like her, you idiot, said a mocking voice in my head. *You just don't want to admit it.*

I told the voice to shut up, put two large handfuls of rice into the now boiling water, and settled down to my essay on the Cuban Missile Crisis.

CHARLIE

"You'll only be given the data you need to complete the task, so you'll have to trust that we have your back. It will be a straight in and out mission, no frills. Got it?" Taylor's green eyes seemed to see right through me.

I held his gaze. "Yes," I said.

"Yes, *sir*," Taylor corrected. He turned to Nat. "You too."

"Yes, sir," Nat said. He seemed calmer than he had yesterday, though just as unwilling to look at me properly.

Why was that? Was he annoyed with me for standing up to Taylor? Was he angry about something else? Or was he just plain uninterested in me?

Whatever, I needed to stop thinking about it and focus on what Taylor was saying.

The van we were in had been crawling along for about twenty minutes now, stopping and starting every few seconds. I assumed we were driving through heavy traffic but it was impossible to tell as we were stuck in the back—empty apart from a couple of thin cushions and the bewildering array of computers and sound equipment set on the low table separating Taylor from me and Nat.

Taylor dug into his backpack and pulled out two earpieces. "You'll be using these," he said. "They mean we can hear you and you can hear us."

"Who's 'we'?" Nat asked. "You and the driver?"

"Classified," Taylor said.

Nat glanced at me. I shrugged. I'd seen the driver of the van as we'd gotten in the back. The driver was dressed in a loose jacket and a baseball cap. I wasn't sure if it was a man or a woman. Taylor, still wearing that expensive cashmere overcoat, had clearly decided to keep the risk of us seeing something revealing to an absolute minimum. I had clocked the van's license plate as we'd gotten inside, but from the extent of the secrecy precautions Taylor had already taken, I was pretty sure it wouldn't be traceable back to Taylor. The thought sent a shiver down my spine.

"Where are we going?" Nat asked.

"Classified," Taylor said.

"You'll have to tell us *something*," I protested. "We don't even know what exactly you want us to steal."

Taylor fixed me with his piercing gaze. The light in the back of the van was harsh, bleaching out half the skin of his face and casting shadows across the other half.

"We are your eyes and ears," he said. "All you have to do is follow instructions."

"Fine, er, sir." Nat sat back with a sigh.

I shifted uneasily on the hard van floor. I wasn't scared at the prospect of breaking into a house, but trusting Taylor enough to guide us through the experience was another thing entirely.

We drove on for another ten minutes. Just before we stopped, Taylor got us to insert the earpieces—they were tiny, smaller than ordinary earbuds, then ran a test using the computer to check both sets were working. He handed each of us a pair of thin latex gloves and gave Nat a memory stick.

"Keep that safe," he said.

The van drew to a halt as we pulled on the gloves.

"Before you get out, I want you to take the EFA oath," Taylor went on. "Even if you don't fully understand what you're saying, the words still have power. Repeat after me."

We did as we were told. Taylor was right that I didn't really understand what we were saying, but there was nothing inherently evil about any part of the oath. It was really just a bunch of words:

"For blood and soil, strength and honor, hope and sacrifice," we said in turn.

Taylor partly opened the van door, then turned back to us, his fingers resting on the door handle. "The house is empty, we're about to disable the CCTV, the electronic locks, and the alarm remotely. But we can only turn them off for ten minutes. You must be outside the gate by then. If you're not, the security system will restart and the alarm will go off."

"How will we know when ten minutes is up?" I asked.

Taylor tapped my earpiece. "I'll be with you the whole

way. Head for the side entrance. The door there should be unlocked." He turned back to the van door and shoved it open. I blinked as the sharp sunlight flared in front of me, a contrast to the dim lighting inside the back of the van. Seconds later Nat and I were outside, on the pavement.

"The alarm is now off," Taylor said. "You've got ten minutes. Go." He slammed the van door shut.

Nat and I turned to face the building behind us. Before, I'd wondered how we would know which house Taylor had meant us to break into, but the detached home in front of us was so huge, it was obvious. The gates were open, surrounded on either side by rows of trees and bushes.

"Get moving," Taylor's voice sounded in my ear. From the way Nat jumped, I was guessing he'd heard Taylor too.

We headed toward the house. It was built over three stories, with a whole row of windows looking down over the gravel driveway. Taylor had said the place was empty, but I wondered how on earth he could know that for sure.

My feet crunched over the gravel as I followed Nat along the side of the house. Looking around, I could see we were completely hidden from the view of the surrounding houses. The side door was immediately up ahead. Nat's gloved hand was already on the doorknob, twisting and pushing. The door remained closed.

"Taylor said it would be unlocked," he said, his eyes widening.

"It should be," Taylor's voice sounded in our ears.

I rushed over and pushed at the door myself. It remained firmly shut. My heart beat faster. We'd hit a problem before we'd even gotten inside. I focused my energy, looking around for another way in.

"What do we do now?" Nat's voice rose.

"Use your initiative," Taylor hissed in my ear. "Nine minutes and counting. Get on with it."

NAT

Taylor's voice echoed in my ear. From the determined look on Charlie's face it was clear she'd heard him too. She was already setting off along the side passage, searching for another entry point. I shoved at the door again, but it was hopeless. It was definitely locked. I gritted my teeth. How were we going to get into the house now? I felt sick with panic.

"Here," Charlie called under her breath. She was pointing to the second of two sash windows set into the side of the house. There was a small gap at the base, easily big enough for us to fit our hands through.

I rushed over and we placed our hands side by side under the window.

"Go," Charlie whispered.

With a grunt, I pushed. The window slid up.

"*Yes.*" Charlie immediately hooked her knee over the window-sill. Within seconds she was through.

"We're in," I muttered to Taylor, as I followed Charlie into a small bathroom. My sick feeling subsided to a low-level queasiness as she tiptoed to the door. No alarm had gone off and the place appeared to be empty. All we had to do now was find the computer, download the data Taylor wanted, and leave.

Charlie was already through the door into the hall. She was looking around, clearly intent on the mission. She disappeared from view.

"Eight minutes," Taylor warned in my ear.

I walked into the hall. It was nicely decorated with polished wood furniture and pale striped wallpaper. Taylor had said a leading League of Iron member lived here, but I couldn't imagine any of the League people I'd seen at the meeting in this house.

"Upstairs," Taylor ordered. "Second floor."

We climbed the wooden stairs to the second floor. Oil paintings hung on the walls and delicate china ornaments were arranged on the wooden table under the landing mirror.

"Is the League member who lives here a man or a woman?" I asked.

"Second door on the left," Taylor said, ignoring my question. "Seven minutes."

Charlie rolled her eyes at Taylor's refusal to answer. A grin flittered across my face. My heart might be hammering, but Charlie looked as if she'd been housebreaking all her life.

"Tell us what you want us to do." I could hear the edge in my voice as I spoke. I hoped Charlie didn't think it was because I was scared.

"Hurry up," Taylor said. "Are you in the room?"

"Yes, sir." Charlie was already through the second door on the left.

I hurried after her. We were in some sort of home office, with a TV screen on the wall, a couple of armchairs, and a long desk containing two computers.

"Go to the Mac," Taylor ordered. "Switch it on. You have six minutes and thirty seconds before the alarm sounds."

Charlie found the on switch right away. Taylor was giving instructions about the password, then the file he wanted her to find. Charlie was nodding, her fingers flying over the keys. If I'd been in her place, I was sure I'd have found it impossible to focus and would probably have missed half of Taylor's rapid-fire orders. But Charlie was concentrating without any problem, following Taylor's complex set of inputs in order to cut through the computer's encryption codes.

"Nat?" Taylor sounded impatient, as if he'd already called my name once.

"Yes," I said quickly. "Yes, sir."

"Get the memory stick ready. Four minutes and forty seconds."

I fished in my pocket for the stick then handed it to Charlie. She slid it expertly into place. I bent closer to the screen to see what she was downloading. It looked like some sort of calendar. Each date was filled with appointment names and times. Most of the entries were written in code. I couldn't make heads or tails of them. I was suddenly aware of how close I was standing to Charlie and took a step away.

"Four minutes and ten seconds." Taylor's voice was terse. "How's it going, guys?"

"Good," Charlie said. She still sounded amazingly calm. "Almost there. Done." She pulled the memory stick out of the computer and handed it to me. I pocketed it while Charlie followed Taylor's instructions for covering her tracks as she closed the various files she had opened. At last she stood up. "All done, sir."

"Two minutes and thirty seconds," Taylor hissed in our ears. "Get out of there."

Charlie sped out into the hallway. I was about to hurry after her when a photograph lying on top of a pile of papers caught my eye. I peered closer. The photo was of a boy walking along a street—and grainy, as if it had been taken through a long lens. The boy was about my own age and clearly unaware he was being photographed. He looked vaguely familiar, but I couldn't place him.

"Come on," Charlie whispered from the door.

I turned away from the photo. Silently, we hurried along the hallway and down the stairs.

"Where are you?" Taylor demanded.

"Ground floor," I said. "Almost."

"Get a move on. You have less than a minute to get outside the front gate."

We raced toward the small bathroom again. A khaki green scarf on a coat rack by the door caught my eye. It had a strange, crisscrossing black and brown pattern along the bottom. I couldn't remember the name of it, but I was sure this was the symbol the League used as their logo.

"You should be outside the gate by now." Taylor swore softly under his breath. "What the hell are you doing? The alarm will go off in forty seconds, thirty-nine, thirty-eight . . ."

"On our way, sir," I said.

Together we raced into the bathroom. Taylor was still counting as I followed Charlie out of the window we'd climbed through earlier. "Twenty-five seconds, twenty-four seconds . . ."

"We're out," I said, breathless.

"Shut the window. Right to the bottom," Taylor hissed. "Then run."

We pressed down on the sill, but it was stuck.

"Fifteen. Fourteen. Thirteen . . ."

Panic rose like vomit into my throat. "Come on," I hissed, tensing every muscle.

With a final shove the sill slid down into place.

"Eleven. Ten."

"Done," I said.

"Get through the gate," Taylor said. "Nine . . . eight . . . seven . . ."

We raced across the gravel driveway. The electronic gate was starting to close. I grabbed Charlie's hand, pulling her along. Faster. Taylor's voice echoed in my ear.

"Five . . . four . . . three . . ."

We squeezed through the closing gate just in time. It clanged shut behind us. As we ran up to the van, the door swung open.

"Get in," Taylor ordered.

I followed Charlie inside and we sank, panting, onto the floor of the van. Taylor thumped on the panel that separated the back of the van from the driver's cab. We sped off.

"Where is it?" Taylor demanded.

I took the stick and handed it over. While Taylor inserted it into the laptop in front of him, I sat back and snatched a look at Charlie. Her cheeks were flushed, her eyes sparkling.

Taylor examined the contents of the memory stick. "This is good," he muttered.

"What does it say, sir?" I asked.

Taylor looked up. "Classified, but it's all useful info on the League of Iron," he said with a smile.

"Is that all you're going to tell us?" Charlie asked.

"Is it another bomb?" I added.

"Classified," Taylor repeated. "And call me *sir*."

"What?" Charlie sounded outraged. "We just risked our necks for you. You owe us more than a freakin' 'classified.'"

"That's enough." Taylor narrowed his eyes. "And you *will* call me *sir*."

"Fine." Charlie folded her arms. "Tell us what we want to know. *Sir*."

Taylor shook his head. "There are plans here but we need to process the codes properly. Once we've done that and I've debriefed the Commander, then we'll see. . . ."

"See what?" I frowned.

"See if the Commander thinks you're ready for training. Once you've completed basic induction, you'll be assigned a cell. Then you'll be trained for missions, at which point I'll be able to tell you not only what the League of Iron and others are planning, but how we're going to stop them."

"What does that mean: 'a cell'?" Charlie asked.

"We operate in small groups called cells," Taylor explained. "It means every group is independent, so there's limited risk of security breaches between groups. It makes it less likely that anyone outside the army will find out what we're doing."

He handed Charlie a phone similar to the one he'd given me before. "You'll be contacted on this. Keep it safe and don't use it to make or take any other calls."

"When will you call us?" she asked.

"Soon. We replace the phones once a month," Taylor said. "We never use the same transport twice or accommodation for more than three months at a time. Each support cell contains someone who deals with all that stuff—admin, then there's someone working on comms . . . communications . . . which is everything from fake IDs to IT manipulation." He paused. "Everyone else is an active or sleeping agent, trained in combat situations so they can defend themselves in event of attack. We only fight in self-defense but sometimes that means lying our way into situations and, occasionally, using force too. So we need frontline soldiers, especially for the new youth army. And that will be you, if the Commander agrees."

"Do you think he'll agree?" Charlie sat back against the steel van wall. Her voice was carefully even. "I mean, will you recommend us?"

Taylor paused for a moment, then a rare grin spread across his face. "Hell yes," he said. "You'll make the best cadets I've ever seen."

I looked down at my lap. I didn't want either Taylor or Charlie to notice but inside I was glowing with pride. After being so scared earlier, the fact that Taylor rated me was beyond brilliant. Lucas's face with its lopsided grin flashed before my mind's eye. If only he could see me now.

"Thanks," I mumbled.

Across the van, Charlie said nothing.

CHARLIE

Taylor dropped us off at a point halfway between our houses. We each hurried home alone. Adrenaline was still pumping through my body. After being so close to one of the League of Iron leaders . . . actually in their house . . . I was more determined than ever to get revenge for Mum's death. And joining the EFA was clearly the best way to do just that. I didn't buy into Taylor's "we only use violence in self-defense" line. From what I'd seen so far, Taylor was quite prepared to lash out when it suited him. But if it brought me closer to taking my revenge I didn't really care.

There was something else too. . . . I didn't want to admit it, but the truth was I'd enjoyed breaking into that house just now. It had been exciting, a thrill. I'd liked being part of an efficient team and Taylor had talked me through every step of that complicated computer job with a calm focus I couldn't help but respect. I wasn't sure what that said about me. Maybe just that my life since Mum died had felt small and dull.

I reached Gail and Brian's house and let myself in. I could see Gail through the kitchen door, chopping vegetables for supper.

I was in no mood to talk, but I knew that if I didn't at least show my face she would pester me later, asking if I was okay, so I made myself cross the hall and stick my head around the door.

"Hello," I said.

"Hi Charlie, love," Gail said, looking up from her pile of carrots with a smile.

I smiled back, then ducked out of the kitchen and went upstairs to my bedroom. In contrast to what Nat and I had just done, life here seemed very boring. As I lay down on the bed, my head spun, wondering exactly what the EFA training Taylor had talked about would involve. I took *Charlotte's Web* off the shelf and curled up on the bed. Just holding the book—one Mum had loved so much she named me after it—felt comforting. But I didn't want to read. I was too excited, so close to getting my revenge on the people who had killed Mum.

I switched on my new laptop. I felt all fired up by the mission Nat and I had just undertaken, and determined to try to find out more about the country's political situation, especially the League of Iron. But all I came across was a video from a local news program on which the mayor of London, George Latimer, was being interviewed by a reporter. It was funny seeing him on-screen after having listened to him talk at the memorial service. I tried to focus on what he was saying—some cliché about Londoners having to pull together and show 'Blitz spirit' in the face of the cuts. I lost interest after a few moments and switched off the video. In the end, all politicians were the same. The mayor was just as big a hypocrite as the rest of them.

I looked around for Nat the next day when Rosa and I arrived at school. He was in our house room, on time for homeroom for once. He was deeply engrossed in some textbook and didn't notice me come in. I felt a twinge of disappointment. Then I noticed Rosa watching me and scuttled away to my locker.

Nat and I barely spoke for the rest of that day, nor the next three that followed. We didn't sit together in any of our shared classes and he never came up to me during break times either. I wasn't sure why he felt it was so important to keep his distance. I guess if people had seen us talking it would have caused gossip. And yet I couldn't help wishing Nat had felt the same bond I had after our housebreaking adventure. But Nat was clearly locked up in his own life. It was obvious that after I had used him to force my way into the EFA, he now didn't want anything to do with me.

I tried to tell myself I didn't care.

But I knew, deep inside, that I did.

Taylor called on the Tuesday evening of the following week. It was mid-November and, after weeks of mild weather, the days had turned cold and damp. I was alone in my room, as usual, when I felt the phone he had given me vibrate in my pocket. I had been carrying it everywhere with me. Just in case.

"Hello?" I said.

"You've been accepted into the English Freedom Army." Taylor's voice was crisp and businesslike.

Yes. I grinned to myself. "Great," I said.

"Induction training is in three weeks," Taylor went on. "You need to make some excuse to get away. Friday after school till

Sunday morning. Figure it out and text me when you're clear."

"Yes, sir."

Taylor hung up. I hesitated, then sent Nat a text: **Did he call u?**

Five minutes later Nat sent a text back: **Yes. I'm in. U?**

So Nat was going to take part in this EFA training weekend too. Well, it didn't matter what he did. I was only interested in revenge on the League of Iron.

I sent Nat another text: *Yes.*

And then I started thinking about how on earth I was going to get away from home for most of a weekend without anyone realizing what I was doing.

NAT

The last week before the training weekend crept by. Every day was wet and gloomy. I hated the lack of light even more than the constant rain. It made the house feel like a tomb: empty, cold, and dark. Meanwhile, Mum was as distracted as ever and Dad was staying at work later and later every night. At least that meant it would be easy for me to slip away unnoticed. I was planning to leave a note explaining that I was going to a party and staying with one of Callum's friends. My only worry was Jas. Apart from the fact that she might bump into Callum himself over the weekend and wonder why I wasn't with him, she had a habit of knowing when I was lying. I could often tell when she wasn't being honest either. It was a twin thing.

I had hardly spoken to Charlie since we broke into that League of Iron member's house. She had made no effort to talk to me either. Which was good. Excellent, in fact. It meant we were linked only by our desire for revenge on the League of Iron. I liked that—it was clear-cut and straightforward.

It was Thursday morning and I was in my house room at school. Taylor sent a text instructing me to be waiting outside the

Featherstone Road building site on Friday at seven p.m. He was going to pick us up and take us to the training venue. I looked up. Had Charlie received the same message? Across the room, I could see her peering down at her own cell phone. As she straightened up, she gazed around, and I knew instinctively that she was looking for me. I kept my eyes on her until she found me. I raised my eyebrows. She nodded.

A mix of excitement and fear thrilled through me—along with a ridiculous desire to impress her. I looked down again, telling myself not to be such an idiot.

Impress Charlie indeed. After the panic I'd nearly given in to when we broke into that League of Iron house, I'd probably be lucky if I got through the training weekend without throwing up.

CHARLIE

Nat was sitting beside me, tapping along to music on his headphones; Taylor and our driver were up front, listening to the radio. I peered through the darkened glass of the 4x4 car. The road ahead was dark and desolate. We'd been driving for over two hours, first along the M1, then on the M6, and now through smaller, slower roads. I didn't recognize the names of any of the places we were passing. It had just started to rain, the light glistening off the deserted pavements.

I glanced at Nat again, wishing he would take off his headphones and talk to me. I was uneasy. For starters, I felt bad about lying to Gail and Brian—they thought I was visiting Aunt Karen for the weekend and I'd been sending both Gail and Karen texts through the evening, reassuring them I was fine. But what bothered me far more was the fact that I was putting so much trust in the EFA.

Nat and I hadn't said much as we'd waited, earlier, for Taylor and his driver—to whom we hadn't been introduced—to arrive at our pickup point. Neither of us really had any idea what to expect. Taylor had told us to wear loose, comfortable clothing, but that was about it. As we drove on, into the dark evening, questions flooded through my head: Where would we sleep? What would we eat? How many other people would be there? What would we be expected to do?

The radio program finished and the news came on. More job and welfare cuts had been announced. The Future Party leader, Roman Riley, was protesting against the changes. Unlike Mayor Latimer who I'd heard the other day, Riley sounded properly sympathetic to what ordinary people were going through.

"I have been hungry," he said. *"I know what it's like to be scared when you don't know how to feed your family. This latest round of cuts is an outrageous—"*

Taylor leaned forward and switched the radio off.

I closed my eyes. Maybe the question I should really be asking was: When there were established political parties to act through, what the hell was I doing in the middle of nowhere with a bunch of strangers who called themselves "soldiers" and belonged to a self-styled "army"?

NAT

I kept my headphones in for most of the long drive. It wasn't that I didn't want to talk, more that I was worried someone might see how scared I was. We were traveling across open countryside; there were no street lamps and the road ahead was dark and lined with low stone walls. Only a few, distant pinpricks of light indicated the existence of other buildings. For a few minutes it felt like we were on another planet, out of time. And then Taylor turned from the front passenger seat and I tugged off my headphones.

"We're nearly there," he growled. "We'll walk the last bit of the way, then there's the introduction meeting, then bed."

Beside me Charlie fidgeted uneasily.

"What happens at the introduction meeting?" I asked.

Taylor frowned. "Well, the first thing it involves is you remembering to call me *sir*."

"Okay, *sir*. What does—?"

"We're here." The driver of the car spoke for the first time. He parked the car in a paved area beside a wood.

"Out," Taylor ordered.

I grabbed my backpack, then scrambled out of the car. The trees alongside us were dark, swaying in the breeze. It wasn't raining right now, but the smell of damp was in the air and a chill wind whipped across our faces. I followed Taylor and Charlie into the trees. Behind me, I heard the car drive off. I shivered. It was stupid, but that car felt like our last link with civilization. I focused on Charlie, striding ahead of me. She gave no sign of being anxious.

We trudged on for about fifteen minutes. A light rain started, pattering softly through the bare branches and onto our heads. It stopped as we emerged from the trees into a field. The moon cast a soft glow through the clouds overhead. A single light shone from a stone farmhouse across the field. There was no sign of any farm equipment. In fact, as we got closer to the house, it was obvious that the building was derelict. Remembering the broken-down place we'd met Taylor in before, I drew level with Charlie, then whispered:

"Do you think the EFA has a thing for houses no one else wants?"

She turned and smiled. For the first time, I caught a hint of vulnerability in her eyes. For some reason this made me feel stronger myself.

"It'll be okay," I whispered.

Charlie nodded. A moment later we reached the cobbled yard of the farmhouse. Taylor strode over to the large wooden door. A man, dressed in black from head to toe, his face obscured with a ski mask, stepped out of the shadow. My heart skipped a beat. The man saluted. As he raised his arm, I caught sight of the gun strapped to his side. I stared, transfixed. Was the English Freedom Army going to train us to shoot? That would be illegal, wouldn't it? A shiver snaked down my spine: part fear, part excitement.

"Evening, sir." The man stared straight ahead, not looking at either me or Charlie.

"Evening, soldier," Taylor growled. He pushed open the door.

With a final glance at the man with the pistol, I stepped inside and followed Taylor and Charlie along a bare, stone hallway to an empty kitchen. There was no table. No chairs. Just a row of cupboards along one wall, a stove, and a sink beneath an uncurtained window. Water dripped from the tap, leaving a yellow stain on the chipped, white china beneath. The room was so cold we could see our breath misting in front of our faces.

"Wait here." Taylor turned and left.

Charlie and I looked at each other.

"What do you think?" I asked.

She shook her head. "It's all—"

But before she could finish, the door swung open again. Taylor was back. Two men followed him into the room. They both wore black ski masks, just like the soldier outside. They stood on either side of the door as four boys and two girls—all in their late teens—came in. The newcomers stared at us, unsmiling. I stared back, taking in each face in turn, as Taylor stepped into the middle of the group.

"You are recruits," he said in a low growl. "Which means you have potential. Each one of you has a special skill, some kind of intelligence, some ability the Commander wants to nurture. The next twenty-four hours will prove—to us and to each of you—whether those abilities can be channeled into something useful. The most important thing is that you do exactly what you're told at all times. Operating as a defense force is often dangerous. Solid training and absolute discipline is what will save your life." He paused. "Get some sleep. You'll be up again as soon as it's light."

I checked the time. It was barely ten p.m. Was Taylor serious about us going to bed so early? It was Friday night, for goodness' sake.

"What will we be doing tomorrow?" Charlie asked.

Taylor threw her a savage look. "I didn't ask for questions. You'll find out when you need to. And this is the last warning to you all about calling me and the other soldiers *sir* or *ma'am*. It may seem odd, even stupid, to you, but it's part of the discipline of being a soldier. Now get some sleep. We start training at daybreak."

He marched out of the room. One of the masked soldiers raised a hand. "Girls over here." She was female.

"Boys with me," the other, male, soldier said.

Charlie and I exchanged a glance, then joined our groups and followed the soldiers out of the room.

CHARLIE

I looked around as I reached the door but Nat was already walking through the hallway with the other boys. I followed the masked female soldier and the other two girl recruits up the stairs. The soldier was about my height and stockily built. I hadn't realized that she was female until she'd spoken. I wondered if she would take off her ski mask at all. She led me and the other girls up a short flight of stairs. Paint was peeling on the walls and the only light came from a naked bulb hanging from the ceiling of the landing above us. It was cold as well—it felt colder inside than it had been outside and we could all see our breath in front of our faces.

The soldier ushered us into the first room on the left. It was as bare as everywhere else, with four thin mattresses laid on the floor and a sleeping bag rolled up on the top of each one. The soldier pointed across the room to another door.

"Bathroom through there," she said. "I'll be back in ten minutes for lights-out."

She left the room. The two girl recruits both looked about

seventeen, just a little older than me. One was tall and skinny, with straggly blond hair. The other had mocha-colored skin, a sleek bob, and fierce, dark eyes.

"Hi," she said, with a quick smile and a London accent. "I'm Parveen."

The skinny blond girl gasped. "Is it okay to give our names?" She sounded northern, a reminder of those girls in my Leeds school who'd teased me about my accent.

"'Course it is." Parveen rolled her eyes. "Taylor's not God, you know."

The blond girl looked crushed.

"I think it's okay," I said. "I'm Charlie, by the way. How do you know Taylor?"

Parveen tilted her head to one side. Her chin, slightly pointy like the rest of her sharp little face, stuck out as she considered my question. I kept eye contact, guessing she was assessing me, wondering how much to say.

"He recruited me from the stupid youth club my foster parents made me go to."

"You're in foster care?" the blond girl asked.

"Yeah, why?"

"Nothing, I was just . . . I'm Nancy. I'm adopted."

"Good for you." Parveen's voice took on a sarcastic edge. "What about you, Charlie? What's your dysfunctional family background?"

"Both my parents are dead," I said. "My mum was killed last year. I live with my aunt and uncle."

"Oh, I'm sorry . . . I mean, about your mum," Nancy said, twisting her fingers through her hair.

"Thanks." I smiled at her.

Across the room, Parveen rolled her eyes again and disappeared into the bathroom. She took ages, leaving Nancy and me only a minute each to wash before our masked soldier returned. She ordered us to get into our sleeping bags and warned us not to talk.

I lay down. There was surely no way I would be able to sleep tonight. My pulse was racing, thoughts about what Taylor had said earlier flooding through my brain. The next thing I knew, someone was shaking my arm, a harsh whisper in my ear.

"Charlie, wake up."

I opened my eyes, staring blearily into the gloom. It was even colder than when we'd gone to bed but, apart from my cheeks and nose, I was warm and snug inside my sleeping bag. The masked soldier—had she *slept* in that mask?—was beside me. Seeing I was awake, she turned to Parveen lying on the ground across the room. I raised my head. It was still dark outside. I blinked, trying to shake the sleep out of my eyes.

The soldier strode to the light switch by the door. She flicked it on. The harsh overhead light nearly blinded me.

"Hey," Parveen complained.

"You have five minutes to get dressed. Your pants and boots are by the door." The soldier vanished.

I scrambled out of my sleeping bag and hurried to the bathroom. As I came out again, I could see Nancy and Parveen, both in black combats, struggling to lace up a pair of heavy army boots. I took the remaining pants and boots and put them on. I'd just tugged a sweater on over my T-shirt when the soldier returned. She led us downstairs and outside into the backyard of the house. It had obviously rained during the night as the yard was squelchy with mud. Taylor strode toward us, the boys at his side. I caught Nat's eye right away. He smiled at me and in spite of everything, my stomach did that strange little skip again.

"Rations." Taylor dug into a bag and handed each of us a roll and a bottle of water. "This is all you get for the next three hours, so make it last."

I pocketed the roll, not feeling hungry, and took a small sip of water. Parveen pointed to the loop on the belt of our combats and showed me how to fasten my bottle to it. Before I could even say thank you, Taylor spoke.

"Five-k run, then combat training." He motioned to the two soldiers. "Get into your teams."

A few moments later, I was picked by the male soldier, along with Parveen, Nat and two other boys. We each gave our name then we started running, following the brisk pace set by the soldier. I glanced at Nat as we ran. His face was set in a determined grimace. The other boys we were with looked fit and muscular. They both moved with power and grace. So, I noticed, did Parveen. I focused on keeping my breathing steady, determined not to get left behind.

We did two laps around a muddy field, then followed our soldier into the trees. He took us on a long run through the woods, stopping only once for a drink break. At last we came to a halt in a clearing. It was still dark, though a silvery light was creeping across the sky. Everyone stood panting, trying to get their breath back.

"In pairs," the soldier ordered. "You. With me." He spun Nat around to face him. This left me with little choice but to partner up with Parveen. We eyed each other warily as the soldier showed us how to attack—and block attacks—by keeping our balance and tipping our opponent off theirs.

"You might be smaller than the enemy," he barked, "but if you put the entire weight of your body behind each strike, that's a fearsome weapon in itself."

Parveen and I dodged and hit at each other for ten minutes as the soldier circled us, watching carefully. We were fairly evenly matched. I was stronger and more precise but Parveen was undeniably faster than me, whipping her arm up to stop my blows before I was even aware of her moving. I redoubled my efforts, concentrating hard. Despite my suspicion of the EFA—not to mention my growing hunger—it felt good to be alive in the crisp morning air. The sun was edging over the horizon now, casting a soft orange glow through the branches of the trees above our heads. And I liked being taught how to fight properly. It made me feel strong, like I was getting ready to avenge Mum's death properly, not just dream about it.

Across the clearing, Nat was working hard too. Sweat beaded on his forehead as he countered the thrusts and punches of his own opponent. The masked soldier was now partnering someone else, so Nat was fighting a tall, thickset boy with a crew cut and biceps that bulged under his T-shirt. We had all removed our long-sleeved tops by this point—and no one had any food or water left.

After an hour or so of combat training, our male soldier led us through the woods again. I had no idea how well I'd done as a fighter. The soldier hadn't singled me out for criticism, but then he hadn't praised me either. The only person he'd actually complimented was Parveen, for a stylish move she'd made earlier: ducking sideways to avoid a full-body thrust from me.

Taylor was waiting for us at what appeared to be some kind of shooting range. A log lay on its side in front of a row of trees, a series of targets rising up like signposts opposite. Was he really going to teach us to shoot? Fighting was one thing, but guns were another. Mum and Karen had always been totally anti guns, but if we were going to get back at the League of Iron we needed access to the same weapons they might use.

"Okay, now I'm not supposed to tell you this but from the preliminary trials, you guys are the elite of the young people we've recruited so far," Taylor said, his green eyes hard and serious. "There are five of you here and I'll be handpicking four to be in my own active cell. That means you *will* be sent into dangerous situations and you *will* have to defend yourselves."

I glanced around the group. Parveen's eyes were shining. All the boys, including Nat, looked thrilled that Taylor had told them they were an elite group. I turned back to Taylor, suddenly full of mistrust again. He couldn't really know how good any of us were at this point. He was surely just trying to make us feel special so we'd do what he said.

"We use the Glock 26 semiautomatic," Taylor said, holding up a gun.

That looked like it packed serious firepower. It struck me that if I came face to face with whoever killed Mum, I would shoot them without hesitation. At least I thought I would. The hairs on the back of my neck prickled.

Taylor put down his gun. "Has anyone here handled a semi-automatic before?" he demanded.

No one spoke.

"Any sort of gun?"

Only the huge biceps guy put up his hand. "I've been to a firing range a few times."

"Right, George, over here."

The big guy, George, swaggered over to Taylor, who picked up the Glock and placed it in his hand. Taylor spent a moment adjusting first George's stance, then his grip. He handed around sets of ear protectors, waited until everyone had placed them over their ears, then told George to shoot. He hit the middle of the target, first time.

A soft, impressed murmur ran around the group.

Taylor nodded. "Good, but firing the gun isn't as important as understanding how to use it." He turned to me. "You. Over here."

My heart raced as I walked up to him. Taylor handed me another pistol from the pile. It was cold in my hands and heavier than I was expecting. "Hold it like this." He placed my hand over the top of the gun, my fingers reaching around the barrel to rest lightly on the trigger. "I'll teach you to load and shoot in a minute. But most of the time convincing the enemy you're *prepared* to shoot is more important. We don't want to hurt people unnecessarily. But if you're going into a dangerous situation, you might need to make people believe you *would* shoot. It could save lives, including your own."

I stared at him. Did he want me to pretend to threaten him?

Taylor pointed to the log at his feet. "Tell me you'll shoot me if I don't step behind that. Go."

I looked into his green eyes. He was totally confident, intimidating as hell. I gritted my teeth.

"*Go,*" Taylor repeated.

I closed my eyes for a second, drawing in a deep breath, then I planted my feet firmly against the damp earth and raised the gun.

NAT

A cool breeze whipped across my face. Charlie raised her arm, the gun in her hand pointing directly at Taylor's forehead.

"Behind the log," she demanded. "Move."

I held my breath. Taylor stared impassively back at her.

Charlie stood, steady as a rock, her gaze unflinching. "I said move." Her expression was icy.

I realized my mouth was gaping open and closed it quickly. The wind was up, swirling twigs and leaves around our feet. The atmosphere in the clearing was tense.

Another beat passed, then Taylor lowered his gaze and stepped over the log. Charlie followed him with the gun. She was utterly focused, completely terrifying. A shiver ran down my spine. I was certain that Charlie would be capable of pulling the trigger should the need arise.

And equally certain that I would not.

"Very good." Taylor nodded his acknowledgment. "I believed you."

"So did I," said George with a grin. "Man, you were scary." He looked at me with his eyebrows raised. "You know this chick?"

"Sure he knows me." Now Charlie was pointing the gun at George. "Who asked *you* about it?"

George blinked rapidly, then put his hands in the air. "You got me, baby." He spoke in a high, silly voice, his hands over his heart. Everyone apart from Taylor and me laughed.

"This is serious," Taylor snapped, lowering Charlie's arm with his hand. "The secret to making the enemy believe you'll shoot is to believe it yourself, that you will shoot if you have to. You need to make your movements definite and precise and to take all emotion out of your voice."

"What about anger?" Parveen asked. "Surely you need to show anger?"

"Only if it's cold and hard," Taylor explained. "No hysterics. No passion. Nothing weak. Just like Charlie."

We each took a turn at threatening the others, forcing them to move. After a few tries it was obvious that no one else was as good as Charlie. George looked threatening, but couldn't get the right emphasis into his voice, while Parveen grew too shrill as she shouted at me to kneel on the ground. I stared back at the gun she was waving in my face. Taylor had been right. Getting all emotional made you sound less powerful. I tried to remember this when it was my turn, but all I could think was that the whole situation was fake and that there was no way I could ever shoot anyone anyway.

I wondered if Lucas had ever taken part in a training session like this?. I would have given anything to know how he had felt about using guns and learning armed combat. I imagined that he had been really good at it.

I badly wanted to be good at it too.

Taylor coached us on gun control and safety procedures for ages before actually explaining how to fire the pistols. I turned out to be the best shot after George. Charlie wasn't bad, nor was Parveen, both getting close to the target on all their attempts, but the other guy missed by miles.

At the end of the session, Taylor took us on a long run back to the farmhouse. A trestle table and two benches had been set in the middle of the kitchen and two masked soldiers served us plates of stew for our lunch. I fell on the food. I couldn't remember ever being hungrier—or colder—in my life. As I ate my way through two large helpings I talked to George, who sat next to me. He told me he lived in south London with his mum and three brothers. Like Lucas, he had once been a big fan of Roman Riley.

"I saw him at a rally," he said, his eyes lighting up. "He was amazing. I just wish he'd go further, you know? Riley really understands what people are going through."

I nodded. There was something about George that reminded me of Lucas. It wasn't just his admiration for Riley and his athletic build—it was also that air of relaxed enthusiasm that Lucas had exuded. Girls had loved it. I could see Parveen and Charlie looking in George's direction several times, laughing as he joked.

Lucas had been like that, full of gentle, flirty teasing—and always with a different girl. He used to tell me that one day soon it would be the same for me, but somehow I doubted that was true.

Toward the end of the meal George leaned over and asked quietly:

"So is Charlie your girlfriend?" The way he said it made it clear he was interested in her himself.

My stomach tied itself into a hot, jealous knot. "Nah, buddy," I said with a nonchalant shrug. "Knock yourself out."

After the meal, Taylor gave us a fifteen-minute break, during which time we were allowed to check our phones. As secrecy was so important, Taylor made it clear that anybody who suspected their parents or guardians were close to seeing through their cover stories should come to him immediately. Much to my relief, there were no calls or texts to deal with from Mum or Dad or Jas.

Afterward, we went outside, into the woods, for another run and a second combat session. I was paired with a boy from a different group. He was wiry but nowhere near as quick as I was and far easier to deal with than George this morning.

By the time we arrived back at the farmhouse again it was dark. This time I wasn't just hungry and cold, but also completely exhausted. We were given more food, then told we had half an hour to relax.

We were shown into a living room with couches, lamps with nice shades, and a fire in the fireplace. George and the wiry boy from combat training both made a beeline for Charlie but, before anyone could speak, Taylor cleared his throat.

"So far we've monitored you closely and all you know about

each other are first names but that can't last and we don't want it to, so we're dividing you into groups now." He reeled off a series of names. "Will those people please go outside now?" The others trooped off, leaving me, Charlie, George, and Parveen. Taylor waited until they were gone, then turned to the four of us.

"The others were good and will be given roles in support cells," he said. "But you four are the best. You'll be joining me in an elite active cell."

"What does that mean exactly?" Parveen asked. She was standing behind the sofa, in front of the fireplace and the unframed mirror above it.

"Being part of an active cell means that you will be properly trained over the coming weeks and months," Taylor explained. "In time we *will* be going after the League of Iron. I can let you know now that, thanks to information we recently received"—he looked, pointedly, at me and Charlie—"we have some preliminary details about the League of Iron's next campaign." He paused. "We still need more information, but I am confident that we *will* stop them." He glanced at Charlie and me again. "Hopefully, we can stop them forever."

The atmosphere tensed. I glanced at Charlie. She was on the sofa next to George, her eyes sparkling with delight. I sank back into my armchair. Lucas had once been put into an active cell too. Now I really was following in his footsteps.

Taylor held up his hand, the five fingers spread. "The four of you—plus me. That's five members." He closed his hand into a fist. "Five members. One cell."

I stared at his fist, feeling myself fill with pride.

"Okay." Taylor lowered his arm. "You have about twenty more minutes to relax and get to know each other before going upstairs to the bedrooms and lights-out. We have an early start back to London in the morning."

He walked out. Charlie and George started talking. I looked across the room to where Parveen was studying her face in the mirror on the wall. It was a huge mirror for what was really quite a small room. I peered closer. The glass was slightly dark and completely unframed. It didn't fit with the home-style décor in the rest of the room at all. Suspicions crowded my head. Was it a two-way mirror? Was there someone on the other side watching us?

I looked down at my lap, not wanting to give my thoughts away, then glanced over at Charlie. I was hoping to catch her eye, but she was laughing at something George had just said. She hadn't noticed the mirror. None of the others had. Or maybe I was wrong. Maybe it was just a regular looking glass. I stood up. I had to find out.

I crossed the room and slipped outside, into the hallway. Pulse racing, I put my hand on the doorknob of the room next door.

Wait. If I just barged in and people were there, Taylor would be angry. I needed an excuse, like maybe saying I was looking for the bathroom. As I hesitated, voices sounded from inside the room. Then footsteps. I backed away from the door. There was an empty room across the hall, the door open. I scurried inside. This room was dark and as bare as most of the others, just floorboards and plaster walls, with a row of cupboards along one wall.

I peered through the crack in the door. Two masked soldiers were emerging into the hallway. One pointed to the room where I was hiding. "See if the boy's in there," he ordered.

So they'd noticed I was missing already. Which meant it *must* be a two-way mirror. Blood thundered in my ears so loudly the soldier would surely hear. I raced over to the nearest cupboard and slid inside, pulling the door after me.

Footsteps sounded in the room. Then a voice.

"The boy's not here," said one of the soldiers.

His footsteps faded away and I crept out of the cupboard. My legs shook as I crept over to the door and peered out into the hallway again. The door to the room with the two-way mirror was open. Taylor was standing just outside it with one of the two masked soldiers. He looked furious.

"You were supposed to be on duty, monitoring the recruits, not letting one of them slip outside without even noticing. And why wasn't the room locked anyway?" he shouted.

"Sorry, sir. I thought it was, sir," the soldier replied.

"Well lock it now," Taylor snarled.

The soldier did as he was told, then Taylor ordered him to check upstairs. As the soldier disappeared from view, Taylor stood back. Another man, this one wearing a dark suit, was approaching in the hallway. I couldn't see his face.

"The situation's under control, Commander," Taylor said. "We'll find Nat and hold him until you're gone."

Goose bumps flared along my arms. The Commander was the head of the English Freedom Army. And he was *here, now,* just a few feet away from me. I strained my eyes, trying to get a good look at the man's face. Taylor was totally blocking my view though I could just make out the low rumble of the Commander's voice. Despite the cold, a bead of sweat trickled down my neck.

Taylor spoke into his phone again, then turned back to the Commander. "No sign of Nat upstairs yet, sir. But he can't be outside. No windows are broken and the door's still locked." He paused. "There's no need for you to wait, sir, if you've finished with your meeting. Shall I get them to bring the car around? We will find Nat, sir. And there's no problem. He hasn't seen you."

Taylor shifted sideways as he spoke, revealing the Commander's face at last.

I saw who it was. My breath caught in my throat. The Commander turned toward the room I was hiding in, as if sensing my presence. He looked straight at the spot where I was crouching behind the door, then raised his arm and pointed.

"I think, Taylor, that you'll find Nat in that room," he said, the slow smile I had seen a thousand times on TV creeping across his face. "I imagine he's watching us right now, in fact."

CHARLIE

Where was Nat? I'd seen him leaving the room about ten minutes ago and assumed he was just going to the bathroom, but he still wasn't back.

George was chatting away at me and Parveen, but I was barely listening anymore. My eyes were on the door, waiting for Nat to return.

But he didn't come.

Another minute passed and I turned to George. "Where d'you think Nat's gone?"

George shrugged. He was in the middle of some story about getting kicked out of his school, but I was too worried about Nat to listen. I went over to the door and pulled at the handle. It didn't open. We were locked in.

"Guys, look!" I rattled the doorknob, then put my ear to the door. I could hear muffled voices, but not who was speaking or what they were saying.

"Hey!" I banged on the door. "Let us out!"

Parveen and George rushed over. They started hammering

against the door too. We yelled our heads off for about ten seconds, then we heard Taylor's voice outside.

"It's just security," he said. "For your own safety. It won't last long."

"Where's Nat, sir?" I asked.

"He'll be back soon," Taylor said.

"When can we leave the room, sir?" Parveen added.

But Taylor had already gone.

The three of us went back to the sofa. George tried to resume our conversation, but all I could think about was Nat. Our phones were all still up in the bedroom so I had absolutely no way of contacting him. Another fifteen minutes passed. I banged on the door several times, but no one came. At last Taylor opened up.

"Security lockdown's over. Go upstairs," Taylor snapped in a voice that made it clear he didn't want to have to deal with any more questions.

"Where's Nat?" I demanded. "If this lockdown or whatever is over, why isn't he back?"

Taylor glared at me.

"Where's Nat, *sir*?"

"Special training," he said.

I stared into his green eyes. Was that true? Taylor's expression was unreadable. He led us up the stairs to the second floor. There was still no sign of Nat anywhere. Taylor led us to a different room from the one we'd slept in last night. Four mattresses were laid on the floor, two on either side of the door. "Lights out in ten. Nobody leaves their mattress except to go to the bathroom. Is that clear?"

"Yes, sir," we chorused.

As soon as Taylor had gone, I peered outside. There were three other rooms off the landing. I crept over and opened the first two doors in turn. The rooms beyond were all empty.

"Get back here," Parveen hissed from the doorway.

"You gonna make me?" I hissed back.

We glared at each other for a moment, then Parveen shrugged and turned away. I checked the next room. Also empty, though more mattresses and sleeping bag rolls were lined against one wall. I went back into the shared room, where Parveen was scowling at me from her mattress. I could hear George whistling in the bathroom. I told myself Nat was about to walk in, but he didn't. As soon as Taylor reappeared I sprang up.

"What's happened to Nat, sir?" I said, feeling sure now that something was very wrong. "Is he okay?"

Taylor studied me for a second, then he folded his arms.

"Who am I, Charlie?"

"You're Taylor, you're a soldier in the EFA."

Taylor pursed his lips. "First and foremost I am your cell leader," he said. "Your captain. Which means *nothing* is more important to me than your life and theirs." He jerked his thumb over his shoulder to indicate Parveen and George, who were watching us with interest. "I realize you are young and untrained and that Nat is your friend and that everything we do seems strange to you right now, but you have to learn to trust me." He paused. "Without trust, we've got nothing. Now, what did I say about Nat before?"

"You said that he was doing special training, sir," I said.

"Exactly." Taylor took a step away from me. "I'm sure you'll do some at some point too. Nat will be back when he's back. For the time being, you need to trust that I have his best interests at heart and that he is absolutely fine." He walked to the door. "Now go to sleep, you'll be up again in five hours." And he switched the light out and left.

I got into my sleeping bag, which was on the floor next to Parveen's. She and George, lying on his own mattress across the room, were talking in low voices: stuff about the training earlier and what we might be expected to do next. I barely listened. All my thoughts were on Nat. It was all very well Taylor insisting I trust him. Surely cell members weren't supposed to have secrets from one another. So why couldn't we be told what this special training of Nat's involved?

Apart from my boots I was still fully clothed under the covers. The sleeping bag was good quality and my body, which had been cold for hours, soon warmed up. I reached for my phone and sent Nat a text. A second later, I heard his phone vibrating as it received the message. It was across the room, under his mattress. I didn't know whether the fact that he didn't have his phone with him was a good or a bad sign. I checked my own phone again. At least I had no missed calls or texts from either Gail or Aunt Karen.

I lay still, listening out for noises outside. Footsteps passed on the landing a couple of times but other than that, nothing. George and Parveen stopped talking after about five minutes. Soon after that I could hear them breathing steadily. They were asleep. It wasn't surprising. We were all exhausted. But there was no way I could sleep myself.

I had to know what had happened to Nat.

I waited another twenty minutes, until I was sure George and Parveen were both deeply asleep. I wriggled out of my sleeping bag and tiptoed to the door. I was half-expecting it to be locked, but it opened with a light creak. I hesitated, listening out for voices. I could hear the low mumble of a conversation from the other bedroom across the landing. A light shone under the door. I crept over and put my ear against the rough, cold wood. I couldn't be certain, but it sounded like two of the masked soldiers we'd been trained by earlier. Definitely not Nat.

I headed for the stairs. He had to be on the ground floor. That's if he was still here at all. I crept down each step, treading as lightly as I could. The floor was cold under my feet, my thin socks providing little protection from the tiles on the floor. I shivered as I edged along the hallway, past the room we'd been left in earlier, past the kitchen. All the doors were open, all the rooms empty.

Where the hell was he? The only light came from outside—a lamp above the front door, I was guessing. As I headed to the back of the house it grew darker indoors. I felt my way along the wall. I'd lost my bearings, but I must surely have checked out every single room in the place by now. And then I came to another door. It was ajar, the room beyond shrouded in darkness. I crept inside and stood still for a second, letting my eyes adjust to the gloom. I was in some kind of office-*cum*-storage room. Crates and bottles lined one wall and there was a desk in front of the window.

I glanced at a row of large diesel cans on the floor.

I had no idea why the EFA would keep diesel in an office, but it wasn't helping me find Nat. I turned around, ready to go back into the hallway. Maybe I'd missed a room somewhere?

And then a footstep sounded by the door and a bright light shone in my eyes.

NAT

I darted away from the door as the Commander walked into the room and switched on the light. He was slighter and shorter than I had expected from seeing him on TV, with dark hair, thinning at the sides, and tanned, smooth skin. He stared at me without speaking. His dark eyes were like magnets, leaving me trapped in their gaze.

"Nat Holloway, it's a pleasure to meet you." The Commander's voice was richer and deeper than it sounded on TV. He held out his arm. I shook his hand, still too shocked to speak.

The Commander smiled. "I assume from the look on your face that you've recognized me, but I like a proper introduction." He paused. "I'm Roman Riley."

I nodded, a million thoughts hurtling around my head. Riley had been Lucas's hero. He was the most charismatic and popular politician in the country, leader of the Future Party, an MP in Parliament and totally against the Government's austerity program.

"You're the *Commander?*" I stammered, finding my voice at last.

Roman Riley raised an eyebrow. There was an incredible

stillness about him, so that each tiny movement he made drew the eye. He watched me carefully.

"I'm Commander-in-Chief of the English Freedom Army, yes." He paused. "I never had the pleasure of meeting your brother but I understand that he was a hero. I'm honored that you have decided to join us too."

A masked soldier appeared in the doorway. "Your car's ready, sir," he said.

"I think I'm going to spend a little time talking with Nat first," Riley said. He hadn't taken his eyes off my face. "I'd like to hear his thoughts, answer any questions he might have."

"Yes, sir."

The soldier left and Riley led me through the hallway and into the kitchen. Another masked soldier was pouring a glass of water at the sink. He jumped to attention as we walked in. Riley saluted him and smiled.

"At ease, soldier," he said. "Door, please."

The soldier sped across the kitchen and tugged at the handle of what I assumed was a cupboard. However, instead of shelves loaded with plates and bowls, the door opened onto a set of narrow stone steps. The soldier reached along the wall and flicked on a light. Then he stood back, holding the door open as Riley strode across the room.

I followed, still feeling completely bewildered.

"Mind these steps, Nat," Riley said. "They're very worn and extremely slippery."

"Yes, sir." The "sir" was out of my mouth before I'd known I was going to say it. I followed Riley down the stairs. Here I was, with one of the best-known faces in the country. My heart raced with fear—and excitement.

The stairs led to a narrow hallway. Riley directed me into a basement room. The walls were covered with maps and a bank of computers stood along a line of tables. A lone masked soldier sat with his feet up at one of the tables. He jumped to his feet as Riley came in, almost knocking over his chair.

"At ease, soldier," Riley said. "We'd like the room, please."

"Of course, sir. Yes, sir." The soldier rushed out.

As his footsteps echoed away up the stone steps, Riley led me to two plastic chairs in the corner of the room. I looked around, trying to take everything in.

"Is this where you monitor what's going on with all the terrorist groups?" I asked.

"Taylor said you were smart," Riley said, turning a chair to face the wall. "Please sit here, Nat. I'm afraid I can't let you look at anything in detail. That's for your own safety. We run a lot of operations from here and I don't want anything compromised."

I forced my gaze back to Riley as I took the seat. Riley drew the other plastic chair up and sat down opposite. "Questions?"

"Is this place the EFA's headquarters?"

"No," Riley said. "HQ is in London, this is just one of our operations centers. We have three in different parts of the country and we're hoping to set up another three over the next six months."

I shook my head. "I don't get it. You're a politician, what are you doing setting up an *army*?"

"I am a politician, that's true, but I used to be a soldier, like my father. He was killed before I was born and I grew up with my mother in terrible poverty until I was seven when she married a successful businessman who gave us both money and opportunities beyond our dreams." He paused. "All of this is well documented, Nat. But what the media have never reported, because I have never told them, is that my stepfather was cruel. He beat me when I disobeyed him, which I did frequently, and told me repeatedly I would never amount to anything. My mother protected me as best she could, but she died of cancer when I was seventeen, just a little older than you are now, and I left his house. I never went back."

I nodded. "So how . . . ?"

"I worked my way through various jobs," Riley went on. "I joined the army for a while, then left again once I'd done my contracted time. Through my twenties I grew increasingly frustrated with the way power was lodged in the hands of a few very self-serving people in this country. There was no party I wanted to join, so, on my thirtieth birthday, I decided to establish the Future Party to fight for the rights and needs of the poor and the downtrodden, for a better future. That was three years ago. When the latest banking disaster happened eighteen months ago we were already establishing a solid base. But since then, as you know, the party has gone from strength to strength and we now have ten MPs in Parliament." He paused. "But political parties are limited in what they can achieve, the police force is riddled with corruption, and extremist violence is increasing every day. A year ago I saw something needed to be done to protect people, but that it would have to be done secretly. I already knew Taylor and a few others who shared my views. Between us, over the past twelve months, we have recruited a hundred or so young men and women, your brother among them, to serve their country by defeating the extreme groups."

"Why does it have to be secret?" I asked, though I was sure I already knew the answer.

"Because politicians are supposed to work within the law and the more successful you are in politics, the more closely the media watch you. We adopted a cell structure to keep our actions secure. Most of our soldiers have no idea that I am their Commander. If I'm honest, I'm rather impressed that you have stumbled upon the truth after just one day."

Riley sat back and folded his arms. His presence, I realized, had changed the atmosphere even in this empty room. The air around us felt charged.

"But the whole point of the EFA is to *stop* illegal violence."

"That's right. We only ever fight in self-defense but many of our activities, from surveillance to counterattacks against known terror-ists, are outside the law. That's the real world, Nat." Riley smiled sadly. "I know you have been brought up to think that adults have all the answers, that our elected representatives carry out our wishes, that democracy works, but none of these things are true. And the EFA is small and poorly funded, so sometimes we need to use fists and threats and even guns. Sometimes, like you yourself said, you have to be prepared to do anything to protect your family, your country. Sometimes carefully targeted force is the only way."

I sat very still, taking in everything Riley had said. The Commander sat still too, watching me with those sharp, compassionate eyes of his. Neither of us spoke. The silence stretched out like an ocean around us. Minutes passed. It struck me that no adult in my life had ever stopped what they were doing and waited like this for me. After a while, I looked up. Riley opened his arms—as if to ask if I had any more questions. There was a tiny open-hand tattoo on the inside of his wrist—the same tattoo I had seen on Lucas and Taylor. I suddenly realized what the hand shape, with its five fingers, stood for.

"Five members, one cell," I murmured.

Riley followed my gaze to the tattoo. "Also 'many people, one cause.'" He made his hand into a fist. "My focus is on young people, because it's their future and right now the older generations around the world are taking it away from them with their greed and their selfishness. But I believe in a better England and I'm prepared to give my life . . . to risk everything, like you said in that League of Iron meeting you went to, to ensure the future is better than the past."

I looked down at my lap. My ambitions weren't anywhere near as noble.

"I just want to get back at the League of Iron," I said. "I want to make sure they can't blow anyone else up."

Riley leaned forward, listening intently. Then he nodded. "So do I."

He waited for me to speak. Another minute ticked past. It

was strange. I felt I was being listened to even though I wasn't speaking, as if Riley were giving me enough time to process what I had heard. At last I shifted in my chair, sitting more upright. I was ready.

"Are you with us, Nat?" Riley stood, his head slightly bowed, as if to honor the solemnity of my decision.

I didn't hesitate. I stood up too, trying to copy the slow, focused way Riley moved. No wonder Lucas had looked up to him. He was amazing, inspiring, everything everyone had ever said.

"Yes, sir," I said. "I'm with you."

CHARLIE

The light in my eyes dipped. Taylor stood in the doorway, a flashlight in his hand.

"What the hell are you doing here?" he demanded.

"Looking for Nat, seeing as nobody will tell me where he is."

Taylor swore. He paced across the room, stopping right in front of me. For a second I thought he might hit me. I flinched, but Taylor's hands stayed at his sides.

"Do you know why I picked you for my cell, Charlie?" he said. His voice was soft, but all the more menacing for that.

"I just want to know where—"

"The others all have skills. They're good shots and good fighters. Nat is smart, George is strong, Parveen is daring. They all have focus and grit. But you, Charlie, you have something much more rare."

I stared up at him.

"But this thing you have, if you don't control it, makes you a liability as much as an asset." He paused. "I already told you that Nat was attending a special training session. He is safe. He will be done soon, back in the bedroom with everyone else. Now, either you believe me and go back to bed, or you insist on defying me and you're out of the EFA. One of my soldiers can drive you home. It's your choice." He stood back, folding his arms.

"Please may I see Nat now, sir?" I said quickly, hoping that deference might get through to Taylor in a way that my disobedience clearly hadn't.

Some hope.

"No," he said, shortly. "Now, you haven't answered my question. Will you stay and obey? Or will you leave?"

What choice did I have? I still didn't trust Taylor or the EFA. It was odd that Nat had been taken off on his own but if I went home now I wouldn't know if he really was okay. And I would also miss my best chance to take revenge on the League of Iron.

"I'll stay, sir."

"Good." Taylor peered out into the hallway. "Okay, let's go. Back upstairs."

I followed him past the kitchen and living room we'd been in before.

"What did you mean about me having something the others don't have?" I asked as we climbed the stairs.

Taylor reached the landing. He turned as I joined him. I could only just make out the outline of his narrow face in the dim light.

"You don't care what people think of you, Charlie," he said quietly. "Now go to bed."

I crept into my room, going over his words. Was it true that I didn't care about other people's opinions?

You care what Nat thinks.

I snuggled down into my sleeping bag, flexing my toes to try to warm up my frozen feet. Parveen and George were both still asleep on their mattresses on either side of the door.

I lay awake, listening. If Taylor had been telling the truth, Nat should be back any moment. Sure enough, after another few minutes, footsteps padded across the landing. The door opened and Nat tiptoed in. He was alone. He didn't look around as he crept to the only free sleeping bag, across the room from mine.

I sat up. "Nat?"

He looked around. Light from outside shone in through the curtainless window, highlighting the dark of his hair and the slope of his nose. He looked breathtakingly handsome.

"Where've you been?" I whispered.

Nat sat down on his mattress and pulled the sleeping bag over him. "I can't tell you," he whispered back.

It felt like a slap in the face. Here I was, awake and worrying, even snooping, risking Taylor's wrath to find out if Nat was okay—and he was shutting me out.

"Is it a mission?" I persisted.

Nat hesitated. "Not exactly," he said. "But don't worry, they're going to let us get back at the League of Iron. You'll get your chance."

He meant for revenge.

That was the only reason he thought I was here.

Well, it was, wasn't it?

"Good," I said, burrowing down into my own sleeping bag.

"Night." Nat turned on his side, away from me. I watched his still body, the edge of the sleeping bag rising and falling with his breath. A few minutes later he was asleep too.

I stayed awake for a long time. I might be in a room with three other people and, together with Taylor, part of a new five-strong cell. But I had never felt more alone in my life.

The hand shaking me was rough and firm.

"What?" I moaned.

"Get up." It was Parveen.

I opened my eyes. She was peering down at me, scowling. "Time to get outta here, baby," she said, making a face. "Get a move on. The rest of us are ready."

I glanced around. Nat and George were standing by the door, rolling up their sleeping bags. It was still dark outside, though lighter than when I'd fallen asleep.

"Come on, girl." Parveen gave me another prod. "Taylor was here two minutes ago. He's expecting us downstairs in three."

I forced myself out of the sleeping bag. I felt terrible, thick with sleep and stiff from sleeping on the thin mattress. I rushed to the bathroom, but there was no mirror and I had no chance to do more than splash water on my face before Taylor was calling out my name and I had to run back to the bedroom. Nat was rolling up my sleeping bag. I shot him a grateful glance as I gathered my backpack and followed the others downstairs.

Outside, the cold air whipped across my face. Suddenly I felt wide-awake. A masked soldier appeared with a flask of tea for Taylor. I eyed it thirstily. A moment later another soldier handed him a bag. Taylor passed the flask and bag to George. "You can share these once we're in the car."

George peered into the bag. "Mmn, rolls," he said.

"Gimme," Parveen insisted.

"Yeah, me too," Nat added.

"Can't you wait?" I meant the words to come out in a jokey way, but they sounded rude and harsh, even to my own ears. "You're like little kids."

Parveen snapped at me to shut up. Nat said nothing, but his face hardened. We walked through the woods in silence. Of course once we were inside the car with Taylor, the tension eased, but that was because Taylor got everyone chatting away, talking about their family situations and work aspirations. I said the least. I knew that Taylor was just trying to get us to bond into the cell unit he had talked about before. The others grew very silent when Nat told them about Lucas being left in a coma. I didn't mention Mum. Neither Taylor nor Nat brought her up either, for which I was grateful.

I fell asleep after an hour or so, waking with a jolt as Taylor stopped the car to let out Parveen. Nat and I were next. We gave the EFA oath: *For blood and soil, strength and honor, hope and sacrifice* and took the fresh disposable phones that Taylor handed us with a final warning not to tell anyone where we had been. Taylor said he'd be in touch soon and that our regular training would begin in a few days.

It was overcast and chilly as Nat and I headed along the pavement. A church bell was ringing nearby. I checked the time. It wasn't even eleven a.m. I knew that when we got to the end of the road, Nat would take a left while I needed to turn right to get to Gail and Brian's. He had barely said three words to me the whole journey home and I didn't want to say good-bye to him without making things better between us.

"I'm sorry if I sounded rude earlier," I said. "I was just worried about you last night."

Nat stopped walking. "Were you?" He sounded genuinely surprised.

"Yes," I said. "I came looking for you after everyone else went to bed."

"You did?"

"Yes, and I found this random room with cans of diesel fuel and other stuff. Then Taylor found me."

Nat grinned. "I bet he was furious."

"He was." I smiled back. "So, can you really not tell me why you got taken off on your own? What the 'special training' you did was about?"

Nat hesitated. "I wish I could." He moved closer. "Honestly, Charlie, but I gave my word and he . . . it . . . the English Freedom Army *needs* to keep stuff secret. There are good reasons and I'd be breaking my promise if I told you." He frowned. "Do you understand?"

I gazed up at him, surprised. He'd been so distant all the way home I'd convinced myself he saw me only as a partner in crime in his desire for revenge on the League of Iron. Yet he was looking at me now with real concern. My throat tightened and my stomach cartwheeled. It was more than the shape of his face and that soft yet tough expression in his blue eyes. There was something inside Nat that echoed inside me. I had never felt anything like it before.

"I'm scared of trusting the EFA." The words blurted out of me before I could stop them. My cheeks burned with embarrassment. Why had I said that?

Nat took my hand. His fingers felt strong and warm. "I'm scared too," he whispered. "But it will be worth it to get back at the League for what they did to Lucas and your mum. And to stop them hurting anyone else."

Up ahead, traffic was roaring along the main road. The church bells were still ringing. The sun was high and bright in a clear sky, the air crisp and cold.

Nat and I stared at each other. Suddenly I very much wanted to be more to him than just his partner in crime. My stomach flipped over and over as he moved closer and I tilted my face up to his.

And we kissed.

NAT

I drew back from the kiss. What the hell was I doing? One minute I'd been walking along, thinking how rude Charlie was, the next I was standing in front of her, unable to stop myself from kissing her.

"Nat?"

I looked away. This was all wrong.

"Nat, what is it?"

I forced myself to look at her. She was gazing up at me, her fierce eyes softer than I'd ever seen them. Man, she looked more beautiful than ever. All I wanted was to kiss her again. But I couldn't and it was impossible to explain why.

"I'm sorry," I mumbled. "Look, we shouldn't do this. We're in a cell together, we need to . . . not . . . just not . . ."

"It's cool," Charlie said. "It was a stupid idea."

"No." My heart was racing. "No, not stupid, just . . ."

"Impractical?"

I laughed, then pulled away. "Right."

We walked to the end of the road. I didn't look at her properly as we said good-bye, just mumbled something about seeing her at school tomorrow.

I hurried home. I was totally right to keep my distance, wasn't I? There were plenty of other girls I could hook up with and I needed to keep a clear head in order to get back at the League of Iron. I was going to be a soldier, fighting in my brother's place, like Roman Riley had said. Soldiers had girls, but never ones they really cared about.

That had been Lucas's way and it was going to be mine, too.

I avoided Charlie for the next couple of days at school. Mum and Dad both asked me if I'd had a good time over the weekend but, as neither of them really listened to my answer, it was easy to lie to them. It struck me that I would have found it much harder to have lied to Riley. He had an air about him that made you *want* to tell him the truth. Mum seemed in a good mood when she got in on Monday evening, which was nice, until it turned out she was happy only because she'd been visiting the chapel in the hospital and was now certain that if she prayed every day, sooner or later God would bring Lucas out of his coma. I said nothing, but inside I despaired. What planet was Mum on? If medical science couldn't cure Lucas, how on earth was prayer going to help?

Every night when I closed my eyes, images of Charlie's face kept floating into my head. I didn't want to think about her. Or our kiss.

On Wednesday, Taylor sent a text giving a time and a place

for a meeting the following evening in a dirty basement on a rundown side street in Archway. Charlie and I talked only about superficial school stuff on the way. Taylor, George, and Parveen were already there when we arrived. I noticed George's eyes light up when Charlie walked into the room. A shard of jealousy lodged itself in my chest. I tried to ignore it.

Taylor spent the next two hours drilling us on combat training. In both cases George and I worked together, separately from the two girls. The session ended at eight p.m. sharp when Charlie and I traveled home saying as little to each other as we had on the way there. Presumably, that was how it was going to be from now on. I told myself I was relieved about this.

There was another training meeting that Saturday afternoon, then a break for Christmas, with sessions beginning again on the first week of January. The five of us soon settled into a routine of three meet-ups a week. Taylor spent several evenings focusing on "exit techniques" or, as Charlie put it, "ways of getting out of trouble."

The simplest of these outlined ways in which we could call in code for help.

"If you can't use words, then you need a distress signal that your cell members will recognize," Taylor explained. He taught us the Morse Code "SOS" signal—a series of taps or light flashes: three short, three long, three short.

After learning basic Morse code we set about studying techniques for slipping and loosening knots. Only Par was any good at that. Next, Taylor showed us how to release a range of door locks using just a credit card or the flat side of a knife. I was use-less at it, but Charlie got the knack right away.

"It's all in the pressure and the angle," she explained.

I shook my head, hoping I would never have to open a door that way.

The sessions were, for the most part, good-humored, though intense. And, whatever else Taylor focused on, he always made sure we spent at least thirty minutes on hand-to-hand fighting. By the middle of February the four of us knew how to disarm an opponent in just three moves (a sidestep, a punch to the guts, and a fast chop to the wrist), then kick his legs from under him. George—and of course Taylor—were still stronger than the rest of us but if we got our balance right and put our body weight behind the moves, we were good fighters.

Taylor did his best to answer our questions too. I noticed that while George was mostly interested in fighting techniques, Parveen and, recently, Charlie wanted to understand more about the political system we were living in.

"It's dog eat dog," Taylor would say with a sigh. "The police cover up for the politicians. Neither of the main parties have got what it takes to lead and the extremist groups, like the League of Iron and the Communists will do anything to get power."

"Including bombing innocent people," Charlie said darkly.

"Yes and its not that hard to make a bomb, that's the scary part," Taylor explained. "You can do it with things like swimming pool cleaner or fertilizer. Get the right mix of basic ingredients and 'boom.'"

Whenever Taylor could organize it, we met at a firing range just outside London. This always meant getting home later than usual but only Jas ever noticed when I was back late, while Charlie invented a bunch of new friends to explain her absences at home. We improved with every session. I could now hit a target on the other side of the room, while Charlie wasn't far behind.

Two more weeks passed. It was the end of February and the pair of us were strolling to the Archway basement where the cell had met many times before, deep in an argument about whether Parveen or George was the better fighter.

"Did you not *see* Par when George got her arm behind her back that third time? She was so quick, the way she ducked away from him. He didn't stand a chance," Charlie argued.

"He's still stronger than she is. I think he *let* her get away because he's into her," I insisted.

"You think George is into everyone," Charlie said with a sniff.

I rolled my eyes. "He *is*."

We were still bickering—this time over my uselessness at opening locks with my student ID card—as we walked into the basement. George and Parveen were deep in conversation with Taylor. They turned to us, all three of their faces strained and serious.

The atmosphere grew tense.

"What's going on?" I asked.

"We've found out what the League of Iron is planning," Taylor explained. "The information you and Charlie stole gave us the first piece of the jigsaw, and since then we've been receiving more data from our undercover agent. We've just gotten our most important clue so far."

"So what is the League planning?" Charlie's eyes hardened. "Is it another bomb?"

"No," Taylor said. "We're pretty sure that they're going to try to assassinate George Latimer."

"The mayor of London?" Parveen asked.

"Exactly," Taylor said.

Charlie whistled. "He was at the memorial service . . ." She turned to me. "Remember? He was with his wife and son."

I nodded.

"The mayor has a high profile," Taylor went on. "He has spoken out against the League several times recently. Killing him would prove that the country really is in chaos. The ramifications would be far wider than just his death."

"Couldn't you . . . or the Commander . . . talk to the police or the mayor about this? Warn them?" I asked. I thought of Roman Riley's calm, assured manner. Surely if he told people what the League was planning they would have to listen?

Taylor threw me a meaningful glance. "As I've told you many times, the police are corrupt," he said. "Almost all senior members of the force are sympathetic to the League of Iron."

"Yes, sir," I said.

"When it comes to the mayor himself, he receives regular threats so it's hard to convince him there's a genuine need to step up his security this time. Plus, he doesn't like to look weak," Taylor went on. "So . . . there are no plans to arrest any

League members or properly investigate our claims."

"Which are what, exactly?" Charlie asked.

"That's the problem," Taylor said. "We know the League is plotting to assassinate Latimer, but we don't have time and place details. Which is where the five of us come in. It's our first mission as a cell so listen up. Everyone has a brief to learn and we have to move fast."

PART THREE

INFILTRATION

(n. military. type of attack in which small groups of soldiers,
or individual soldiers, penetrate the enemy's
defenses where they are weakest)

CHARLIE

"This *so* wasn't what I thought I'd be doing when I joined the EFA," I muttered.

Beside me, Parveen stifled a snort. It was the day after Taylor had told us about our mission to prevent the Mayor of London's assassination. Everyone had their own role to play and I was decidedly unimpressed with mine. The five of us were gathered for a full briefing. Taylor had just told Nat and George that their job was to infiltrate the League of Iron with a view to getting the details about the assassination that we needed. Now *that* sounded like a mission. Taylor went on to explain that Parveen would also have a role in what the boys were doing. Parveen looked positively smug as he outlined the daring plan.

"What about me?" I had asked.

In answer, Taylor had held up a picture of the mayor at a formal function, his wife and son on either side of him. I recognized Aaron, with his ruddy cheeks and his thick, fair hair from the memorial service. As the picture was passed around, Nat gasped.

"I saw that boy in a black-and-white photo at the League of Iron house we broke into," he said. "I forgot afterward, but it was there, in a pile of papers on the desk. I'm sure it was him."

Taylor nodded. "That fits with the plans we found on the coded material you downloaded. His name is Aaron, he's the Latimers' only child. And he's where you come in, Charlie."

"What do you want me to do, sir?" I asked.

"The mayor refuses to stop working just because of possible threats to his life. And, if anything, his wife is even more stubborn. So it's proving difficult to get close to the family, to work out the times in their upcoming schedule when the mayor is most likely to be at risk."

"You'd think they'd be grateful people were trying to protect them," Parveen said with a sniff.

"We know that you, Charlie, talked to Aaron Latimer at the memorial service a few months ago," Taylor went on, ignoring her.

The others all turned to look at me. Parveen gave me a nudge. I could feel Nat's eyes boring into me with that intense gaze of his. What did he care if I talked to some other boy? The memory of our kiss all those weeks ago still haunted me. But I had buried the feelings I had felt back then. Nat wasn't interested in me. He said that his reluctance to get involved was down to us working in Taylor's cell together, but that was obviously just to save my feelings.

"So what, sir?" I said, crossing my arms and leaning back against the wall of the Archway basement. "I talked to Aaron for about a minute. I'm sure he spoke to a lot of other people at that service too."

"Yes, but he remembered you specifically. The Commander's contact tells us that he's been asking questions, trying to find out who you are, where you live." A smile curled around Taylor's lips. "Seems like he's taken quite a shine to you."

"Oooh." George and Parveen both made silly noises.

Nat stared at the floor.

I blushed, feeling annoyed. "What are you saying?"

"The plan is to engineer a meeting between you and Aaron. Something 'accidental.' Then we want you to get an invite to his sixteenth birthday party which is happening on Saturday. It's a chance to start getting to know Aaron better, to become friends, get invited to his house, get to know the family."

"And find out, from the inside, when the mayor is going to be in public so you can protect him?" I asked.

"Exactly," Taylor confirmed with a nod.

"Great," I said sarcastically. What a waste of time. Not that I wished anything bad on the mayor, but spying on his son wasn't going to help me take revenge on the League of Iron.

"Do you have a problem, Charlie?" Taylor asked.

"Yes, sir." The others looked at me. "When are we actually going to get the League back for all these bad things they're doing? I mean, why don't we just take out the leaders, the people who planned the market bombing?"

A silence fell across the group. Taylor shook his head. "Our job is to *protect* people, not take the law into our own hands. If the police force wasn't riddled with corrupt officers, then maybe we could get the League leadership arrested, but as things stand . . ."

I looked at the others. None of them met my eye. I shuffled uncomfortably from side to side.

"Right, sir," I said. "So we just let the League do their thing and—"

"No," Taylor interrupted. "We *stop* the League. If we do our job properly we should be able to stop them permanently." He paused. "In the meantime, your assignment is to get information from Aaron Latimer. Do you hear me, Charlie?"

"Yes, sir," I said with a sigh. I glanced at Nat, wondering if he would mind me getting all chummy with Aaron, but he was still staring at the floor, evidently lost in his own thoughts.

NAT

I didn't like it. Not just the danger Charlie might be in if she got close to a high-profile family where the father was the subject of a League of Iron plot, but the fact that she was obviously going to have to flirt with Aaron Latimer in order to do so. At first I wondered why Riley couldn't warn the mayor himself. They were both politicians, after all. Then I remembered that Riley belonged to a different party. If I'd learned one thing about how politics worked over the past few months, it was that for all the surface talk about 'coming together in the national interest,' none of the political parties were genuinely prepared to cooperate with each other.

I went up to Charlie after the briefing. She was chatting in the corner of the room with Parveen.

"What did Aaron say to you at the memorial service?" I asked.

Charlie shrugged. "Just some stuff about hoping to meet girls. Nothing really."

Parveen narrowed her eyes. "I'd keep your focus on your own mission, Nat," she said sharply. "Charlie's got the easy part.

You're the one infiltrating the League of Iron. And if you're not convincing, I'm the one who'll suffer."

I turned away, not wanting to show Parveen that her words had sent a shiver down my spine. I didn't feel confident about what I was being asked to do. The English Freedom Army already had an undercover agent in the League of Iron, the same guy who had reported on my own appearance there a few months ago. This agent, whose user name was Lionheart, was going to look out for us, which at least offered some protection. But, as the only cell member with a previous connection to the League, I knew that the whole operation centered on me. And that it was an important step, taking Charlie and me closer to the point where we could get our revenge on the League.

Taylor talked us through the EFA oath with a greater solemnity than usual that night: *Blood and soil. Strength and honor. Hope and sacrifice.* But as I looked around at the others, their eyes shining with excitement, their faces lit with determination, I felt uneasy. The oath was just words. It wasn't going to help us prepare for the action we were about to take. Not that there was time to prepare anyway.

This mission was going to take place the very next day.

CHARLIE

Parveen had persuaded me to put on lipstick and eyeliner and I felt stupid.

"I'm only going to be seeing Aaron outside his school. It'll make me look out of place," I argued.

"Don't be ridiculous," Parveen snapped, tactful as ever. "You'd look out of place *without* makeup. Most girls wear it."

I rolled my eyes. "*You* don't."

Parveen batted her dark eyelashes at me. "I have *natural* makeup," she said. Her pointy little face was indeed blessed with perfect skin and her eyes framed with velvet lashes.

"Fine." I let her stroke a black eye pencil over the skin around my eyes, then looked in the mirror. My face was transformed, the slant of my eyes deeper than before and their chocolate color heightened by the eyeliner. I hated the fact that I didn't look like me anymore but, though I didn't want to admit it, the effect was actually quite pretty. I didn't say this, of course, just smeared a little pink gloss across my lips.

I rode in the back of the van with Taylor. He was busy,

hunched over his laptop. I stared at the tiny hand-shaped tattoo on the inside of his wrist. It was hard to remember how I'd been so obsessed with tattoos last year . . . how I'd begged Mum to let me get one and how we'd argued about it just before the bomb went off. That all felt like a million years ago.

The van stopped and I got out, having first inserted an earpiece so Taylor could keep in contact while Aaron and I talked. I hadn't really had time to feel nervous before, but now, waiting on the corner of the street with Taylor's voice in my ear telling me to hold back until Aaron appeared from his school gate, butterflies were zooming around my stomach.

I took a few deep breaths. All I had to do was smile and maybe mention how much I loved parties. Taylor had insisted that Aaron *wanted* to see me and the way he'd flirted at the memorial service suggested that it shouldn't be too hard to get him chatting. Still . . .

"Time to go, Charlie," Taylor said in my ear. "He's heading your way. If you start walking now, you'll see him as soon as you're around the corner."

"Okay." I sauntered off, trying to look casual and relaxed. Out of the corner of my eye I could see the van where Taylor was parked with all his monitoring equipment. Aaron appeared up ahead.

I gave a horrified gasp. I'd only ever envisaged speaking with Aaron on his own. Now what did I do? I stared down at my shoes, feeling my face flush.

"Take it easy, Charlie," Taylor warned, a low murmur in my ear. "He's a boy, not a bomb."

I swore under my breath. "Well you get out here and do this, then," I muttered.

Taylor chuckled in my ear. "I somehow don't think I'd have the same effect that you're having. Look up."

I looked up. Aaron and his friends had caught sight of me and stopped walking. So had all the boys behind them and to the sides. At least fifteen pairs of eyes were staring at me. I glanced down at my clothes. I had changed out of my school uniform into jeans and a sweater. Granted, the sweater was Parveen's—she'd insisted I borrow it—and therefore smaller and tighter than the baggy tops I normally wore, but what on earth was making them all stare at me like that?

"Hey, Charlie?" It was Aaron. He walked toward me, the dimple in his left cheek showing as he beamed at me. "What are you doing here?"

I smiled. Much to my relief, several of the boys watching melted away. Plenty were still standing around, though.

"I was visiting a friend then I was trying to get to the tube," I said, the lie that Taylor had coached me in running surprisingly easily off my lips. I made a face. "I think I'm lost."

"No problem." Aaron's grin deepened. His eyes twinkled. He was actually quite cute looking, I realized. Not gorgeous, like Nat, but still quite attractive, with his small, snubby nose and an air of mischief about him. "I can show you to the tube. In fact, I can show you all the way home if you like?"

"Me too," said one of the boys watching us.

"Yeah, and me," said another.

Suddenly they were all arguing about who was going to come with Aaron to take me home. I frowned. This so wasn't going as I'd imagined.

"No need for a posse." Aaron looked me in the eye. "Can you run?"

"Yes," I said. "Why?"

For an answer, Aaron grabbed my wrist and yanked me around and along the pavement. I could hear the sound of feet pounding behind us, but Aaron and I ran fast and, soon, the footsteps fell away. We kept running, Aaron darting this way and that through the crowds on the hill, until we reached Highgate underground station. We raced inside, then stood catching our breath. Aaron, I was pleased to see, was panting harder than I was. He bent over, clutching his side, then stood up. His eyes shone with excitement.

"You are *fast*," he said. "I'm, like, four-hundred-yard-dash champion at my school. That's why they stopped chasing us. They knew we'd get away. I didn't think you'd be able to keep up the whole way here."

I bridled at this. "If I could be bothered to run stupid school races, I bet I'd win them, too." As soon as I'd spoken I winced. I'd sounded haughty and rude. Not the best way to get myself an invite to Aaron's party. In my ear Taylor muttered a warning. But Aaron, to my surprise, laughed out loud.

"I bet you would," he said, clearly unbothered by my tone. "So, can I see you home?"

I hesitated. "Don't you have to get home yourself?"

Aaron shrugged. "I let myself in. Mum's never back until

sixish. Dad's . . . well, you know what he does. He's at work till eight or nine, usually."

Another thought struck me. "Don't you have a bodyguard?" I asked, looking around. "I thought the mayor of London and his family would have proper protection?"

"Nicely done," Taylor murmured approvingly in my ear. I'd been told to ask about the mayor's security arrangements in case our information was out of date.

Aaron made a face. "We have security for big events, when there's some special public occasion, but not every day. Dad said he didn't want it. Anyway, there are so many cuts, it wouldn't look good for us to use taxpayers' money to protect ourselves."

I nodded. There was a silence. Aaron was still looking at me, his expression suddenly uncertain. I realized I still hadn't answered his question about seeing me home. It was the last thing I wanted. I was supposed to be meeting Jas and some of her friends at the Nutmeg Café on Park Street. However, as I didn't yet have an invite to Aaron's party, I couldn't see how I could get out of it.

"Go on, Charlie," Taylor urged in my ear.

"Sure." I smiled. "Though I'm not going straight home. I've got to meet some friends first."

Aaron raised his eyebrows. "Girl friends?" he asked.

I rolled my eyes. "I guess, yes, mostly."

"Excellent." Aaron rubbed his hands together. "Let's go."

NAT

George, Parveen, and I hurried along the street. We were heading for an alley near the building where a League of Iron meeting was apparently due to take place. It was almost 5:30 p.m. and my thoughts kept straying to Charlie. She should have met up with Aaron by now. In fact, she should have already had her conversation with him, received an invitation to his party, and be safely on her way home.

"We should put in the earpieces," George said. "Taylor said to do it at five thirty, that he'd be finished with Charlie by then."

My fingers trembled slightly as I slid my earpiece into place.

"Did Charlie seem okay when you saw her?" I asked Par.

"Her usual charming self," Parveen said with a roll of the eyes. "Snapped at me when I suggested a little eye makeup, but otherwise totally cool." She paused. "So long as Aaron isn't into warm, fluffy girls, she'll be fine."

"She'll be fine anyway," George said loyally. "And she doesn't need makeup."

"For goodness' sake, you're pathetic," muttered Parveen. She turned to Nat. "*Both* of you."

I had no idea what she was talking about but then that was often the case with Parveen, who was serially grouchy about practically everything. Anyway, it was stupid to worry about Charlie. My own mission was going to be far harder to pull off; I should focus on that.

"Are you there?" Taylor's voice sounded in my ear.

"Yes, sir," Parveen muttered.

"Yes, sir," George said.

"Nat?"

"Yes, sir." I shook myself. "Did Charlie do okay?"

"We don't know yet," Taylor said. "She got on the underground with Aaron Latimer so we lost contact. He wanted to see her home. It's good, makes it more likely he'll want to be friends."

"More than friends, I bet." George chuckled.

"Focus, guys," Taylor warned.

I said nothing. I didn't like the fact Charlie was still with Aaron and cut off from Taylor's support. On the other hand, Aaron wasn't one of the bad guys. I was about to meet some of those. And I was going to need all my wits about me to deal with them.

We walked on. It had been a mild day, but as darkness closed in, the air grew colder. I shivered in my thin jacket. I had changed out of my school uniform before meeting up with the others. Parveen had done the same. George, who had dropped out of school more than two years ago, was in his trademark combats and T-shirt, despite the weather. We reached the rundown alley just off Caledonian Road where Taylor had told us to wait. The alley walls were high. No one could see in from either side. The stink of rotting meat filled the air from a nearby garbage bag, its contents spilling onto the grubby concrete ground.

Another fifteen minutes passed and my thoughts strayed again to Charlie. She must be almost home by now. Was she still with Aaron? Suppose he tried to kiss her? Suppose Charlie kissed him back? I couldn't bear the thought of it. Which was ridiculous. I'd already kissed Charlie myself then pulled away. I'd made my decision about her.

"Nat, are you listening to me?" Taylor's irritated voice sounded through my earpiece.

"Er, yes, sir," I said.

"Good. Our inside man tells me WhiteRaven is on her way to the meeting. She'll be passing the alley in about ten seconds. Get started."

"Yes, sir." WhiteRaven was the Goth-looking woman I'd seen at the League of Iron meeting I'd gone to before. Taylor said she was a central member of the group—so had almost certainly been involved in planning the Canal street market bomb.

"Go on, Par," George said.

"Okay, okay." Parveen started groaning and clutching at her stomach. She rubbed her hand on the dirty ground, then smeared some of the dust on her face. "No," she cried, "stop, please."

"Louder," whispered George.

"Make it sound real," I added.

Parveen made a face. "Well attack me, then," she muttered.

"Fine." I stepped forward and gave Par a gentle shove in the stomach. It was the lightest of taps, barely making contact, but Par doubled over, yelping with fake pain.

"Serves you right, you stupid Paki bitch," George shouted.

I glanced to the top of the alley. No sign yet of WhiteRaven, but she must be about to appear. I edged closer to Par again and shoved her shoulder. She collapsed onto the floor.

"Don't hurt me," she begged.

She sounded completely convincing. A wave of nausea washed over me. How could people do this for real?

"Why shouldn't we hurt you?" George snarled.

"Yeah, you're nothing," I shouted. "Not even really human. Like an animal."

"No, please." Parveen curled up on the ground. She was sobbing, her hands over her face.

Out of the corner of my eye I could see WhiteRaven come into view. She stood a couple of yards away, watching us. I aimed a careful kick at Parveen's thigh, making sure I pulled my boot short of actually thudding into her.

"What you need is a freakin' lesson," I yelled.

"More," Taylor urged in his ear. "Make it bigger."

I swore loudly then carried on, timing each curse with each kick of my boot.

"Stupid bitch." George joined in the kicking, aiming his foot over and over at Par's stomach. She writhed and groaned with each strike. Her pain and fear were totally believable, even though I was close enough to see George was barely touching her.

"What's going on?" WhiteRaven called.

I turned. She was walking over. This was it.

"Get lost," I shouted.

Beside me, George stopped his pretend kicking of Parveen and clenched his fists. "We're not doing anything wrong," he mumbled.

"What did she do?" WhiteRaven asked.

I steeled myself. "She was born," I spat. "Then she had the nerve to ask us for a light."

George nodded. "Yeah, stupid bitch."

WhiteRaven laughed. I held my breath. The biggest risk of our mission was that the League members who found us might want to join in our attack on Parveen. Much to my relief, however, WhiteRaven wasn't focusing on Parveen.

She seemed more interested in me. "Haven't I seen you before?" she asked.

"Don't know," I said, "I did go to one League meeting but I haven't been for a while. . . ."

"Why's that?" WhiteRaven's small, dark eyes bored into me.

"Wasn't sure it was my thing," I went on. "But I heard about tonight. It's in some place called Totton House, isn't it?" I glanced at Parveen, who was now crawling away from us. Fake blood— from the sachet Taylor had given her to bite on—trickled from her lip. "This bitch got in our way."

"You're doing well," Taylor whispered in my ear. "Give WhiteRaven a chance to think about you."

I held my breath. A beat passed. WhiteRaven folded her

arms. "So, do you think the League is your 'thing' now?"

I glanced at Parveen. She was on her feet and staggering away holding her stomach.

"Yeah, I do," I said. "I didn't really get it before, but I do now."

"Are *you* in the League?" George said. Unlike the kicks, which he'd faked convincingly, his tone of admiration sounded slightly forced to my ears. Would WhiteRaven notice?

"I am." She cast George a quick, dismissive glance, then turned to me again.

"How did you hear there was a meeting?" she asked.

"Same way as before," I said with a shrug. "Forums."

"Good," Taylor breathed in his ear. "Now shut up and let her decide."

At the end of the alley, Parveen was limping away out of sight. George was watching her, but I kept my gaze on WhiteRaven's face.

"Okay, you can come in with me," she said.

"Really?" Again, George's enthusiasm sounded a little over-done to my ears.

"Yeah, really," WhiteRaven sneered. "We only use usernames inside. You got yours?"

"Sure," I said. "I'm AngelOfFire." I indicated George. "This is Rioter."

"Right, I'm WhiteRaven." She offered us a thin-lipped smile. "Come on, then, if you're coming. We'll see what Saxon66 has to say about you. Decide if you'll make it as League members."

"That's great, thank you," George said.

Again, I winced at the fake enthusiasm in his voice. I hoped George wasn't making WhiteRaven wary. She didn't look like she suspected us of trying to infiltrate the League, but there was no way I could know for sure.

CHARLIE

Aaron chatted away as we left the tube and walked along Park Street to the Nutmeg Café. It was almost six and I found my thoughts straying again to Nat. Parveen had been right that Nat and George's mission—to fake a racist attack on her and convince the League of Iron to let them join a meeting—was far harder than mine.

Was Nat okay? Had he and George gotten into the League? Did anyone there suspect them? I knew that the meeting was to start at six, so presumably their faked beating of poor Par had either succeeded by now or it hadn't.

"Hey, Charlie?" Aaron's voice drew me back to the present moment. "Before we go inside, I just want to say I'm sorry about your mum."

"Oh." I felt awkward. Back at the memorial service Aaron clearly hadn't known who I was which meant someone must have told him since. "How did you find out?"

"I checked the press cuttings in Dad's home office afterward," Aaron said matter-of-factly. "Why didn't you tell me at the service?"

I shrugged. "You didn't ask. You seemed more interested in impressing me than anything else."

"Ouch." Aaron made a face. "I'm sorry if I was rude or . . . or thoughtless or whatever." He paused. "I asked about you afterward too. You live with your aunt and uncle, don't you?"

I nodded.

We were almost at the Nutmeg Café. Several of the small cafés and shops on this road had shut down in the past year and most doorways were filled with tramps. We passed an old woman with straggly hair, asleep under a bit of old blanket. Was Par writhing on the ground right now, still pretending to be hurt? Or had all three of them been exposed as frauds? Was Nat okay, or was he lying, beaten, somewhere?

"So who are you meeting at this café?" Aaron asked.

"I don't know exactly who'll be here," I said, feeling distracted. "Jas, I guess. Her brother's in a coma from the same bomb that killed my mum." I threw him a sharp look. "Just in case you feel like being less rude and thoughtless today."

"Right, okay, sorry." Aaron shrank into himself a little, hunching over and folding his arms.

I inwardly cursed myself. What was I doing? I was supposed to be flirting, getting Aaron to invite me to his stupid party. I braced myself, ready for Taylor to mutter something about my attitude in my ear. But Taylor didn't speak. It suddenly occurred to me he was almost certainly listening in to whatever Nat, George, and Parveen were doing. He was leaving me to my own devices, trusting I would bring back the invitation we needed. And I shouldn't let him down. Not because I particularly cared about the League's plot to assassinate Aaron's dad, but because foiling it would bring me another step closer to getting my revenge on the League. I took a deep breath and turned to Aaron.

"I'm sorry," I said with a rueful smile. "I just get really uncomfortable when people talk about Mum. It's not your fault."

"No worries." Aaron grinned. "I get it."

We reached the Nutmeg Café. Rosa and several of her friends were sitting by the window. That was all I needed. At least Jas and our friends were here too, toward the back of the café.

"This is it," I said, and pushed open the door.

After the chilly late-afternoon air, the Nutmeg Café was warm and inviting, rich with the scents of toffee and cinnamon and buzzing with excited chatter. It was my favorite place for Jas and me to meet, mainly because the hot chocolate was delicious and the young guy who ran the place gave discounts on every drink. Rosa spotted me immediately. She came rushing over, one of her giggly friends in tow.

"Hi, Charlie, wow, is that *makeup?*"

I winced. I'd forgotten about the eyeliner Par had made me put on.

Rosa turned to Aaron. For goodness' sake, she was practically batting her eyelashes at him. "And *who* is *this?*"

I gritted my teeth. Rosa was clearly trying to sound all seductive and sophisticated but she was coming across as a total idiot. Swallowing the impulse to tell her this, I tried to speak as calmly as I could.

"This is Aaron. We met at the memorial service the other day, then bumped into each other just now."

"Oh, how *awful.* I was there too. It was *really* moving." Rosa's face crumpled with concern. Her silly friend whose name was Milly or Minnie or something copied her expression. Now the pair of them looked like someone had just drowned their pet kittens. I shuddered with embarrassment. "Were you related to one of the victims too?" Rosa asked.

Aaron's rosy cheeks flushed a deeper shade of red. "Er, no," he said. "I was there because my dad was there, er, for his job."

"Aaron's dad is the mayor of london," I added.

Rosa's eyes now widened into circles, the concern on her face morphing into the kind of look she normally reserved for her favorite boy band.

"Wow," she said.

"Yeah, totally, *wow,*" Milly/Minnie added fervently.

This time I couldn't resist. "I don't know why you're both so impressed," I snapped. "He's just somebody's son, it's not like he won a gold medal at the Olympics."

Too harsh, Charlie.

An awkward silence descended. Rosa and Milly/Minnie looked completely offended. Aaron was now an even deeper shade of red. I bit my lip, wishing I were anywhere but here. My thoughts skittered to Nat. Was he inside the League of Iron yet? Was he okay? It struck me that I'd rather be facing a bunch of racist thugs than the situation I was in now.

I stared at the floor.

Aaron cleared his throat. "Can I buy anyone a drink? I have a gold medal at spending my allowance."

I forced myself to look up. Aaron's face was still flushed, but he was grinning, the dimple showing in his cheek. I had to admit he was pretty cool for not being offended by me.

"Hey, I'm sorry."

"No need for that." Aaron waved his hand. His eyes sparkled. "I've been told a lot worse."

"Well, I'd *love* a caramel cappuccino," Rosa said. "Thank you, Aaron." She took his arm and walked him to the counter.

I followed, telling myself to be more careful with what I said. *Just act nice*, I told myself. *How hard can it be?*

The end of the counter was near the back of the café, where Jas and two of our friends were sitting. Jas sidled up as Rosa pointed out a display of iced cupcakes to Aaron.

"Hey," I said.

"Hi." Jas grinned. "I was beginning to think you weren't going to make it." She lowered her voice to a whisper. "You look gorgeous with that makeup on. Come over, we're sitting in the corner."

"Thanks, er, I had to bring someone," I said, pointing to Aaron.

Jas's eyes widened. "Where did you find him?" she asked.

I shrugged. "Just bumped into him. We've met him before."

"Yeah, at the memorial service," Jas said. "I remember. Is he going to come and sit with us?"

"I guess, if I can get Rosa away from him." I lowered my voice. "I'm not into him, okay? But he's actually really nice."

"Okay." Jas nodded, then scuttled off to her table. Aaron was at the counter, still talking with Rosa, but he was looking around, taking in the whole café. I hurried over, determined to reclaim him.

"Our table's at the back," I said pointedly.

"But I've asked Aaron to sit with *us*." Rosa pouted.

I was on the verge of snapping at her again, but Aaron spoke before I had a chance.

"I came here with Charlie, so I should really sit with her. Maybe you could join us?"

Rosa looked at me hopefully.

"Sorry, but there's not much room." For a moment I wasn't sure Rosa would take the hint, then she turned on her heel and stalked off to Milly/Minnie and their friends.

Gail's warning about trying to get along better with Rosa flashed into my mind. Well, there was nothing I could do about it. I *had* to get Aaron to invite me to his party and he was hardly likely to do so with Rosa hanging on his every word.

To my relief, Aaron didn't seem all that bothered I'd blown Rosa off. He quickly put in an order for some drinks. They arrived all together at the end of the counter. I immediately snatched up Rosa and Milly/Minnie's caramel caps and took them over. I expected Aaron would still be waiting when I returned to the counter, but he was already sitting at the table with Jas, her two friends, and both our hot chocolates. I hurried over and sat down.

Aaron was smiling at something Jas had said. She was laughing, self-conscious even for Jas. I felt a stab of guilt, for imposing Aaron on the group. I liked Jas and it really wasn't fair to inflict him on her. On the other hand, Aaron was actually being quite charming, asking her about the black-and-cream check coat she was wearing over her school uniform. I knew she'd made it herself, and when Aaron found out, he sounded genuinely impressed, complimenting her with a surprising level of fashion knowledge.

"It's kind of Prada, with a dash of Kate Spade," he said. "But then it's totally original too."

I stared at him. So did Jas.

"My mum wears a lot of designers so I've picked a few things up," he said modestly. "She usually asks me to help her choose what she wears to functions. My dad's too busy."

"Does she ever wear Versace?" Jas asked.

"Actually, there is one evening dress . . . ," Aaron said.

I sat back, letting the two of them chatter on. A few minutes later, Jas's two friends left and, after politely saying good-bye to them, Aaron turned back to Jas and asked her something about school. In a minute I'd try to bring the subject around to birthdays and parties. My thoughts drifted to Nat again. It was a quarter past six now and I was itching to find out what was happening in that League of Iron meeting and whether he and the others were okay. I couldn't send Nat a text while he was in the middle of an operation, but if all had gone according to plan, Parveen should be free now. She could tell me if Nat and George were inside the meeting at least.

I sent a quick text, then got up and headed for the bathroom. Par replied even before I reached it.

They're in. All good, esp my fake blood. ;)

I smiled to myself as I went into the ladies' room. Well, that was a relief, at least. I took my time in the bathroom, washing the makeup off my face as best I could. I didn't care what Aaron thought, I didn't like how I felt with all that eyeliner. It just wasn't me. I came out into the café, intending to get Aaron talking about his birthday party immediately but when I got back to the table he was gone.

I looked around, but there was no sign of his tousled fair hair anywhere in the café.

"Where did Aaron go?" I asked, sitting back down next to Jas.

"He got a message from his mum," she explained, her face reddening. "Said he had to leave right away."

My mouth fell open. *No.* This was a disaster. We hadn't even mentioned the birthday party. Taylor would be *furious.*

"But he didn't say good-bye," I blurted out.

Jas looked really uncomfortable now. "He asked me to say good-bye to you, to thank you for bringing him here." She hesitated.

I groaned, putting my head in my hands. Aaron had gone back to Highgate. I'd completely blown my only opportunity to get an invite to his party.

"Hey, Charlie." Jas tugged at my arm.

I looked up at her. "What?"

"He . . . he said it was his birthday this weekend," she stammered.

"And?" I clutched at her hand.

"He asked if we'd like to go his party," Jas went on.

I stared at her, filling up with relief. Oh, thank goodness.

Jas frowned. "Aaron said his parents had been strict about the numbers but he was sure he could get four more people in. I think he wanted it to be the four of us who were originally here at the table, but Rosa came over when he was leaving and she dropped such a massive hint about coming that he was forced to invite her. Which means it's just you, me, and her." A tiny smile curled around Jas's lips at the memory. "Though I suppose we could still bring *one* of the others as well."

"Right." My head spun. I'd gotten my invite, which was great. But Jas and Rosa were invited too, which was seriously not great. Still, I had nearly two whole days to work out a way of stopping them both from coming. "You don't have to go if you don't want to," I said to Jas. "I'm sorry I had to bring Aaron with me this evening."

"It's fine," Jas said, giving her hot chocolate a careful stir. "His party sounds like it might be fun."

"Right," I said. Whatever else the party might involve, the prospect of trying to make friends with Aaron—with Rosa annoying me and Jas watching in that quiet way of hers—certainly didn't sound like fun to me.

NAT

We were inside. George was nervous, I could feel the anxiety coming off him in waves.

"Calm down," I whispered as we crossed the echoey entrance hall and followed WhiteRaven into the League of Iron meeting room. Curtains had been drawn at all the windows and the only lighting came from a series of wall lamps that gave off a dim glow. The effect was probably supposed to be mysterious and atmospheric, but to me it seemed sinister. It was noisy, too. Music was playing—some loud, heavy rock track—on top of which WhiteRaven's arrival was greeted with a chorus of deep cheers and shouts from about half of the thirty or so people gathered in the room. As on my previous encounter with the League of Iron, most of those present were men dressed in black T-shirts. Nobody seemed to have noticed me and George arrive. We stood, hesitating, in the doorway. Our instructions from Taylor were clear: wait for the undercover EFA agent, Lionheart, to make contact, then do what he ordered to get information on the assassination plot.

I had no idea why Lionheart hadn't been able to get the info by himself, but Taylor said Saxon66 kept all the data on paper to avoid hacking and data cloning and was incredibly security conscious.

"Nat? George?" A very tall man with fair skin and white-blond hair appeared in front of them. He didn't look much older than George, but there was a still and steely quality to him that I immediately associated with Taylor—and, of course, Roman Riley. For a moment, I wished Riley were here; his calm focus was just what I needed right now.

I stared at the man. "Who's asking?"

"Lionheart," he whispered.

I nodded, pressing the earpiece inside my ear. Taylor had been silent since the end of the fake fight with Par. I knew he was holding back, letting the agent on the ground take control, but I felt nervous without Taylor's reassuring bark in my ear.

"They won't talk openly about their plans," Lionheart hissed. "You're going to have to steal the file."

"What?" George's mouth gaped. *"How?"*

"Cool it, soldier." Taylor's authoritative voice murmured in our ears. "Don't draw attention to yourself."

Even though the comment had clearly been aimed at George, and was hardly a positive one, I felt suddenly more confident. Knowing Taylor was there made everything seem possible.

"Where is the file?" I asked Lionheart.

"Back room," he said. "Saxon stores his papers in a locked safe when he's here. The combination is on his phone. That's why I need your help."

"What do you m—?" George began.

"Quiet," whispered Lionheart. He spun around, an easy smile on his face as WhiteRaven approached us, a man at her side. "Saxon," he said, opening his arms toward the man. "Good to see you."

The two guys clapped each other on the back. I stared at Saxon66's square, muscular face, remembering the evil words he had spoken at the previous meeting. This was the person who was to blame for Lucas being in a coma.

I clenched my fists.

"So these are the boys you found?" Saxon66 asked WhiteRaven.

"Yeah." WhiteRaven pointed at me. "This one says he came to a meeting once before."

"Is that right?" Saxon66 looked at me. "I don't remember you. What's your user name?"

"AngelOfFire," I said, releasing my fists.

"What made you think of that?" Saxon66 asked.

I shrugged. I'd actually gotten the name from Mum's book about angels in which my own name, Nathan, belonged to the angel of fire, but I didn't want to explain that to Saxon66.

"So how come you haven't been to a meeting for a while?" he said, eyeing me shrewdly.

"Not sure; had some growing up to do," I said, meeting his gaze.

Saxon66 nodded.

"I found the pair of 'em kicking the stuffing out of some Paki girl," WhiteRaven said. "Thought it would be okay to let them come. I mean, tonight's just a social really, isn't it?"

"Absolutely," Saxon66 said. There was a bruise on his jaw, presumably from a fight. "Nice work on the Paki girl, anyway," he added approvingly.

I felt sick at the casual hate of his words. It was *Par* they were talking about. I shrugged, trying to hide my anger. "She had it coming," I said gruffly.

"Good," Taylor whispered in my ear. "You're doing well."

"So do you think you might stick around this time?" WhiteRaven asked.

"Sure," I said.

Saxon66 shook his head. "Teenagers," he said with a grin. "They have commitment issues."

WhiteRaven laughed, but I sensed she was doing so only because it was Saxon66 who had spoken, not because she thought he was funny.

"And you are?" Saxon66 turned to George.

George gave the username, Rioter, that Taylor had assigned him. He looked scared, in awe of Saxon66 and the others. Still that wasn't a bad thing. Saxon was a forceful presence without any of Riley's easy charm. Even genuine League of Iron supporters would surely find him intimidating.

A few moments later Saxon66 and WhiteRaven wandered off. Lionheart leaned in close and whispered in my ear, "Wait for a 'go' from Taylor." He turned to George. "You, stay here. If anyone asks say Nat's gone to the bathroom."

George and I nodded, and then the room fell silent as Saxon began speaking.

"Welcome," he boomed. "It's good to see you all here tonight." He pumped the air with his fist. "Iron Will forever!"

As Lionheart crossed the room to join the cheering crowd, Taylor spoke in my ear.

"Lionheart will get the code then tell me what it is so I can tell you. You need to head toward the back room without making it obvious. Get ready to act on my command."

"Yes, sir." I edged around the wall of the room. Almost everyone else was gathered in the center, listening to Saxon66 speak the same angry, ugly ignorance that I had heard at the previous meeting.

"We're not going to take this lying down." Saxon's voice rose. "We are going to use our Iron Will to resist. Are you with me?"

The crowd roared and cheered.

George moved nearer to the main group. Everyone was focused on Saxon in the middle.

I kept back. I was close to the door of the back room now, waiting. My heart pounded and I rubbed my clammy palms down the front of my jeans. I suddenly thought of Charlie. Was she okay? Had she managed to get close to Aaron? How close?

"Are you inside yet?" Taylor's voice hissed in my ear, bringing me back to the present.

I slid silently into the back room. "Yes, sir." I peered around the door. Nobody was looking in my direction. No one had seen me.

"The safe's in the corner, behind the desk," Taylor whispered.

I turned and focused on the room. It was lit with wall lights that gave off a ghostly glow. Coats had been dumped on the floor beside a battered old filing cabinet. I headed for the desk. The steel safe was set into the wall behind.

I knelt in front of it. I'd been shown how safes like this worked on one of our many training sessions. I just had to match the arrow on the knob to the numbers that Taylor gave me.

"Ready?" Taylor whispered.

"Go."

"Nine. One. Eight. Six. One. Five." Taylor repeated the numbers.

I turned the knob, finding each number in turn. Sweat beaded on my forehead but I resisted the temptation to wipe it away.

"You're doing fine, soldier," Taylor's reassuring voice murmured.

"Done, sir." I turned the knob to the final number. The safe door gave a click, releasing under my hand.

"Open it. Take the file," Taylor urged.

My heart drummed loudly as I pulled a worn paper folder out of the safe.

Footsteps sounded outside. I froze, ducking down behind the desk. The room grew lighter as the door to the room beyond opened. Someone was there. I held my breath, listening as yells rose up from the main room and the footsteps went away again.

"Hurry," Taylor urged. "Copy the pages. Now."

I took the smartphone Taylor had given me earlier and quickly clicked on each of the three pages. My mind was jumping about too fast to register properly what I was looking at but I couldn't see the mayor's name anywhere. In fact, there were hardly any words. All three sheets were covered with numbers; they looked like accounts of some kind.

"Get out of there, Nat." The sudden anxiety in Taylor's voice gave me a jolt.

"What is it?"

"Just get out."

I slid the phone back in my pocket and the pages back in the folder. A second later the folder was inside the safe and its door shut. I spun the knob, listening for the soft click that indicated it was locked again. *There.* It was done. I stood up, feeling triumphant, and crept to the door that led back to the main room. People were still shouting, but what had earlier been incoherent yells had now settled into the chanting of a single word:

"Fight. Fight. Fight."

I peered into the room. Everyone had their backs to me. I couldn't see either Lionheart or George. I slipped into the room. What was happening?

I crept to the edge of the crowd and pushed my way through. The atmosphere was electric, almost pulsating around me. And then I saw what it was all about: Lionheart and George were fighting in the middle of the group. And George was getting the worst of it, by far. His big fists were in front of his face, but Lionheart was too fast. He swung a punch. It connected with

George's jaw with a sickening crack. George staggered backward. Blood was already trickling from the corner of his mouth.

I stared in horror.

"They had to fight to stop WhiteRaven going in the back room," Taylor whispered in my ear. "Make sure they see you now."

I didn't need to be told twice. George was putting himself through this for my sake. And, unlike our fake beating of Par outside, the fight he was having with Lionheart was clearly hurting. The onlookers were too close for Lionheart to pull his punches.

"Hey, stop it." I rushed forward.

Lionheart ignored me but instead of another punch, he gave George a push and George let himself fall over, onto his side, with a groan.

I rushed over. "Are you all right?" I asked, bending down.

"You took your time," George whispered. He gave a convincing moan.

I lifted him up and hooked George's arm over my shoulder.

"Your friend needs to learn some manners," Lionheart spat. "He should stay away from us."

I looked around at the angry faces. I didn't know what to say, but I sensed if I didn't get George out of here now, the fight could escalate.

"I'll take him out," I said tersely.

I helped George to the door. "How bad are you?" I whispered.

"Bad enough," George muttered. "The big guy packs a mean punch."

"Get outside. Turn left," Taylor snapped in my ear.

A minute later we were on the steps of Totton House. I helped George limp along the pavement. We'd only just turned the corner onto the next road when Taylor pulled up in the van. We got inside and I sat back as Taylor examined George's injuries. George was hyper by now, all full of the stunt he'd pulled with Lionheart to provoke the fight.

I let him have his moment. A minute later Taylor pronounced George fine other than a few bruises and asked me for the smartphone. I handed it over, hoping I'd been wrong about the assassination data not being in the folder. If that was so, then all our stress and effort and pain had been for nothing.

I watched Taylor's face as he clicked on the pages, studying them hard.

His expression fell.

"It's not there, is it?" I said, feeling glum. "The assassination information."

"No," Taylor acknowledged, "it's not. But we got you through the door and what is here may be useful later anyway." I looked up. "And we've got Charlie on the inside with Aaron too."

My stomach gave a jealous twist. "She's going to his party?"

Taylor nodded. "Aaron invited her and two others."

"What?" That hadn't been part of the plan. "Which two others?" My mind ran through the friends Charlie would have been with when Aaron asked her. I gasped, as the obvious thought occurred. "He didn't ask my sister, did he?"

"Your sister is one of the invited, yes," Taylor said smoothly.

"But don't worry, Nat, the party's just a chance for Charlie to get to know the family. Nothing's going to happen there. Jas will be fine."

"Yes, sir." I sat back again, feeling sullen. No way could Taylor be certain of that.

CHARLIE

Before I knew it, the Saturday of the party arrived. Aaron had texted Jas all the details. "He says the venue is a nightclub in Camden," she told me excitedly. No alcohol officially, obviously, but as Aaron had apparently hinted, we were free to smuggle in our own.

Alcohol was the last thing on my mind. I was more worried about how I was going to develop my friendship with Aaron when I'd been so awkward and rude the other day and with Jas and Rosa in tow. Thanks to their text chats, it was clear that my original plan to stop Jas coming to the party wasn't going to work—and Rosa was determined to be there too.

Then, on Saturday afternoon, as I was getting ready for the party at home, another bombshell dropped. My cell rang—my actual phone, not the latest disposable Taylor had given me. It was Nat.

"Hi," I said, instantly self-conscious.

"Hi." He sounded worried.

"What's up?" I asked.

"I've told Jas I'm coming to the party with you guys and Rosa.

Aaron said he could fit in four people. There shouldn't be a problem and I don't like the idea of Jas being there with Aaron and all
his friends otherwise."

"Right." I tried to work out what he meant. Was he saying
Jas needed some kind of special protection? What from? "Aaron's
cool. I don't think he would—"

"You know what I mean. It's a party. The boys'll be all over
her. And Jas, well, she's not kick-ass like you. She . . . they could
take advantage of her."

A miserable hollow feeling swelled inside me. Nat was basically saying he wanted to keep Jas safe from male attention, which
meant either that he didn't think I'd get any myself or, worse, that
he didn't care.

"I get it," I said.

"Okay, well I'll see you there. You-know-who wants me to run
some errand for him in an hour or so, before I get to the club."

Nat meant Taylor. He sounded distracted, presumably torn
between worry over Jas and irritation over having to do something for Taylor. Either way, he was clearly completely uncon-
cerned about me.

"See you later, then," I said.

We said good-bye and I sat down on my bed. I'd been planning
on wearing a glittery top with my jeans and maybe even a dab of
makeup, but now I felt too depressed to bother. An hour passed. It
was almost 7 p.m. Maybe I'd head on over to Jas's. Nat had said he
would be out running some errand for Taylor, so there was no danger of bumping into him and I couldn't bear the thought of having

to wait any longer at home, with Rosa getting all overexcited across the landing.

There was a rap at the door. Gail stuck her head around.

"You looking forward to going out, Charlie?" she asked.

"Sure." I forced a smile onto my face. "I think I'll head over to Jas's actually."

I didn't think this would be a problem. Brian had offered to give all of us a lift into Camden and drop us at the club for the party start time of eight thirty. I'd rather have gone by myself and arrived a little bit later, but Brian was adamant—he'd even said he'd pick Jas up from her house on the way, so it surely wouldn't matter if I left from there too.

Gail frowned. "What about Rosa?"

"What d'you mean?"

Gail came in. She closed my bedroom door softly behind her and sat down beside me on the bed. "Do you remember what we talked about a few months ago, when you said you wanted to stay here? About making an effort to get to know Rosa better? I thought going to this party together was a sign things were changing. I imagined the two of you getting ready to go with each other."

I stared at the carpet. Not this again. Why couldn't Gail see that Rosa and I were never going to be friends in a million years?

"Jas needs me to help her choose what to wear," I lied. If Gail had known Jas better, she would, of course, have seen straight through that. Jas was a total queen of design and had probably already picked out the perfect outfit.

"Okay." Gail sighed. "I suppose I can't force you. Brian will call for you and Jas later. Just please don't ignore Rosa once you are at the party, all right?"

I resisted the temptation to roll my eyes. What with trying to spend time getting to know Aaron and trying not to feel bothered as Nat paid me absolutely no attention whatsoever, I couldn't imagine having much inclination left to pretend to be all chummy with Rosa.

"Of course," I said.

I left the house soon after, a thin cotton top on in place of the glittery T-shirt I'd planned to wear. I caught a glimpse of Rosa in front of her mirror before I left. Made up to the nines, she was wearing a hideous hot pink rah-rah skirt. It looked like something a six-year-old might choose to annoy her mother. She didn't see me looking as she carefully inserted some bright pink hoop earrings that matched her skirt.

I shuddered and ran off to Jas's house. It was drizzling and, despite the hooded jacket I was wearing, I got soaked as I jogged. Jas did a double take as she opened her front door and saw me.

"That's so weird," she said. "I was about to call you to come over. How did you know?"

"Know what?" I said, coming inside. Jas's house felt as cold and empty as usual, but I knew, once we were up in her cozy bedroom, I'd feel better.

"That I just finished your dress," Jas said excitedly. "I didn't say anything because I wasn't sure I'd get it done in time, but you can wear it tonight."

She was already on the stairs. I followed, more depressed than ever. A dress was the last thing I felt like wearing. Still, I didn't want to hurt Jas's feelings.

"Oh, right," I said. "That's great. I was just going to wear what I've got on."

Jas turned from the top step of the stairs, her mouth open. "You weren't thinking of going to a birthday party in a club in that?" she said, staring at my jeans and hoodie. "You're wearing *sneakers* for goodness' sake."

I shrugged. Why couldn't everyone just leave me alone?

"Come on," Jas said, running on to her room. "You'll love the dress. I worked half the night getting it ready."

Steeling myself to be appreciative, I followed her into her room. The blue fabric Jas had chosen all those weeks ago was hanging from her wardrobe. Except that it was no longer just a bit of fabric. It was a dress: short and simple, with just a little line of beads around the neck. It was so pretty and so perfect that I actually gasped.

"Try it on," Jas urged.

Forgetting my earlier despondency, I wriggled out of my damp jeans and hoodie and slid the dress on. It fit beautifully, clinging to my waist then draping gently over my hips.

"Your legs look, like, ten feet long," Jas said admiringly. "It *really* suits you."

I turned in her mirror. She was right. I'd never worn anything that suited me better.

"Now we just need to do something about your hair, your makeup, and your shoes," Jas said firmly.

I let her spend most of the next thirty minutes fussing over me, styling my hair with her curling iron and selecting a pair of her own vintage heels to go with my dress. After Parveen's use of the heavy eyeliner last week, I was wary about Jas doing my makeup but she actually did a great job, emphasizing the slant and size of my eyes with just a touch of pencil and mascara.

All my worries about Aaron and Rosa—and even Nat—disappeared as I transformed into a girl who looked like she was going to a party. After I was ready, I helped Jas with her own long, silky hair. At the last minute she slipped on a gauzy green tunic dress. The tunic was covered with embroidery and tiny sequins. It suited Jas perfectly, making her somehow both less skinny and more ethereal than ever.

We had only just finished when Brian called to say he was waiting in the car outside. He did a double take when he saw me.

"Gosh, I hardly recognized you, Charlie," he said with an approving smile. "Very pretty."

"Come on, Dad," Rosa said, rather sulkily, as Jas and I got into the backseat of the car. She had braided her hair into two short plaits and applied a cake load of silver eye makeup.

"That's an interesting look, Rosa," Jas said politely.

"Uh, yeah," I echoed.

"Oh, it's nothing," Rosa said in an affected voice. She didn't say anything about what either of us were wearing but I knew, thanks to Jas, that I looked okay. Which meant it hopefully wouldn't be too hard to do my job for the EFA and get Aaron talking to me. Who cared if Nat wasn't remotely interested? I had work to do.

NAT

Charlie hadn't sounded in the slightest bit pleased that I was coming to the party. I tried to put this out of my mind as I opened the EFA e-mail account. The army had a clever system for passing messages when members needed to communicate something more complex than a text. It worked like this: everyone was given the password to the same e-mail account. You logged in, then checked the draft folder for your message. It was a great way of communicating because nothing was actually ever sent online, so nothing could ever be tracked.

I opened the e-mail Taylor had left for me. It contained a floor plan of a building. Or, to be more accurate, a single floor of a massive building. It was a warren of rooms and interconnecting passageways.

I was certain Taylor was going to ask me to go there tonight—that's why he wanted me to collect one of the miked-up earpieces the EFA used. Whatever I had to do later, I was determined at least to show my face at Aaron Latimer's party. Jas had looked bewildered when I'd insisted on coming. I wasn't sure why *she* was connecting with Aaron when it was Charlie who had sought him out, but I was determined to keep an eye on both of them. I particularly wanted to make sure Aaron didn't mistake friendliness on Charlie's part for anything more.

I checked that the floor plan was readable on my phone, then shoved my cell into my pants pocket. I debated swapping my T-shirt for a fancier shirt—I didn't want to look out of place at what Jas had insisted would be a classy party. In the end, I took one of Lucas's shirts—dark gray and slim fitting. It looked good over my jeans yet would still be easy to move around in if Taylor needed me to work later. I smoothed down my hair, then set off. Jas was fussing over a length of blue material and barely noticed me leave. I made my way to the derelict house on Featherstone Road where Taylor had left an earpiece under a brick. Once it was in place, I listened as Taylor directed me to take a very specific and circuitous route across north London. It was frustrating, traveling around for no reason I could understand. But at last I was free—though Taylor warned I would definitely be needed again within the hour.

I slid the earpiece into my pocket and set off for the party. It was almost nine p.m. when I arrived; Charlie and Jas had probably been here for half an hour already. The bouncer on the door checked my name off, and I walked into the party. The room was heaving, music throbbing through my feet. Lights flickered everywhere from hundreds of tiny lamps and a huge throng was dancing, leaving just a few groups and couples talking on the outskirts of the room. I stood near the doorway, trying to spot Charlie or Jas. There were loads of people here—girls dressed up in heels and pretty dresses, most of the boys in tuxedos. This was easily the fanciest party I had ever been to. I looked down at my shirt and jeans. What had seemed relatively dressed-up in my bedroom now looked very casual. It didn't matter. I wasn't likely to be here for long and, anyway, I didn't care what anyone else thought.

Except Charlie.

I pushed the thought away and moved closer to the dancers. I saw Rosa almost immediately. She was dancing energetically with a group I didn't recognize, her face almost as pink as her skirt. I edged away, aiming to put some distance between us; Rosa was really the last person I wanted to deal with right now.

A moment later I saw Jas. She was dancing in a dreamy, Jas-like way wearing something floaty and green. She was also with a group of people I didn't know, though I recognized the boy immediately opposite her, with thick, fair hair and red cheeks, as Aaron Latimer. So where was Charlie? She was supposed to be spending the evening talking to Aaron.

I just had time to feel a wave of relief that I hadn't found them all over each other, when a group on the edge of the dance floor parted and Charlie came into view. She was laughing, her whole face lit up with her smile, and surrounded by boys.

I stared. The blue material Jas had been working on was now covering Charlie. It clung to and swayed around her body, softening everything about her. It was short, with a low back, showing off her long, slim legs. I was still staring, my heart pounding, as my phone vibrated in my pocket. That was probably Taylor with instructions on the next part of his evening's assignment. I ignored the text. I still couldn't take my eyes off Charlie. Any second now she was going to turn and see me. And I realized that I didn't have any choice anymore. There were lots of other pretty girls in the room but, as I stood on the edge of the dancers, I knew there was one thing wrong with all of them.

They weren't her.

CHARLIE

I looked up and Nat was standing there, staring at me with those ice-chip blue eyes of his. The music soared and the floor pulsed and the air filled with the scents of perfume and sweat and we looked at each other. It was weird, like the whole world shifted forever in that moment. There were other boys around me, still laughing and talking and dancing. One called my name, but Nat was all I could see. He walked toward me and took my hand. We stood there for a second or two, then Nat led me deep into the dancing where the bodies were close together and the music was fast and the world whirled around us. Nat bent his face to mine and we kissed and it was different from before. I knew this time he was going to stay and keep kissing me and my heart filled with a feeling I hadn't felt for what seemed like a million years.

Joy.

We pulled apart. People were still dancing all around us. All strangers. I couldn't see Jas or Aaron or Rosa. Nat took my hand again and led me through the crowd, past the groups at the edge of the room and out to the top of the stairs. Another couple were leaning against the wall, deep in their own kiss.

"Hi." Nat smiled at me and my stomach somersaulted over and over.

"Hi." I smiled back.

"Before . . ." He hesitated. And in that moment I saw in his eyes what he couldn't put into words: that he had liked me and he had been scared.

"I know," I said. "I was the same."

"Now . . ." Nat stopped again. He leaned forward and rested his forehead against mine. His fingers trailed down my cheek. My heart raced with fear and excitement.

"Me too," I said softly.

Nat drew back. He was still smiling and staring at me. "You look amazing," he said.

I blushed, my chest almost bursting with how wonderful it felt to have him look at me and say such things.

"Not so bad yourself," I murmured.

Nat laughed. "I didn't think you'd noticed."

"It was *you* who didn't notice," I said.

"No," he said, frowning. "I did, I just . . ."

I put my finger against his lips. There was no need to explain anything. I put my hands on his face and drew him into another kiss. I don't know how much time passed. I forgot Taylor and Aaron and why I was supposed to be at this party. I lost track of everything except Nat and our kissing. I didn't want it to end. And then the door behind us banged open and a crowd of people surged out of the party room and as Nat was pushed against me, I felt his phone vibrate.

"I think someone's texting you," I muttered.

Nat's eyes widened. "Man, that'll be Taylor. I think he texted me about twenty minutes ago too." He took out his cell and checked it. "Yeah, I've got to go."

"Where?" I asked.

Nat frowned. "Says here to go to Covent Garden tube."

"What for?" I asked.

"No idea," Nat said. He hesitated. "I don't want to leave."

I reached up and kissed him again. "I could come with you?"

"Yes." Nat's eyes brightened, then dulled. "Yes, except you're supposed to be here, getting to know Aaron Latimer." He made a face. "Don't get to know him too well, okay?"

I grinned. "Why? Would you mind?"

Nat met my gaze, his expression growing darker. "Yes," he growled.

My grin felt like it would split my face. He was jealous. Because he liked me. I felt so happy I could burst.

"What's so funny?" Nat grunted.

"Nothing." I hugged him. "I guess you'd better go, and I'll try to find Aaron."

Nat nodded. The people who'd passed us before were starting to come back from the bathroom. Nat gave me a swift kiss. "I'll call you later, when I've done whatever Taylor wants."

"Sure." I watched him race down the steps and out of sight, then went back into the party room. Aaron was busy, in the middle of a large group. Jas was nowhere to be seen. I wanted to be on my own for a bit, anyway. I drifted around the outskirts of the party for a while, thinking about what had just happened. I could hardly believe Nat had kissed me, that he liked me. I almost wanted to shout out to the whole party how great it felt. But of course I didn't. I kept my eyes on Aaron the whole time, waiting for a moment when I could wander over and start chatting.

I was just about to make my move, when my EFA phone buzzed. I opened Taylor's text, expecting a request for an update. Then I stood, staring at the screen.

That was odd. That was *really* odd.

NAT

I took the earpiece from my pocket and put it in my ear as I hurried out into the freezing cold. It was going to take me another fifteen minutes at least to get to Covent Garden tube. Taylor would expect me to be already there.

"Hello?" I said, feeling guilty.

"Where are you?" Taylor snapped in my ear.

"Almost there, sir," I lied.

Taylor swore. "I needed you outside the tube five minutes ago. Let me know when you get there."

"Yes, sir." I broke into a run. It felt good to pound along the street, dodging the passersby. A huge wave of happiness washed over me. Charlie liked me. The way she'd looked at me . . . the way she'd looked . . . I drifted into a daydream about that blue dress and Charlie's face as she'd drawn away from our kiss.

She liked me. I hardly dared believe it was true, but she had made it clear. I darted into the tube and down to the platform, my head still buzzing. I couldn't believe something so fantastic had actually happened to me. I bounced into the last car of the train that had just pulled up at the platform. Man, everything was going better than it had for ages. Okay, so Mum and Dad were still all over the place and Lucas was still in his coma but at least I knew he had been one of the good guys, a soldier on the side of right.

And now, here I was, actually following in his footsteps, a soldier myself, with Charlie beside me.

Yes, life was definitely looking up.

I changed to the Piccadilly line and my train sped to Covent Garden. Up in the elevator to street level and I contacted Taylor again for instructions.

"You're very, very late," Taylor said tersely.

"Sorry, sir." I tried to sound like I meant it. After all, Taylor had drilled the importance of discipline into us over and over again. But the truth was that I didn't care about being late.

Charlie liked me. What else mattered?

"Outside," Taylor ordered. "There's a guy in a blue sweatshirt sitting against the wall. Go over. Give the oath. Take the package he offers you."

I sighed. It sounded like a pointless game of pass the parcel. Still, I knew better than to complain.

"This is important, Nat," Taylor went on. "The package contains vital League of Iron information. Something we might be able to use to expose them to the public, destroy them once and for all."

"Yes, sir." Feeling suddenly more enthusiastic about the mission, I went outside, onto the street. The air was cool and the pavement crowded, but I saw the guy in the blue sweatshirt right away. He was sitting, hunched against the wall, his hood pulled low over his face and a ratty backpack clutched in his lap.

He looked like a tramp but as I squatted down beside him I noticed that his hands were clean and his fingernails carefully cut. Clearly this was another EFA agent.

"Blood and soil," I whispered.

"Strength and honor," came the man's hoarse reply.

"Hope and sacrifice," I finished.

I expected the man to take something out of his backpack and give it to me. Instead, he shoved the entire bag into my hands, then jogged away. I stood up, slung it over my shoulder, and walked back into the underground station.

"Got it, sir," I said, keeping my head bowed so no one passing by would see me talking. Maybe if Taylor didn't want me to take the bag far, I would still have time to get back to Charlie at Aaron Latimer's party.

"Good work," Taylor said. "Now take it down to the south-bound platform."

Southbound? My heart sank. If I was ordered to travel to south London, it would take me ages to get back.

"Which station d'you want me to go to, sir?" I asked.

"You're not getting on a tube," Taylor said. "Lionheart will get off an incoming train, meet you on the platform, collect the bag, then get back on again. After that, you're free to go."

"Yes, sir." My heart leaped for joy. If that was all I had to do, I could be back at the party with Charlie in less than half an hour.

"Go," Taylor urged. "We'll lose contact once you're

belowground, but you have to wait for Lionheart. Stay on the platform until he gets there."

"So how long will—?"

"Just follow the freaking order, Nat. Do you have the floor plan on your phone?"

"Yes, sir." Muttering under my breath, I headed into the elevator. The bag weighed heavily on my back. I wondered what kind of important information on the League of Iron was inside it. There was no point asking. All I'd get out of Taylor would be an irritated: 'Classified.' My thoughts drifted to Charlie again as I walked to the southbound platform then stood waiting. There was no sign of Lionheart on the first tube. Or the next. Or the one after that.

I waited as people got on and off each train.

And I waited.

Ten minutes passed and still Lionheart didn't appear.

I started to worry. I wanted, more than anything, to head up to ground level and ask Taylor what was going on, but I didn't dare. Taylor had told me to wait down on the platform and if I left I was likely to miss Lionheart's arrival. Another train stopped. Still no sign of him. The platform cleared. What had happened? I decided to give Lionheart another five minutes, then I was going up to ground level and I didn't care what Taylor said.

"Nat!"

I turned to see George flying along the platform toward me, his face consumed with panic. He rushed up, panting for breath.

"What is it?" I asked.

"The mission's been compromised," George gasped. "The League of Iron has found out about the information you've gotten. They know about Lionheart, too. They're on their way down here right now. Taylor says we have to get out of the station."

My heart thudded violently. Steadying the backpack on my shoulder, I took a step toward the exit.

"Not that way," George said, grabbing my arm. "Taylor said we had to go through the door at the end of the platform. He says you've got a map? A floor plan?"

I stared at him. "What's that got to—?"

"Taylor knew it was a high-risk mission so he made sure you had a fallback, just in case," George explained. He tugged at my arm and pointed along the platform. It was filling up fast. The next train was signaled to arrive in two minutes.

"Why don't we just wait? Or get on a tube?"

"No time," George insisted. "Don't you get it? Saxon66 and his men *know* about us. They're *here*, trying to find us. *Now.*"

He raced off. Steadying the backpack again, I charged after him, along the platform to the door at the end.

CHARLIE

Taylor's text told me to go to the ladies' room—which was just along the hallway—and retrieve a package from the end stall. Mystified, I hurried along to the bathroom. I checked my face in the mirror as I passed. My cheeks were flushed, my eyes shining.

It was because of Nat.

I could still feel his fingers on my face and the soft touch of his lips. I had never felt like this in my life. I wanted to yell out, to tell the girl emerging from the middle cubicle that the most amazing thing had just happened. I almost couldn't contain it—but of course I did, simply scurrying over to the end stall and shutting the door. I felt for the package, which was, as Taylor had said it would be, taped to the underside of the cistern, hidden from view. I pulled it free from the tape that held it in place and brought a large padded envelope out into the light.

The envelope contained something hard. I ripped off the end and pulled out a slim black box with an earpiece taped to the top. The box was locked with a number combination, so I tucked it under my arm. I peered outside as I put the tiny earpiece in my ear. The bathroom was empty, the doors of all five other stalls swinging open, no one at the sinks.

"Taylor?" I whispered. "Are you there, sir?"

"I'm here," Taylor said. He sounded tense. "Do you have the package?"

"The box?" I said. "Yes, sir. What's this ab—?"

"The assassination is tonight," Taylor interrupted.

"What?"

"The League of Iron is sending someone to kill the mayor, his wife, *and* their son. Tonight."

"*What?*" My head spun. "Kill Aaron? Are you—?"

"Sure? Yes," Taylor snapped. "We don't know who they're sending—probably three separate hitters—and we don't know exactly when or how. But it will take place in the next hour."

I sat down hard on the toilet seat behind me. How could this be happening? We were at a *party* for goodness sake. Nat had *kissed* me. Aaron was in the next room *dancing*.

"Charlie?" Taylor's voice was like steel.

"Yes, sir."

"You need to focus."

"Yes, sir. What do you want me to do?"

"Get hold of Aaron. Tell him he has to leave."

"But what about the police?" I said, my stomach shrinking inside me. "What about Aaron's parents? Where are they?"

"The police are compromised, they won't move against the League of Iron. Or rather, they'll deliberately wait until it's too late. I have an agent on her way to get the mayor and his wife. But there's no time to wait for her to get to you, too."

"There's a bouncer at the door. I could get him to help. He—"

"For all we know he could be one of the hit men. It's down to *you*, Charlie. Our agents are getting the proof we need to expose the League of Iron right now. But we have to stop them from getting to Aaron. Which means you taking him out the fire exit at the back, down the fire escape. I'll meet you there. *Hurry*, there's no time. It could already be too late."

I stood up, my legs shaking. "How am I going to get Aaron to leave his own birthday party?" I asked.

"You'll have to force him. Use what's in the box, your birthday date and month is the combination: 259," Taylor said. "Now, *go*. I'll be listening in. *Run*."

I raced out of the cubicle, barged past a posse of giggling girls, and ran back into the party. The music hit me as soon as I entered the room—and the air, hot and crackling with excitement and energy.

The black box was still in my hand. Clutching it tightly, I circled the dance floor. There was no sign of Aaron. I pushed my way into the crowd of heaving bodies, earning myself angry glances as I shoved dancers aside. I passed Rosa, gyrating alongside a group of other girls I didn't know. For a second I felt a stab of protective anxiety. For Gail and Brian's sake, I needed to make sure Rosa didn't get caught up in the assassination attempt. Rosa saw me and waved. Ignoring her, I turned and pushed my way out of the throng. I circled the room once more. Still no Aaron.

"I can't see him," I yelled over the music.

"Try the back." Taylor's voice was urgent in my ear.

I darted past the dancers and raced through the door marked STAFF ONLY. The fire door Taylor had mentioned was just a few yards away, but no Aaron. I ran along the hallway and around the corner. I stopped in my tracks.

There was Aaron. He was kissing someone . . . a girl with long dark hair. They were so close together I couldn't see her face. Then Aaron stood back and I realized who it was.

Jas.

My mouth fell open. Jas opened her eyes and saw me. She shrieked. Aaron turned and his already-red cheeks blushed scarlet.

"Charlie," he said, running his hand over his tousled hair. "Er . . ."

"You have to leave," I said, trying to focus on my mission, rather than the fact that Jas and Aaron had just been eating each other's faces.

"What?" Aaron frowned.

"Leave. *Now*," I said. "There are people coming to kill you."

"*What?*" Aaron repeated. A smile faltered on his lips. "You're joking."

"Charlie, what's—?" Jas started.

"I'm serious. You have to go." I took a step toward them. Aaron put his hand around Jas's shoulders, pulling her close. It was a protective gesture, as if *I* were the enemy. Didn't he get it? I was trying to save his life. "Come *on!*"

"Calm down, Charlie." Aaron smiled for real now, his dimple appearing in his left cheek. "I get it. Good joke. But enough, already, okay?"

"I'm not joking. I—"

"It only just happened, Charlie," Jas butted in. "I'm sorry, I guessed how you felt about him, but . . ." She trailed off, looking close to tears.

What was she talking about? Aaron patted her shoulder. Oh my goodness. They thought I was telling Aaron to leave because I'd caught him with Jas, because I was jealous.

"This isn't about *me*," I pleaded. I turned to Aaron. "It's the League of Iron. They want to take you out. And your parents. You have to come with me now."

"Don't be crazy," Aaron said. "I'm not going anywhere."

Jas shook her head. "How could you possibly know what the League of Iron is doing?" she asked.

"Do not mention the EFA," Taylor warned in a terse whisper.

"I can't tell you." Panic rose inside me. I was painfully aware of the seconds ticking away. Any moment, an assassin could burst in.

"Box." Taylor's low growl reminded me of the small black package in my hand. "Use what's in the box."

"We're going back to the party," Aaron said firmly.

"No. Wait." My fingers fumbled as I rolled the numbers on the combination to the day and month of my birthday—259—and lifted the lid of the box. I blinked with shock at the small, black Glock pistol that met my eyes.

Aaron took a small step toward me, his arm still around Jas's shoulders.

"Stop." There was no more time. I took the gun out of the box and pointed it straight at Aaron's forehead.

Aaron's eyes widened. Jas gasped.

They both looked utterly terrified. I hardened my heart. They would understand when they were safe. I had no choice. Drawing on all my training, knowing that I had to make them believe I would use the gun, I narrowed my eyes and pointed toward the fire exit.

"Outside. Now," I ordered. "Or I'll shoot."

NAT

The door at the end of the tube platform would surely be locked. Even as I watched George reach for the handle, I was convinced it would remain shut, that there was no way through. But to my surprise the door opened easily. I glanced over my shoulder, back along the platform. Saxon66 and two other, black-shirted men appeared at the far end. They were looking around.

"They're here." I tightened my grip on the backpack. My palms felt clammy with sweat.

"Go." George stood back, holding the door open. "Taylor says to follow the tunnels using your map. You're in room three now. Someone will meet you in room forty-six. You have fifteen minutes to get there."

"Aren't you coming?" I said.

"I'm the decoy." George smiled. Then he shoved a tiny flashlight into my hand, turned, and raced away, disappearing into the oncoming crowd.

I watched him go, feeling uneasy. The platform was full of people now, mostly either looking down at their phones or up at the electronic destinations board. I slipped through the door and closed it swiftly behind me. I was in a dark room that smelled of dust and damp. A breeze blew around my legs. I switched on the small flashlight George had given me. The room was square, with metal pipes running along the walls. I focused on the map on my phone. It showed a series of lines and boxes. Each box had a number. I found "3." George had said that was *this* room. I searched for the number "46." There it was. That was where I had to head for. Man, it looked miles away. How was I going to get there in just fifteen minutes?

I set off. The network of tunnels I was following seemed to be completely separate from the tube line, though at first I could still hear the trains rumbling past on the other side of the thick, damp, brick walls. The bag over my shoulder grew heavier and heavier as I walked. Soon the draft around my legs died away, and then the sound of the tube trains faded too. Several of the doors had, clearly, once been boarded up or padlocked. In two cases the padlocks hung off chains that had been cut clean through with bolt cutters.

Questions raced through my head. Who had come down here ahead of me and opened all these doors? Where did the tunnels lead? And what was in the bag I was carrying? If I hadn't been under such time pressure, I would have stopped and looked, but I had only a few minutes now to reach room 46. Who was going to meet me? Was it Taylor himself? I had to admire him. He might be irritatingly officious sometimes, but tonight his thoroughness in having prepared a backup plan had probably saved me from being caught by the League of Iron.

I just hoped that George was all right—and Charlie too, back at the party. I checked the time again. Only a couple of minutes until I had to be in room 46. I sped up, jogging through the next dusty tunnel. The bag with the package felt heavier than ever, a solid weight against my back. If the next part of my mission went smoothly, maybe there was still a chance I could see Charlie again this evening.

The underground world was dark and silent. My flashlight caught a couple of mice scuttling out of the way as I reached room 39. Yet despite the shadowy gloom down here, I didn't feel scared. Just preoccupied with concern for George and a desire to be with Charlie as soon as possible.

I kept running. I stopped for a second in room 44 to catch my breath. I could hear traffic immediately above my head. I must have been walking gradually uphill for a while to be so close to the surface. It felt weird to think I was under roads. I shone my light around the room. Metal pipes ran along one wall. The light glinted off iron rungs that led up to a rusty manhole cover in the ceiling.

I shuddered, imagining the asphalt and all the cars and the buildings on either side pressing down on me. Then I moved through another tiny room and into my final destination, room 46.

No one was here. The traffic noises had subsided too. Did that mean I was underneath a building now? I shone my light around the room. There wasn't much to see: the same bare floor and brick walls as elsewhere.

Where was my contact? George had said that I should get here within fifteen minutes, implying that whoever was meeting me was operating on a deadline. I frowned. I had made the journey through the tunnels within the given quarter of an hour, so my contact should already be here, shouldn't he?

What was I supposed to do now? Just wait? I peered around the room. I seemed to have reached the end of the tunnels. How was the person meeting me going to get here except along the same underground network I had just run through?

I laid the backpack carefully on the floor. I wondered again what exactly was inside it. Taylor had said that it contained information that could potentially bring down the League of Iron. What on earth did that mean? The information certainly wasn't paper-based. The bag was too heavy for that.

I shone the light around the room again. There was definitely no sign that anyone else had been here. I was supposed to wait to hand over the bag, but what if something had happened to whoever was due to meet me? No way was I going to retrace my steps carrying that heavy backpack without at least taking a peek inside it. It was totally against the rules, of course, but I was quite alone here. No one would know that I'd taken a look.

Without thinking about it any more, I opened the top of the bag and peered inside. The package inside was wrapped in some kind of green material. I shone my light more closely. It was a scarf . . . with the League of Iron's emblem printed across it in blacks and browns. I had seen one just like it in the house Charlie and I had broken into.

My heart beat faster. I hadn't expected that. Did this mean the package inside the scarf had been stolen from a League member? I had to see what it was. Holding the flashlight between my teeth, I drew the heavy package gently out of the backpack, placed it on the floor, and peeled the edge of the scarf away. Some sort of metal container was underneath. I folded back the rest of the scarf, freeing a cube of metal about the width of a shoe box. Two wires poked out of the side. I turned the box over. A display screen was running some kind of countdown.

2:24 . . . 2:23 . . . 2:22 . . .

What the hell was this?

A split second later, I realized. It was a bomb.

I stared at the numbers, numb with horror.

2:13 . . . 2:12 . . . 2:11

The box was a bomb. And it was going to go off in two minutes.

CHARLIE

I held the Glock steady, the barrel pointed at Aaron's head. "Move," I ordered.

"What are you doing?" Jas's hands flew to her mouth.

"Come on, Charlie, this isn't funny," Aaron protested.

"I'm not laughing." I *had* to get Aaron out of here *now*. I turned the gun on Jas. "If you don't move now, I'll shoot her."

Jas gasped.

"Okay." Aaron grinned, though the smile didn't reach his eyes. "Whatever, I'm moving."

I kept my gaze on him steady. In the distance the party music changed to a bass-heavy dance track. Aaron edged past me to the fire exit.

"Please, stop, Charlie," Jas pleaded.

"It's for his own safety," I said.

"Where are you going?" She was crying. I kept my eyes on Aaron who had reached the door.

I bit hard on my lip, trying to block the feelings of guilt that swamped me. I wanted to run over and put my arms around Jas and explain properly, but I knew I had to stay focused on the mission. I *had* to get Aaron out of here.

"You're doing well," Taylor murmured in my ear.

My resolve strengthened. I could explain to Jas later.

"Take me, too," she sobbed.

"No," Taylor snapped in my ear.

"No," I said. Aaron was the target. Until he was safe, anyone anywhere near him was in danger. "I can't, Jas. You have to trust me."

"I don't understand." She wept.

I snatched a look at her. Her hands were clasped so tightly together that the knuckles were white. Her eyes were round and scared, tears streaming down her face.

"Open the door." I turned back to Aaron, hardening my voice.

Aaron pushed the metal bar down and the fire exit opened. The night air rushed in around us. I shivered, cold in my blue dress. Aaron walked out, onto the fire escape.

"Down the steps," I ordered.

"You're nearly there," Taylor murmured. "My car will meet you outside."

I followed Aaron down the iron fire escape. We were in an alleyway. Music from inside the club filled the air.

"What the hell are you doing?" Aaron demanded.

Ignoring him, I glanced toward the busy street just a few yards away. As I watched, Taylor's car swerved off the street and along the alley. It pulled up alongside us with a jolt.

"Get in," Taylor said. His darkened window was slightly down so I could hear him both live and through my earpiece.

Relief swamped me. Now Taylor could explain everything to Aaron so that he would understand.

I opened the back door. "In here," I ordered Aaron.

"No way." He stepped back.

"We are out of time, Charlie," Taylor barked.

I pressed the Glock against Aaron's side. *"In."*

With a final and despairing look, Aaron crawled onto the backseat. "You're freaking *kidnapping* me?" he protested.

"It's to keep you safe," I said, scrambling in after him. "Trust me."

I slammed the door shut. Taylor was sitting in the passenger seat, next to the driver. Both wore masks, but I recognized Taylor from the shape of his head. A moment later the car roared off.

I removed my earpiece and sat back, feeling my entire body relax. I'd done it. Aaron was out and safe.

"What's going on?" Aaron said. His voice shook.

"It's okay," I said. "You're safe now." I turned to Taylor, wondering why he didn't take off the mask. Was it really that important Aaron didn't see his face? "What's happened to Mr. and Mrs. Latimer? Are they okay?"

"My mum and dad?" Aaron paled. "What have you done with them?"

"I don't have an update," Taylor said.

"Where are you taking me?" Aaron asked.

"Don't worry, I'm sure your parents are fine," I insisted, wondering why Taylor wasn't attempting to be more reassuring. "We're just taking you somewhere safe."

"Where?" Aaron's voice cracked. "*Why?* What is this?"

"Give me your phone," Taylor ordered.

I stared at him. Why was he asking for that? Surely it was a good thing if Aaron had the chance to reassure his parents that he was safe?

"You are *kidding*," Aaron said.

"*Now.*"

Aaron handed over his cell. Taylor removed the SIM card and dropped it out of the window.

I wriggled uneasily in my seat. Either Taylor was being totally unnecessarily security-conscious, which was of course eminently possible, or something was very, very wrong. Outside the busy street was passing in a blur of storefronts and lights.

"Now *your* phone, Charlie," Taylor ordered.

"What, sir?" This, surely, was too much.

"You heard."

"Why, sir? Why do you need my phone?"

Taylor said nothing. Something was definitely wrong.

"Where are we going?" I asked.

"Phone," Taylor repeated.

"No." I gripped the gun at my side.

"You will follow my orders, Charlie, like you've been trained to," Taylor insisted.

I glanced through the window. The streets of Camden were giving way to those of Kentish Town and Tufnell Park. Beside me, Aaron clutched his seat. I could hear his breath, all jagged and shallow.

Then I held the Glock up and pointed it at Taylor.

"Tell me where we're going," I said.

Taylor laughed and the sound chilled my blood. "It's not loaded," he said.

I checked the gun Taylor was right. I hadn't noticed before, but the indicator showed that the chamber was empty. I reached for the car door, but it was centrally locked. Heart pounding, I looked up at Taylor. What the hell was he playing at?

Taylor shook his head. "You did well, Charlie, but you can stop now. Aaron is exactly where he's supposed to be. Now give me your phone." He held up his own gun. He didn't point it at me. He didn't have to. I knew how fast and how accurate Taylor was with a pistol.

I handed him my phone.

"Now sit back," Taylor said. "I'm sure you'd rather I didn't tie you up, so keep still and shut up, both of you." He turned around to face the front.

I sat, frozen. I could feel the blood draining from my face as the horrific realization filled me. Taylor had betrayed the EFA. Betrayed *me*.

"You made it up," I said, my voice hoarse. "There was no assassination plot. You just wanted Aaron."

"And he's here now," Taylor said. "Which is thanks to you, so well done."

My head spun with confusion. What was going on?

Across the backseat, huddled in his corner, Aaron looked at me with wide, terror-stricken eyes. Outside we were zooming along a fast road. I could see people on the distant pavements but I knew they couldn't see in at us.

Aaron is exactly where he's supposed to be. . . . Well done.

I still had no idea what was going on, but one thing was clear: Taylor had kidnapped Aaron.

And I had helped.

No. I sank back in my seat, my head in my hands. The truth was far worse.

I had done the kidnapping.

PART FOUR

INSURRECTION

(n. a violent uprising or rebellion against an authority.)

NAT

I laid the bomb back on the floor. The numbers of the countdown blinked at me.

1:57 . . . 1:56 . . . 1:55 . . .

How was it possible that I had been carrying a bomb? Had someone switched the package I was supposed to take?

1:52 . . . 1:51 . . . 1:50 . . .

Less than two minutes left. I had to stop the countdown. I stared at the bomb, panic rising inside me. Should I pull the wires out of the side? I reached for them, then stopped. Attempting to yank the thing apart was insanely risky.

I stood up, trying to force my brain to focus. I couldn't stop the bomb. So I had to get away from it. I shone my flashlight around the room. There was definitely no way out except back through the tunnels.

I glanced down at the bomb again.

1:36 . . . 1:35 . . . 1:34 . . .

I turned and pelted away from room 46, through room 45, into room 44. Traffic sounds roared overhead. The beam from my flashlight danced off the walls, glinting on the iron rungs in the corner. I glanced up at the manhole cover in the ceiling. Should I try to escape that way? Or should I run for it? There was only just over a minute to go. If I tried to run, I wouldn't get far. And down here, in this confined space, the fire would get me, no matter how fast I went.

This manhole was my only possible way out of the tunnel system. I raced over. Flashlight in my mouth, I scrambled up the metal rungs. The hatch above was rusty and fixed with a bolt. Balancing precariously on the top rung, I pulled at the bolt. It was stiff. Old. Heavy. I took a breath, my heart hammering. How much of the countdown was left? Fifty seconds? Less?

I took my phone from my pocket and drove it hard against the end of the bolt. With a smash, the phone broke into two pieces. It flew out of my hands, onto the floor, the battery and two sections of the plastic cover skittering away in different directions.

I took the flashlight from my mouth. Swearing loudly, I whacked it against the bolt. The metal creaked and shifted slightly. I drove the flashlight against the bolt again. The light went out. I stood for a moment in total darkness, the sound of my ragged breathing harsh in my ears. My fingers trembled as I felt for the bolt. It was almost free.

I dropped the flashlight. It clattered to the floor. Surely there could only be a few seconds left. I pulled at the bolt with both hands, almost slipping off the metal rungs. *Again.* I summoned every ounce of strength to my arms. Another pull. *Yes.* The bolt scraped back. I pushed at the hatch. It was heavy. *So* heavy. And awkward to raise, especially from where I was standing, directly below it. I shoved at the metal again, roaring out in fear and frustration.

I was not going to die here. I had to live. For Jas. And Lucas. And Mum and Dad.

And for Charlie.

With another shove, the hatch opened enough for me to force my hands through. I raised myself up, pushing at the metal with my shoulders. The hatch slid sideways. Cold night air rushed across my face. The scream of traffic was all around. Man, I was right in the middle of a road. I turned toward the oncoming cars. A black Audi was almost on top of me. I ducked down, nearly losing my balance. The car passed. Sweat was pouring out of me. How much time? Surely less than ten seconds. More cars were heading toward me. I couldn't wait. With another roar, I pushed up from the metal rung beneath me, letting my arms take all my weight. I hauled myself up and out of the hatch, then scrambled to my feet. I stood in the road, arms open wide, and yelled.

A car swerved to miss me. I raced to the pavement. Another car screeched to a halt. I turned and yelled.

"Bomb. It's a bomb. Get away."

People all around stared at me.

I looked past the traffic. My mouth gaped as I saw what was on the other side of the road, directly above the room where I had left the bomb.

The Houses of Parliament.

"Run! Run! It's a bomb!" There were only seconds left. I turned, still yelling, and ran, hoping people would copy me. My throat burned with the cold air as I rounded the corner.

Bam!

My feet flew out from under me. I crashed against the cold pavement. Eyes tight shut. All the breath knocked out of me.

CHARLIE

Aaron was still huddled in his corner of the backseat. Why had Taylor made me kidnap him? It was a total betrayal of the English Freedom Army and everything it stood for.

"Why are you doing this?" I demanded.

"Calm down, Charlie." Taylor turned around from the front to meet my angry stare. "This won't be a problem for you, so long as you keep following my orders."

"What's he talking about?" Aaron asked. "Why are you taking *orders* from him?"

I looked out of the window. We were zooming past open fields, the outline of distant trees black against the dark navy night sky. I'd seen enough road signs to know we were on the M1, heading north, but what for?

"Where are we going?" I asked.

"Quiet." Taylor turned to the driver. "I can't get a signal here. Turn on the radio."

The driver muttered something as he reached forward and pressed a button on the dashboard.

"There should be something on the ten o'clock news," Taylor replied.

I glanced at Aaron. He caught my eye, his expression a mix of fear and disgust, then turned away again. The radio fizzed into life. An ad was coming to an end. Then the station jingle. And then an announcer:

"The news at ten o'clock. Reports of an explosion at the Houses of Parliament are just reaching us. Details are hazy, but emergency services are heading for the scene. The explosion appears to have been initiated from the warren of tunnels linked to the tube network beneath the edge of the building. The explosion is feared to have left at least two fatalities and many in—"

Taylor switched off the radio with a grunt.

My mind raced. When I'd last seen Nat, he'd been heading to Covent Garden tube station. Was it possible that the errand Taylor had told him to run was linked to this explosion?

"Was that a bomb?" I asked, leaning forward. "Was Nat there? Is he okay?"

Taylor said nothing.

"Nat?" Aaron sounded horrified. "You mean *Jas's* brother Nat? Is he involved in all this?"

"No," I said. "At least I don't know."

I sat back as a new fear wormed its way through my head. Suppose Taylor had manipulated Nat, like he had me? Suppose Nat was caught up in a bomb blast? I steeled myself. As soon as the car stopped, I was going to get myself and Aaron away from Taylor. Whatever it took.

NAT

I lay against the pavement, hands over my head. For one terrible moment I was in the Canal Street market, trying to find Lucas. Then the shrieks and the car alarms brought me back to reality.

I staggered to my feet and walked around the corner. The scene was one of devastation. A huge hole had been blown in the side wall of the Parliament building opposite. Bricks and cables had been shot outward and lay strewn across the road. Smoke rose among the debris. Worst of all, people were lying, motionless, on the street.

Horror filled me. I felt for my earpiece. It should work now that I was aboveground, but it was gone. It must have fallen out as I hauled myself out of the metal hatch in the road. My phone was gone too, of course. I leaned against the wall behind me, watching the ambulances arrive and some of the people lying on the ground ease themselves up and limp away.

Nothing made sense. Had Taylor known about the bomb? He *must* have. He gave George instructions to tell me where to take it, and he'd left the floor plan for me to use too. But why? I thought it through. There could be only one possible explanation. Taylor must be working with the League of Iron—as a double agent. A bomb under the Parliament building, close to the House of Commons, was just the sort of action the League would take.

Images from the market bomb flashed into my mind's eye. I thought of Lucas, in his hospital bed, then I thought of how close I had just come to being killed.

Killing me had been part of Taylor's plan.

What about Charlie? And Jas? Taylor had sent Charlie to make friends with Aaron. Presumably that was all part of some bigger plan too. I had to warn her. I set off, walking toward the embankment. I could follow the river to the nearest station, then head north to the West End and the party where Charlie was. I still felt dazed, the past hour a surreal blur.

I walked down to the river. The city was buzzing, alive with the screech of sirens and people hurrying away from the blast site. It was funny how bombs and wars looked so thrilling in movies and computer games, when the reality was so heart-stoppingly ter-rifying. The air was colder than ever by the water and, as I turned along the pavement, I started to feel the chill. A minute later I was shivering so much, I ducked into a newsstand to keep warm.

The Asian man behind the counter frowned as he saw me.

"Go take your drugs somewhere else," he snapped.

Man, he thought I was a junkie. I shook my head, still trying to stop shivering. I didn't dare go farther into the shop, but stood in the doorway, hugging my chest and trying to get warm.

The TV that hung from the far wall caught my eye. It was

showing pictures of the carnage from the bomb blast: smoke and broken brick and victims with blankets over their shoulders being helped away. I wished I had a blanket too. I wasn't so cold now I was inside the store, but I still couldn't stop shivering.

Ignoring the shopkeeper glaring from the counter, I watched the TV as the camera focused shakily on a female reporter.

". . . all tube stations have been closed as a precaution and the security services have ordered Parliamentary staff down to the bunkers," she said, her hair blowing across her face. "The latest reports we're receiving suggest this was a terrorist attack. A bomb."

I gulped. The camera turned to a familiar face.

"And now we have Roman Riley, leader of the Future Party," the reporter said. "Mr. Riley, you were one of the few MPs actually in the House during the explosion. Why are you not in the bunkers now?"

Riley's face was pale with cold, his eyes strained. "The emergency services are here, the press is here, the public is here. I'm not running away in the face of this violence, this cowardice, this horrific attempt to intimidate our freely elected officials."

"Who do you think is responsible?" the reporter asked.

"What matters now is saving lives. A bomb here, in this place, is an ugly and brutal attack on the very foundations of our democracy. Whoever did this, we have to show them they will not succeed. I suggest that you and I stop talking right now and see what help we can offer. The police will get to the bottom of the bomb in due course. Let's focus now on helping all those caught in the blast."

"You, get out of my store." The shopkeeper was out from behind his counter, fist raised.

I scuttled outside. The air was still cold, but at least I wasn't shivering quite so badly. I stood on the pavement for a second. I had no phone and barely any money. The reporter had just said all the tube stations were closed. It would take me at least twenty minutes to walk back to Aaron's party. Maybe longer. A fire engine sounded in the distance. Roman Riley was at the bomb scene. He probably had no idea that Taylor had betrayed him and the English Freedom Army. It was, after all, pure chance that I had survived.

Roman Riley was only a couple of minutes away. I had to warn him. Telling Riley what had really happened was not just the right thing to do, it was also the fastest way to get hold of Charlie and warn her, too. Riley would have a phone. Probably also a car. Perhaps I could persuade him to drive me to the party. He'd seemed so kind and concerned when I'd met him before, I was sure he'd want to help me. And he would certainly want to catch Taylor.

I set off at a run.

CHARLIE

"Okay, I have a signal now," Taylor said. "Stop the car."

The driver pulled over by the side of the road. We were on a country lane, on the outskirts of a village. It was dark outside, the sky above pitch black with a sprinkling of stars. We had just passed two pubs and plenty of houses. Help wasn't far away, if I could only get away from the car.

Taylor opened his door and got out. As he slammed it shut again, the driver pressed the dashboard button twice, relocking the car. Taylor wandered along the lane, speaking into his cell. I thought fast. When he came back, the driver was going to have to unlock the door again. He could, of course, reach across and open Taylor's door manually, but it was more likely he'd unlock the door centrally, in the same way as he'd just locked it. Which would hopefully give me and Aaron enough time to escape.

I looked through the window at Taylor again. He was still deep in conversation.

I edged across the backseat toward Aaron. He drew away.

"Aaron," I whispered.

"Get off me," he said, his voice full of contempt.

"Please." I wriggled closer.

He put out his hand to push me away, but I darted right next to him and leaned my head over so my mouth was hot on his ear. "Get ready to run when the door unlocks," I whispered.

Aaron hesitated. The driver turned his head, clearly sensing the change in atmosphere.

"Fine, I'll get off you," I said, as if in response to Aaron. I slid across the backseat again and slipped off my shoes. These heels would be impossible to run in.

The driver turned to face the front. For a second I considered trying to get past him to the lock control on the dashboard. No, there was no point. It was too far away for me to reach easily, I'd be at an awkward angle, and the driver was almost certainly armed. Even if he wasn't, he would be quick—all EFA soldiers were fast.

It was my own speed I was banking on, after all.

I looked at Aaron. How quickly could he run? He met my eyes and gave me a swift nod. His hand rested on the car door handle next to him. Good. He was ready. And what had he told me that time I met him outside his school? Hadn't he said he was his school's four-hundred-yard champion?

I had to hope that wasn't just some idle boast designed to impress me. Not that Aaron was interested in me. For a moment my thoughts drifted to his kiss with Jas . . . then to mine with Nat . . . then to the report of that bomb in central London. . . . Was Nat okay? Had he been hurt? Worse?

I couldn't bear the thought of losing him.

Aaron cleared his throat. I looked up. Taylor was heading

back toward the car. I couldn't read his expression. I glanced at Aaron. He nodded again. He was ready. I rested my fingers on the door handle. Waiting.

Taylor reached the car. He tapped at the window.

The driver leaned forward to the central lock control. I held my breath. The driver pressed the control. The doors clicked open.

Now.

I pressed down on the handle, opening the door beside me. Across the car, I could hear Aaron's door opening too, but all my focus was on Taylor. He turned as I leaped out of the backseat. I made a fist. Threw my punch into his gut. All my body weight was behind the strike, just as Taylor himself had taught me.

Caught by surprise, Taylor staggered back. I turned and ran. Around the car, Aaron was struggling with the driver, his arm twisted behind his back. He let out a roar of pain. The driver slapped his free hand over Aaron's mouth. Summoning all my strength, I punched the man's back, landing two blows, one after the other, directly on his kidneys. The driver yelled. Turned. Reached for me. I shoved my knee up, hard, between his legs.

He doubled over with pain. I darted past him, grabbed Aaron by the wrist, and yanked him after me. A second later we were both running, hard and fast, up the road. The asphalt was rough and cold under my bare feet but I pushed myself on. It was only a few yards more back to the houses and the village and to help.

"Aaagh!" Aaron cried out.

I heard a thud behind me and turned. Taylor had tackled

Aaron to the ground. I stopped running. Aaron's face was pressed into the asphalt.

Taylor looked up at me. "Enough, Charlie. Come here. *Now.*"

I hesitated. The driver was still doubled over by the car. I could run. I could get away. Bring back help for Aaron.

Then Taylor drew a gun out of his pocket. "This . . . ," he said, looking me in the eye. "This one's loaded."

My breath misted in front of my face.

"Back to the car, Charlie." Taylor dragged Aaron to his feet. He pressed the gun against his temple. "Or I shoot him."

A beat passed. Aaron's eyes were wide with fear.

"You wouldn't," I said.

Taylor raised his eyebrows. "Want to take that chance?"

I hesitated again. But there was no choice.

Gritting my teeth, I walked slowly back to the car.

NAT

I stopped running as the Houses of Parliament came into view.
The smoke had settled now, though the scene was even more
chaotic than it had been a few minutes earlier. From where I
was standing, I could see two ambulances over the heads of
the crowd. A bright light was shining beyond them. Guessing
that was the light from the TV news crew that had just been
interviewing Roman Riley, I ran on. I pushed my way to the front
of the growing crowd. Someone—the police, presumably—had
put up a crime scene cordon while I had been gone. I pressed
against the tape, searching the devastated area in front of me.
Two people were still lying on the pavement. A third was being
lifted into one of the two ambulances by paramedics. Police
swarmed everywhere but I still couldn't see Riley.

I edged around the cordon. *There.* Riley was crouching down
on the other side of the ambulance. He was bent over a young
woman who lay on the ground, her foot twisted at a strange
angle. Two paramedics were examining her ankle. Riley was holding the woman's hand. She was crying and he was speaking softly,
an expression of sympathy and concern on his face.

I moved closer, hoping that Riley would look up and see me. But he was totally focused on the girl. I reached the bright light of the news team. The news reporter I had seen on TV just minutes before was pressed up against the cordon, though a couple of people were holding the rest of the crowd back as the cameraman focused on her face and the scene behind.

"The scene here is one of shock and carnage," the reporter said. "We have received no reports of casualties from inside the building but there are many injured people out here. The police have confirmed two fatalities, but there may be more. As a precaution, security officers have ordered the prime minister and the cabinet to be taken to a secure location. The nation is on red alert. Few politicians were in the building this evening. One exception is Future Party leader, Roman Riley, who was in a meeting on the other side of the House. You can see him behind me. . . ." The reporter turned to indicate Riley, now standing as the paramedics lifted the woman with the broken ankle onto a stretcher. "Riley has refused security commands to take shelter, instead choosing to offer comfort to the victims of . . ."

As Riley, still holding the girl's hand, walked beside her stretcher to the nearest ambulance, I edged past the news crew so I could keep him in my sights. The girl was loaded into the back of the ambulance and Riley turned away. People from the crowd called out, but Riley, grim-faced, was walking toward the point where the police cordon reached the Parliament building wall, his back to the crowds.

This was my chance. Ducking under the cordon, I rushed toward Riley.

"Hey!" I called.

"Get back." A policeman stepped in front of me.

"I need to speak to Mr. Riley," I said. "I've got information about the bomb."

The policeman stared at me. His eyes registered alarm—and something else. Man, he looked *guilty*. I suddenly remembered the endless warnings we'd been given about the police force being riddled with corrupt officers secretly working for the League of Iron. I'd always wondered if perhaps the EFA exaggerated the extent to which the police were dishonest, but maybe it was true. Maybe this policeman in front of me already knew about the bomb—and that the League was behind it.

I darted around him. "Mr. Riley!" I cried. "Roman."

Ahead of me Roman Riley stopped. He spun around to face me and his look of surprise morphed into one of recognition.

I ran up to him. "Mr. Riley." I lowered my voice. "Commander Riley, *please* sir, I need to speak to you."

"Come here!" The policeman lumbered toward me.

I dived sideways, away from the man's outstretched hand. I ducked under the cordon and ran back, into the crowd. After a few seconds I risked a look over my shoulder. The policeman was nowhere to be seen. Neither was Riley. I backed away, out of the crowd. Where had he gone?

"Nat?"

I spun around. Riley was in front of me, a look of real concern on his face.

"What on earth are you doing here?" He looked me up and down, taking in the dust on my pants and in my hair. "Were you caught up in this?"

I moved closer. My throat was choked. "Commander Riley, it was me. I mean, it was . . . I don't know . . . Taylor sent me with a package, but it turned out to be the bomb. I just managed to get away."

"*What?*" A look of consternation came over Riley's face. "*Taylor did this?*"

"I don't know but he made me take the bomb and told me to go to the room where it went off." It was a massive relief to talk, to tell Riley everything. Huge emotions bubbled up inside me as I described how I'd fled from the League of Iron along the tunnel network. "Do you think Taylor is working for the League?" I said. "It's the only thing that makes sense. Unless someone switched the package. I'm really worried about what's happened to George. And to Charlie. She was on an assignment for Taylor too, and my sister was there with her and—"

"I hear you, Nat." Riley put his hand on my shoulder. "You've done really well." He lowered his voice. "We need to take all this to the police. But there are only one or two senior officers we can trust. We have to be careful who we talk to."

I nodded. "That policeman who tried to stop me talking to you," I said. "He looked like he already knew all about the bomb."

"Highly likely," Riley said. He looked around. "If the League of Iron is really behind this explosion, then your life is in danger. They will want you dead."

"They probably think I already am dead." My voice shook as I spoke. It was hard to face the thought that Taylor, who I had trusted so completely, could have sacrificed me so easily.

Riley took off his coat and put it around my shoulders. "Okay, this is what we will do," he said firmly. "I'm going to take you to one of the few police officers I know we can rely on. You can talk freely with him. Does that sound okay?"

I nodded. "What about George? And we should check on Parveen, too. And . . . and definitely Charlie."

"Of course. I'll get my driver to go straight to the club Charlie is at, make sure she's all right. When you speak to the police officer we'll tell him about George, get him to put out a call. And for Parveen, too. Come on, you need to get warm before you go into shock." He paused. "Unless you're hurt? Do you need to see one of the paramedics?"

"No, I'm fine."

Riley led me away from the crime scene area. His car was parked around the corner. The man leaning against the driver's door stood to attention as Riley strode up. As he saluted I caught a glimpse of the open-hand tattoo on the inside of his wrist. He was obviously another EFA soldier.

"Get in the warm, Nat," Riley ordered.

I slid gratefully into the passenger seat of the car. It was a sharp Mercedes and, any other time, I would have enjoyed taking a better look at the stylish body and sleek interior. Right now, though, I was too upset. All those people dead or injured. And what about Charlie and Jas—were they okay? And poor George?

Outside the car Riley spoke to the soldier for a few seconds, then the soldier took off at a brisk jog. Riley pulled out his phone and made a call. I took a few deep breaths, trying to calm down.

I should call Mum or Dad. They were likely to have seen news of the explosion on TV by now and though they thought Jas and I were at a party miles away from Parliament, after the Canal Street market explosion all terrorist attacks made them anxious.

A minute passed. The soldier who had taken off at a jog was returning at a brisk walk, a polystyrene cup in his hands. As he walked up, Riley got off the phone and took the cup. He spoke to the soldier, clearly giving another order. The man ran off immediately.

Riley came back to the car and got into the driver's seat. He handed me the cup. "Drink this, it's some sweet tea. I'm going to drive us to the police officer I told you about. He's expecting us at his house in the next ten minutes."

"I'd like to call home," I said.

"Of course." Riley started the car's engine. "Drink the tea first. You don't want your teeth chattering when you talk to your mum." He glanced at me. "And we need to work out what you're going to say. Telling your parents about the EFA will only put them at risk."

"Right," I said, sitting back as Riley started the engine. I sipped slowly at the tea. It was hot and sweet and, though I didn't usually like sugary drinks, I had to admit the effect was definitely soothing.

We drove for about ten minutes. I didn't know the streets we passed through, but the road signs indicated we were heading westward. Riley asked me questions about Taylor as we drove— and about the bomb. His voice was steady and calming. I answered as best I could, feeling my body release with each sip of tea.

At last Riley turned onto a residential street. He pulled up outside a large, gated house. As the car stopped, the gates opened, and he drove on, into the driveway.

The car was warm now and the tea had relaxed me so much that, when I opened the door, the cold air came as a shock. I reeled as I got out of the car, then staggered sideways. Riley caught my arm.

"Steady," he said. "Let's get you inside."

I looked up at the house. It seemed vaguely familiar, but for some reason I was having difficulty focusing properly. Was that from shock? *Surely* I'd been here before? Riley led me carefully over to the front door. My legs were barely able to hold me up as we went inside. I blinked as the hall lights came on, but everything was blurry. Something was wrong. Very wrong. Black spots appeared at the edge of my vision. I looked around the hall, straining again to focus on what I was seeing.

I had definitely been here before.

My eyes lit on the hat stand next to the front door. I had seen that before too. Back then a scarf had dangled from the peg: a green scarf, with a tiny brown and black pattern.

I turned to Riley. "No," I said. "This is . . ." My voice slurred, my brain searching for the name. "The League . . . this house . . ."

My legs gave way again and I slumped against Riley, who let me fall, down to the floor. I lay on the cold ground. Images of the scarf, the bomb it had been wrapped around, Charlie's face flashed before my eyes. The darkness was crowding in.

"League of Iron." I forced the words out. "Someone . . . League . . . lives here."

"No, Nat." Riley's voice sounded as if it were coming from far away. But his next words sank deep into my brain as my eyes closed and I let the darkness take me.

"*I* live here," Riley said. "This is *my* house."

CHARLIE

Another hour passed, mostly in silence. After our escape attempt, Taylor bound our wrists and ankles for the rest of the journey. I kept watch out of the window, but we were driving through small roads, where the signs for turnings were few and far between and mostly flashed past too quickly to read.

At last the driver stopped beside a stretch of woodland. I stared out of the window. This was the same place that we'd come to for the induction weekend. My guts twisted. Did that mean the English Freedom Army was behind everything that had happened tonight? My head spun as Taylor undid our ankle bindings and ordered us out of the car. Over the past couple of months, I'd let go of my suspicions about the EFA. Now I almost groaned out loud. It looked like I'd been right about them all along.

"Does the EFA know what you're doing?" I demanded.

Taylor didn't answer. He made me put on a sweatshirt and some boots, then refastened my wrists and led me and Aaron through the trees toward the derelict farmhouse I'd stayed in all those months ago and which served as one of the EFA's operations bases. I had no idea what time it was, but it must have been past midnight. I tried to focus on my surroundings, so that I could find my way back to the road if we managed to escape.

It was a big "if."

Aaron had asked several times what Taylor was planning to do with him. I kept quiet, knowing that once Taylor had refused to answer, there was no point pushing him. The EFA soldier on the door of the farmhouse saluted as Taylor passed him.

Taylor locked both of us in the room with the diesel cans where I'd searched for Nat all those months ago. Our hands were still bound but Aaron and I could speak freely and, as soon as Taylor had gone, Aaron bombarded me with questions: Who was Taylor? Why had he been kidnapped? Why was I involved?

I answered as honestly as I could, explaining that the EFA had presented itself as a nonviolent organization set up to combat terrorism.

"I don't know why Taylor took you," I admitted. "But it looks like the EFA was behind it."

"I know why they took me," Aaron said bitterly. "It's obvious what they're doing."

I stared at him. "What d'you mean?"

"They're going to try to get a ransom off my dad," he said. "Probably as a way of funding themselves."

I fell silent. Was that true?

Hours passed. I couldn't see the time, but it must have been the middle of the night. Brian and Gail would be desperately worried about me. I wondered what on earth Jas had told them.

Another hour or so passed. And then Taylor was back. "Come with me, Charlie," he ordered.

I shot a quick look at Aaron, then followed Taylor along the hall to the kitchen. He opened what I'd thought was a cupboard door to reveal a short flight of steps. Down these to the basement and some kind of operational center, empty of people but complete with filing cabinets, desks, and banks of computers. My attention was caught by the computer in the corner. The sound was off but the news screen quite clearly showed smoke rising from rubble at the edge of the Houses of Parliament. Was that the bomb we'd heard about on the radio news earlier?

"Hello, Charlie."

I spun around. My mouth fell open as I came face to face with Roman Riley. What was a politician doing here? Taylor stood beside him.

"It's good to meet you at last," Riley said. He extended his hand. "I'm Roman Riley."

I backed away. "What's going on?" I demanded.

Riley smiled that warm grin of his I was so familiar with from TV. "I'm the EFA Commander. I'm the one who ordered Aaron Latimer's kidnapping. I'm the one who insisted you were brought here tonight."

"*What?*" I glanced at Taylor, then back to Riley. "I don't understand."

Riley smiled again. "The chain of command is pretty simple, Charlie. I order Taylor to act. He orders you. And you've both performed wonderfully tonight." He paused. "Taylor, you can go now."

"Yes, sir." Without looking at me, Taylor left the basement room.

"I still don't understand," I said.

Riley sighed. "I hear you tried to escape earlier," he said. "So I thought it was time for a full explanation. I'm sorry we didn't bring you in earlier, but you are very young. And what we were doing required absolute secrecy."

"You mean the kidnapping?" I asked. "I thought the EFA was *against* violence?"

Riley considered this for a moment. "It's about seeing the bigger picture, Charlie," he said. "We took Aaron so we'd have some leverage over his father."

"You mean so you can *blackmail* him? Why?" I frowned. "I thought you . . . I thought your party was a *democratic* party? I thought you did everything inside the law?"

"The party does. That's why I had to set up the English Freedom Army to deal with the country's more . . . challenging problems." Riley sighed. "The mayor of London is a weak man. He doesn't always act in the country's best interests."

"And you do?" I shook my head. "This isn't right. Whichever way you look at it, blackmailing the mayor by threatening Aaron is going too far. You're making Aaron suffer. None of this is his fault."

Riley raised an eyebrow. "Perhaps not," he said. "But you know from your training, Charlie, that power requires ruthlessness." He paused, his eyes alive with cold intelligence. "Don't you think that sometimes the end justifies the means?"

"Nothing justifies terrifying and threatening a teenage boy," I insisted. I pointed to the computer screen in the corner, still showing footage of the explosion at the Houses of Parliament. "Did you do that, too? Was Nat caught up in it? Is he okay?"

Riley sighed. "I'm afraid I can't talk to you about that right now."

My chest tightened.

"Was Nat there?" I persisted. "Is he hurt?"

"Let's not dwell on collateral damage," Riley said quietly.

I dug my fingernails into my palms. What was he saying? That Nat was gone?

"Where is Nat now?"

Riley said nothing. His silence oozed menace. Then he cleared his throat.

"I want you to join my inner circle, Charlie," he said.

"What?" I said, startled. I certainly hadn't expected that.

"I know the pain that lives inside you," Riley went on, his voice soft. "I see you better than you see yourself. You have no fear, you are smart, a good fighter. In fact, I see a lot of myself in you."

"I don't see how—"

"Like you I never knew my father. He was, like yours, a soldier who died fighting for his country before I was born. And, like you, I lost my mother when I was a teenager." He paused. "You're the real deal, Charlie. Most people need to belong but you, you aren't afraid to be on the outside . . . you need no one. That makes you unbelievably powerful and, if you agree to work with me, I can help you become more powerful still."

My stomach twisted into knots. There was some truth in what he said. At least, maybe there had been. I had kept myself separate from everyone in my life since Mum died: from Aunt Karen, from Brian and Gail and Rosa, even from Jas.

But not from Nat. He had gotten right under my skin, almost as if he was a part of me.

"I don't accept your offer," I said, drawing myself up. "I don't want to work with you. I don't think it's okay to kidnap and black-mail people."

Another silence. Riley waited, as if expecting me to say more. But all I wanted now was to leave. Riley didn't stop me. But as I walked to the door, Taylor appeared, blocking my way, his gun in his hand. He looked at Riley.

"Sir?"

"Charlie needs time to think," Riley said smoothly. "Put her in the Hole."

"No—," I started, but Taylor had already grabbed my arm and was marching me out of the room. I struggled, but he pressed the gun against my ribs. A few moments later I was shoved inside a dark room. I fell to the stone floor, landing heavily on my side as the door slammed shut. The ground beneath me was cold and hard, the room pitch-black.

I sat for a moment in the darkness. I could see nothing, not even my hand in front of my face. And all I could hear was the sound of my own harsh, shallow breathing.

I was utterly alone.

NAT

My head felt thick, like someone had stuffed it full of padding. I was lying on something hard and cold, my body stiff and frozen. I opened my eyes. White plasterboard loomed up in front of me: a wall. Where was I? I struggled to move and the world seemed to tilt sideways. I lay still for a few moments. What had happened?

Like a wave of cold water, the whole thing crashed, shockingly, over me. I remembered the bomb, Taylor's betrayal . . . and that Roman Riley was behind it all.

Suddenly awake, I sat bolt upright. I was in a tiny room, dark and bare. A streak of moonlight streamed in through the only window, which was set in the sloping roof. I scrambled to my feet. The room spun around me again and I clutched at the wall. I could barely stand upright here, under the slope. I staggered into the middle of the room.

Where the hell was I?

Slowly, easing my stiff muscles into action, I made it to the window across the room. It was dark outside and raining, but I could just see the woods in the distance. It was all horribly familiar. This was where Charlie and I had come for our first EFA training. Riley or one of his men must have driven me here from London. Which meant I must have been unconscious for hours.

Where was Charlie? Was she okay? And what about George? I staggered over to the door. It was locked. I banged on the wood. Footsteps sounded outside, but no one came. I tried to cry out, but my mouth was so dry that all that emerged was a hoarse gasp. I turned back to the window. I pushed at the catch, but it held. I made a fist, intending to break the glass, then realized I would cut myself if I just punched at the window. I looked around for something to wrap my fist in, to protect my hand. But just then the door opened and Taylor walked in.

We stared at each other. Taylor raised his gun. "Out," he ordered.

I stumbled to the door. Taylor pushed me outside, onto a small landing. I must be in the attic of the farmhouse.

"What's going on?" I asked, my head clearing. "Why did you make me take that bomb? Riley ordered it, didn't he? Where's George? Is he okay? What about Charlie?"

"Quiet." Taylor pushed me toward the stairs.

"I don't understand." An intense fury started to build inside me as I remembered how proud I had once felt of being part of the army. "What happened to 'strength and honor,' sir? You said the EFA was nonviolent, that we only fought in self-defense, but you gave me a bomb to set off, people died, you . . . you . . ." I stopped, my throat choking with the realization of how close I had come to dying earlier.

And how little this had mattered to Taylor.

"I didn't *want* you to die," Taylor muttered, his gun still in his hand. "I was just following orders. The bomb had to happen. Which meant someone had to be seen near a known League of Iron house earlier in the evening—that's why I sent you all over north London before going on the tube to Covent Garden." He paused. "Then someone had to take the bomb to . . . to where it needed to be."

"You used me . . . and George and Charlie . . . you used *all* of us." My guts gave a sickening twist. "You used my brother for the Canal Street market bomb too, didn't you?"

Taylor cleared his throat, then prodded me down the stairs to the first floor. "I already told you a long time ago, Lucas made a noble sacrifice."

"Oh, God." I felt sick as I remembered the text I'd seen on Lucas's phone.

Take package—Canal St market, 3pm

Lucas had taken his "package" *to* the market after all. Like me, he hadn't known what he was really doing. Like me, he had been left for dead. How ironic, I thought bitterly. I truly had followed in my brother's footsteps, in the worst possible way.

"Why?" I asked. "*Why* did there have to be a bomb?"

"It's part of the Commander's theory of Chaos to Order," Taylor said. "You set off bombs, get others to claim them, to scare people."

"What does scaring them achieve?"

"When the public is scared, they look for strong leadership," Taylor explained. "In a civilized society, only a minority of people will follow an openly violent leader but if you keep yourself separate from the violence, then you allow them to feel good about themselves *and* you do what needs to be done: discrediting the extremists and allowing the right people into power."

"Roman Riley being 'the right people,' I suppose." I threw Taylor a scathing look as we reached the landing. This was where we had slept during the induction weekend.

"Commander Riley has a *lot* of support," Taylor said. "Huge sections of the police, for instance."

"Right." My mind flashed back to the officer I'd gone up to just after the bombing. No wonder he'd looked guilty. He'd been working for Roman Riley. In fact, I realized with a jolt, when Taylor had kept emphasizing how corrupt the police were he hadn't been exaggerating the extent of their dishonesty, just lying about who they supported. "So Commander Riley has brainwashed the police into thinking he's a big deal too."

Taylor flashed an angry glance at me. "He *is* a big deal, Nat. He's going to save this country."

I shook my head as we headed down the stairs to the ground floor. For a second I considered making a grab for Taylor's gun. But that would be stupid. I knew only too well that Taylor was faster and stronger than I was. "What about George and Parveen and . . . and Charlie?" I asked instead. "Are they okay?"

"Information on George and Parveen is classified, but Charlie is fine."

"Are you sure?" I asked. "Is she really all right?"

Taylor snorted. "Oh, you don't need to worry about *Charlie*. She's here, with the Commander."

"Here?" My stomach clenched as we reached the ground floor. I had hoped Charlie was still back in London, safe from harm.

"Yes. The Commander's chosen to bring her into his inner circle. Now, she's kidnapped Aaron Latimer for him, she'll be trained as—"

"She kidnapped Aaron?" My mouth fell open. "No way. I saw her at his party. She was briefed to get to know him, that's all. Those were *your* orders."

We walked through the hallway. The house was quiet. No sign of either Charlie or Riley. Then a masked soldier appeared from the kitchen. He was carrying a spade.

"The orders changed," Taylor snapped. "Charlie is now working directly for Roman Riley. I'd forget all about her if I were you."

I stared at him. That couldn't be true. I knew Charlie. There was no way she would go along with Roman Riley's plans, not once she knew what he was really up to.

The soldier with the spade saluted Taylor, then opened the front door, holding it for Taylor and me to walk through. Outside, the cold wind whipped at my face, but I barely felt it. All I could think about was that Charlie was here somewhere.

"Why would Riley want to bring Charlie into his 'inner circle'?" I demanded.

Taylor said nothing. Just led me and the soldier across the grass to the edge of the woods. He turned to the soldier.

"Are you armed?" he barked.

"Yes, sir." The soldier stood to attention.

"Give him the spade; get him digging."

The soldier handed me the spade. "Make a hole in the earth," he ordered.

I knew better than to ask why. This was probably just some

random task designed to keep me busy—or maybe Taylor needed a place to store weapons outside the house. Either way, I was too preoccupied with how I was going to escape and find Charlie to pay much notice.

Feeling numb, I thrust the spade into the earth. It was softer than I expected, damp from the rain, which still pattered lightly down on my shoulders and back.

"Good-bye, Nat." Taylor strode away without looking back.

I kept digging. The masked soldier stood, watching me. Moonlight glinted off the gun in his holster. Part of me was tempted to lunge for the weapon, but I knew how fast EFA soldiers could move. A lurch and a grab wouldn't work.

I had shifted all the topsoil now. "How much deeper do you want me to dig?" I asked.

"A few more feet yet," the soldier said with a nasty smirk. "Enough to cover a body."

I looked up. Reality hit me like a punch to the guts. This hole in the earth was no storage space.

I was digging my own grave.

CHARLIE

I sat for a while, hoping my eyes would adjust to the gloom, but the room barely lightened. I had to get my bearings; at least work out how big a space I was in. I edged forward on the floor until I reached a wall. I kept moving, keeping the wall on my right until I reached the corner of the room, then following the next wall along. Once I'd found all four corners I crossed the room diagonally. Then I did it all again, this time on foot, pacing the distance. After about fifteen minutes I'd discovered that the room was empty and roughly eight paces wide and ten paces long, with the only door about halfway down one of the long walls. I was certain there was no window because there had been lights on outside the house when I'd arrived, plus a nearly full moon in a clear sky, yet I still couldn't see anything. However, a breeze was blowing in from somewhere. . . . I edged around the room again, feeling up the wall and down to the floor with every step. The draft wasn't coming from the door. So what was bringing it into the room? After another minute I found the source of the cold air: a tiny gap in the brickwork around a length of pipe at the top of one of the side walls.

I stood on tiptoe and opened my mouth, ready to yell for help. I stopped. What was the point of calling out? Apart from Aaron, still trapped upstairs, nobody here would want to help me. In fact, if I made a noise shouting, they'd almost certainly send someone in to gag me.

No, I needed to be more subtle. I thought back to my EFA training. Taylor had taught us some basic Morse code, including how to sound an SOS: three short notes, three long, then three short again. I took off my shoe and tapped it against the pipe. I stopped. Waited. Silence. I tapped again. And again.

And over and over again.

But no one came.

NAT

Palms sweating, I pushed the spade into the earth again. The grave was nearly dug. *My* grave. Which meant I didn't have much time. I gripped the spade more tightly. I had to escape and find Charlie. I had to get her away from here.

"Keep at it, I'm freezing my ass off out here," grunted the soldier.

"Yes, sir." I gritted my teeth. I would get only one chance. I needed to be strong. And fast.

I lifted the spade as if about to thrust it down into the earth again. Instead, I raised it up and sideways. I drove it—*wham*—against the soldier's head.

He fell to the ground with a thud.

I stood over him, panting, then reached down and felt for a pulse. The soldier groaned; he was alive. I whipped his belt off and fastened it around his ankles. I tore a length off my own shirt to tie the soldier's wrists. Then I tugged off the soldier's mask, ripped it along the seam, and bound it tightly around his mouth so that he couldn't shout for help.

The soldier's eyes opened just as I finished. He writhed on

the ground, trying to get free. I looked for his gun. He had been holding it when I hit him. It must have skittered away, toward the trees.

Damn. I didn't have time to look for it. Surely the soldier must have another weapon? I patted down his jacket, feeling the pockets. *There.* A short, flat-bladed knife was attached to his belt. I removed it from its sheath, then straightened up and raced toward the farmhouse.

Lights were on in just one of the downstairs rooms, revealing a group of men gathered inside. I veered to the side of the house to avoid being seen, then slowed to a walk as I reached the gravel by the back wall. The rooms here were in darkness. I crossed the gravel, wincing as my feet crunched over the stones. Treading as lightly as I could, I crept to the nearest window and peered through. It was the kitchen. Moonlight reflected off the metal on the stove, casting soft shadows across the floor. The room was empty; the door that led down to the basement was shut. I pushed at the bottom of the sash window, but it remained firmly locked. I tiptoed on. The next room was in darkness. And the next. Their windows were locked too. I crept around to the other side of the building.

I found myself outside some kind of office-*cum*-storage room. There was a desk and shelves containing bottles and boxes. I peered into the shadowy depths of the room. A hunched figure sat in darkness on the floor near the door. Was that Charlie? I stared harder, my pulse racing. Surely it *had* to be her. I rapped softly on the glass, ducking back as the figure looked up.

Not Charlie, but a boy with tousled hair and ruddy cheeks. It was Aaron Latimer. What was he doing here? Aaron's eyes widened as he saw me. He struggled to his feet, holding up his hands to show me they were bound together with a rope that was, in turn, fastened to the desk. I nodded to acknowledge that I'd seen he was tied up. Then I turned to the window. It was locked. I was going to have to break in. I slipped off my jacket and wrapped my hand in the material. With a swift punch I smashed through the glass. It shattered onto the floor, echoing loudly in the air around me. My heart raced. I had to hope that the soldiers I'd seen on the other side of the house had been too far away to hear it.

Aaron watched, his face full of anxiety as I pulled the larger pieces of glass out of the frame, then crawled over the window ledge. My pants tore on a jagged edge, the glass piercing through to my skin. The pain was sharp. I stifled the yelp that rose inside me then leaped down, into the room.

"You're Nat, aren't you?" Aaron gasped. "Jas's brother?"

"Shh, yes," I whispered, feeling for the tear in my pants. The skin beneath was broken, but not bleeding. I took my knife and sliced through the rope around Aaron's wrists. "Do you know where Charlie is?"

"No. Nat, she *kidnapped* me. Forced me into—"

"Shh." I hesitated. Charlie could be anywhere in the house. If I was going to find her, I'd be better on my own than with Aaron slowing me down. "Over here." I led him to the window and pointed through the broken glass to the trees.

"Where are we?" Aaron whispered.

"EFA operations base," I said.

Aaron stared at me blankly.

"Never mind, I'll explain later. Head over there, to that dip in the trees. I'm going to find Charlie, then meet you there."

"*What?* You have to be *kidding*," Aaron hissed. "We need to get away from here as fast as—"

"I've got to find Charlie," I said stubbornly. "If I don't make it out in ten minutes, then head west, through the trees. There's a road about fifteen minutes away."

Aaron opened his mouth as if to protest again, then clearly thought better of it. He nodded. "Okay."

I searched the room for anything that might help find Charlie. A thin beam of moonlight shone across the bottles and cans on the shelves and floor. I scanned them quickly: bleach, diesel fuel, ammonium nitrate. I frowned. Those last two would make a powerful explosive. They had probably been used to create the bomb I had set off. I shuddered, pushing the memory away. There was no point looking at these bottles. They were of no use in helping me work out where Charlie was.

Aaron had crawled out of the window and was running across the field toward the trees. I crept to the door and opened it a crack. The hallway outside was empty, though I could see lights on at the other end. Voices drifted toward me from the hallway. Charlie could be in any of these rooms. I had to search them.

I tiptoed through the hallway, checking the rooms on either side. They were all dark and empty. I came to the kitchen. Peered inside. Also empty. I crept over to the door that led down to the floor below, then hesitated. For all I knew this door was the only way into and out of the basement. There certainly weren't any windows down there. It would make sense to try the other rooms in the house first, rather than risk going belowground, where I could easily be trapped.

As I turned away I heard a faint tapping sound. I stopped. The sound ended, then started again.

Three short taps, then three long ones, then three short again.

It was the Morse code distress signal that Taylor had taught us all those months ago.

Charlie.

I held my breath. The tapping sound was very faint. Where was it coming from? I crouched on the floor, my ear next to the pipes that ran along the kitchen baseboard. The tapping was more distinct now.

It was coming from the basement. I crept back to the door that led downstairs and pressed my ear against the wood. I couldn't hear anything now but then I wouldn't if Charlie was sending out her SOS through the pipes. Gently, I eased open the door. The stairs below were shrouded in darkness. I tiptoed down. Down. I reached the stone floor at the bottom. I was in the basement.

Light seeped out from under the door of the operations room on the left. The dim rumble of voices drifted toward me. I turned right. The air was much colder down here. My breath misted in front of me. I concentrated on moving as swiftly and silently as possible. The first two doors I passed were open, the rooms beyond empty. Around the corner I reached the third.

It was so dark down here I could barely see the door in front of me but as I stood and listened, the tapping sound was audible again. I felt for the handle. It was locked. I scratched at the wood, pressing my ear against the door, listening hard for movement inside.

The tapping stopped. Footsteps sounded inside the room.

I scratched the wood again.

"Hello?" The whisper from inside the room was faint, but unmistakable.

I had found her.

"It's Nat," I hissed, relief mingling with anxiety as I wondered how on earth I was going to get through the door.

"Oh." Charlie made a sound: half gasp, half sob.

I felt for the door handle again. My fingers traced down the wood, to the metal lock, then along to the gap between the door and the frame.

If I had a gun I could have blasted the lock away.

But I didn't.

I would have to use my knife.

"I'm going to get you out," I whispered.

But, even as I took out the knife and slid the thin blade between the gap, footsteps sounded on the stairs above.

CHARLIE

I backed away from the door, holding my breath. Nat had found me. I couldn't even begin to think how he had managed it. I could hear him pressing something metallic against the lock of the door. I thought back to our training sessions on "exit techniques." Nat was a great shot with a gun, but had found it virtually impossible to open locks using the flat of a school ID.

"Press the top of the lock," I whispered. "Use the tip of—"

"Yes, thanks, I've got it," Nat muttered.

I stood back, chewing on my lip. An agonizing few seconds passed—he was surely taking too long—and then the door swung open. Nat stood in the dim light, a dusting of rain on his hair and a dirty smudge on his face. It was unbelievably good to see him. And then footsteps sounded nearby. There was no time. Nat held out his hand. I raced out of my prison, toward him.

He grabbed my arm, pulling me through the hallway. I gasped. Two male soldiers were running toward us.

"Get away," Nat ordered. He held out the knife in front of him.

The soldiers hesitated. Then the one on the left lurched forward. He grabbed Nat's wrist, twisting it. Nat yelped with pain. The knife clattered to the floor. The second soldier was coming for me. I ducked under his arm, then spun around, fists raised. I steadied myself, focused, then punched. My fist met the man's stomach, my entire body weight behind the blow. He doubled over, just as Nat slid out from the first soldier's grip.

We raced along. Up the stairs to the kitchen. Nat grabbed my hand as we pounded through the hallway. He tugged me after him. Seconds later we were in the office-*cum*-storage room where Taylor had brought me and Aaron earlier. Aaron's bindings, sliced through, lay on the floor.

"This is how I got in," Nat said, rushing over to the window. The glass was broken, cold air sweeping in. "Aaron's already out."

I stared at him, overwhelmed that he'd risked so much to save us. "Where is he?" I asked.

"In the trees."

I headed for the window. Voices rang out behind us from the hallway.

"The boy's got a knife, sir."

"Charlie's out of the Hole."

"Where are they?" That was Roman Riley. He sounded furious. And only yards away.

I hauled myself onto the ledge, pushing away a large piece of glass.

Out in the hallway, Riley was giving orders. He was sending

some of the soldiers upstairs, others into the field outside the farmhouse. I raised my knee to the sill.

"Stop." It was Riley.

I looked around.

Riley stood, panting, in the doorway. He had a furious scowl on his face and a Glock pistol in his hand.

"Come here, Charlie," he said.

"No," I said.

"Please, Charlie," Riley said. "I don't want to hurt you. I already explained that I want you to join us."

"And I already explained that I don't want to join *you*," I said.

Riley pointed his gun at Nat. "If you don't come with me now, I'll kill him."

I gasped. Nat was blinking furiously, his focus on the gun in Riley's hands.

"If you kill him," I said, trying to keep my voice even, "then I will never join you. In fact, I will make it my life's mission to track you down and kill you, wherever you go, whatever you do."

"Charlie, please." Riley gave a wry laugh. "Okay, okay, calm down." He lowered his arm and placed his gun carefully on the stone floor in front of him. "Listen to me, I haven't told you every-thing yet. When you hear the truth, you'll *want* to stay."

"Charlie's not staying," Nat said and I could hear the slight tremble in his voice. "You tried to kill me earlier. You'll do the same to her."

"No." Riley met his gaze. "No, she's safe . . . she's going to stay with the EFA, it's where she belongs."

"Don't listen to him," Nat urged. "Go. Get out of here."

I hesitated, half in, half out of the window. Riley made no move to pick up his gun. He wasn't going to kill me. And he meant it when he said he wanted me to be part of the EFA, though I didn't understand why. But Nat wasn't safe. And he had risked everything to find me. I couldn't leave him now.

I swung my legs off the window ledge and jumped back down, into the office. I stood next to Nat.

"If I stay, will you let Nat go?" I said.

"No way," Nat protested. "You're coming with me. We're both leaving."

"It's a weakness to care so much about this boy, Charlie," Riley said. "He will lie to you, just like all the other people you've ever trusted."

"Shut up," I said.

"It's the truth," Riley insisted. "For example, Nat's known I was the EFA Commander for a long time. Ever since the induction training. He didn't tell you the truth about that, did he?"

"I only kept that secret because I trusted you," Nat spat. He turned to me. "He made me believe everything about the EFA *needed* to be secret so that it could defend and protect people when the law couldn't."

"Which it does," Riley said smoothly.

"No," Nat insisted. "You don't care about people or the law. You just care about being powerful. That's why you secretly plant bombs—to make people afraid, so that you can pretend you're some big hero, looking after them." He paused. "You did the bomb tonight and . . . and you did the Canal Street market bombing last year too, didn't you?"

I stared at Riley's face. He was looking intently at Nat. Then he glanced across to me.

"Yes," he said.

A beat passed. I sucked in my breath. "You killed my mother," I said. "You're actually admitting to *murdering* her."

Riley sighed. "I'm sorry about your mother, Charlie. And about Lucas. Sometimes difficult decisions have to be made . . . and innocent people get hurt."

"That's not good enough," I said, my voice shaking with emotion.

"Charlie, we can talk about all this later." Riley took a step toward me. "As a show of good faith, I will let Nat go, but I need you to stay."

"Fine." I moved closer to him. If I could just get that gun from the floor . . .

Then what? A little voice sounded in my head. *Are you really prepared to shoot Riley?*

"It's a lie. A trap," Nat insisted. "He's going to kill us both."

"No." Riley held my gaze. "I told you, Charlie, I value you. I want you to join us. And there's something else . . . something that makes you special. . . . We didn't know until a week ago, but it makes all the difference. . . ."

I glanced at Nat. His gaze flickered to the gun, then over to the diesel cans on the floor and to the bottles of ammonium nitrate on the shelf above.

"You should stay with Riley," he said. "Riley's got a gun."

I looked at him. What was he saying? Nat shot me a quick glance.

He wanted me to make a grab for the gun. I could see it in his eyes. I didn't know what his plan was after that, but he was asking me to trust him.

I turned back to Riley and took a deep breath.

"Okay," I said, raising my hands in a gesture of surrender. I kept my eyes off the gun on the floor but took a step toward it.

"I'll stay with you," I said. "On the condition that you let Nat go."

I took another step toward Riley. I was just inches away from the gun now. Riley eyed me warily. I could feel Nat watching and my guts twisted into a knot. I was going to get only one chance to make this work.

"So what's the big secret?" I asked. "What's this thing that makes me so spec—" As I spoke, I dropped to the floor. In one, swift move, my hand darted toward the gun. Riley saw what I was doing. He made a grab for the pistol himself.

He was too late. My fingers curled around the cold metal. Quick as a flash I darted up again and jumped backward, away from Riley's outstretched arm.

"Don't." His mouth fell open in horror.

"Shut up." I pointed the gun at his face. My heart thudded in my chest.

This was it. My chance to take revenge for Mum. The man behind the Canal Street market bomb was finally at my mercy. All I had to do was pull the trigger. Behind me I could hear Nat moving around the room. Unscrewing something. Pouring liquid onto the floor.

"Nearly there, Charlie," he said.

I took a step away from Riley. All I had to do was pull the trigger.

"The EFA is just one branch of a larger organization." Riley spoke fast, urgently. "There are other groups. And their leader, *my* leader, is an ex-soldier like me . . . someone who has a deep desire to meet you, to keep you safe. . . ."

I stared at him. What was he talking about?

"Give me that, Charlie," Nat said, appearing beside me. He took the gun from my hands. "Get over to the window."

I backed across the room, my eyes still on Riley. What was Nat going to do? Was *he* going to shoot Riley?

"Outside, Charlie," Nat urged. "Now."

Still watching Riley, I hooked my leg over the window ledge, then crawled onto the sill. I could hear Riley's men across the field, shouting instructions to one another. Riley kept his gaze on me.

"If you go, you won't meet him," he hissed.

"Shut up, Riley." Nat turned to me. "Don't listen to his lies."

He was right, wasn't he? They *were* lies. Riley was just trying to keep me here, to manipulate me again. I jumped down outside, landing on the gravel with a crunch. Right away Nat clambered onto the ledge, still pointing the gun at Riley. A second later he, too, was outside. Riley watched me. He met my gaze and shook his head, like he was telling me I was making a huge mistake. For a moment, I doubted myself. Maybe he *was* telling the truth after all?

"Who is it?" I asked, suddenly full of fear "Who wants to meet me?"

Riley kept his eyes on mine.

"It's your father, Charlie," he said. "He's still alive."

NAT

I barely heard what Riley said. I focused on the diesel and the ammonium nitrate, now pooling together on the floor in front of the desk. Then I steadied the gun and took aim.

"Go," I whispered to Charlie. "Head for the trees."

I fired. With a flash, the pool of liquid exploded into fire.

I turned as Riley, on the other side of the fire, roared out in fury. Charlie hadn't moved. I grabbed her hand.

"Run!" I shouted.

For a second I was dragging her after me, then Charlie found her stride and we raced, hand in hand, across the field. Behind us, shouts echoed into the air. I headed for the woods. Shots fired all around us. We let go of each other's hands and ran harder, away from the soldiers. Seconds later, we reached the cover of trees. I darted along, weaving in and out of the trees, looking for Aaron.

But Aaron was nowhere to be seen. I stopped running. Charlie raced up, panting.

"Where is he?" she hissed.

"I don't know." I swore under my breath. Through the trees I could just make out the dark silhouettes of three soldiers entering the woods only yards away. Across the field, fire blazed from the farmhouse.

"Aaron must be hiding from the soldiers. Come on," I whispered.

We crept over the fallen leaves, trying to make our steps as light as possible.

"Did you hear what Riley said about my father?" Charlie whispered. Even in the dark of the woods I could see her face was pale, her eyes full of shock.

"It was a lie," I whispered back. "Don't you think your mum or your uncle would have said something if your dad was really alive? Riley was just trying to manipulate us again." A twig snapped to our left. I stopped walking. "Who's there?" I hissed.

Silence.

Tensing, I raised the gun.

A figure emerged from behind a tree. It was Aaron, his scared eyes glinting in the moonlight.

"Let's go." I shoved the gun in my pocket and the three of us raced through the trees toward the road.

I tried to keep my footsteps as soft as possible. Charlie was making barely any sound, but Aaron was heavy-footed, his steps echoing loudly around the wood. We ran on. I tripped. Fell. Forced myself up. My lungs strained for breath. I gripped Charlie's hand as she sped along beside me. We had to make it to the road before the soldiers found us.

A shot rang out, loud in the night air. It came from the left.

I swerved to the right, dragging Charlie after me. I could hear Aaron's breath, raw and ragged, as he turned too.

We raced on.

The men chasing us crashed through the trees. They were close. Too close. The trees thinned. The roar of a truck filled the air. We must be near the road now. I sped up, Charlie on one side, Aaron on the other. I flew past the last tree. A truck was thundering along the road toward us. It passed a masked soldier emerging from the woods just thirty yards away.

I reached for Riley's pistol. It was gone. It must have fallen out of my pocket when I tripped and fell. The truck was approaching fast. Down the road, the soldier raised his gun. "Hands up," he shouted. "Or I shoot."

There was no time to think. The truck was about to pass us. If I didn't make it stop, we would all be caught and taken back to Riley.

I flung myself into the road. Arms waving, I yelled at the truck driver.

"Stop! Stop!"

The truck kept coming. It was huge, towering up in front of me. I caught a glimpse of the driver's face, his mouth open with shock. I closed my eyes as it roared right up to me.

It screeched to a halt just inches away from my outstretched arms. I stood, trembling, for a second.

"Get in!" Charlie yelled. She was already dragging Aaron toward the driver's cab.

I ran around to the far side, scrambling in next to the

shocked driver before the man could protest. Aaron and Charlie hurled themselves in on his other side. A shot fired out.

"Drive!" I shouted.

The truck driver—still open-mouthed—roared away at top speed. I struggled with the door, slamming it shut, then peered out of the window. The masked soldier was running after us, gun poised, ready to shoot again. Then the truck swerved—far too fast—around a corner and the soldier disappeared.

I sat back, squashed between the door and the driver.

"What the hell?" the driver shouted. He was middle-aged, with a lined, weather-beaten face. "What is this?"

Charlie and I exchanged a glance. We shouldn't say anything, not until we knew we were safe.

"We . . . I was taken—" Aaron started.

"Quiet," I ordered.

Aaron stopped talking.

I sat back. Where on earth did we go now? The enormity of getting—and staying—away from Riley and Taylor was over-whelming.

"Whatever it is, I don't want to get involved," the driver said. I glanced at the speedometer. The truck was still traveling at over sixty miles an hour. We turned onto a main road. Other cars were passing. The driver slowed slightly. "I'm dropping you here." He indicated a traffic circle up ahead.

I nodded. We needed to get out of the truck anyway. The EFA soldiers had seen us get inside and were probably already looking for it. We were better off on our own. A few moments

later the driver pulled up. Charlie, Aaron, and I got out opposite the circle and the truck zoomed off again.

I pulled the others into the cover of the trees. Two roads led
off from the circle: one was signposted to the highway, the other
led downhill, to a town called Hilmarton.

"That driver could have taken us farther," Aaron said. He was
white-faced, his whole body shaking.

"Better we're away from anything Riley's men can trace,"
Charlie said.

She slipped her hand into mine and squeezed. I squeezed
back. In spite of everything I felt better, stronger somehow.

Cars roared past us. There was no sign yet of Riley's men but
they couldn't be far away.

"We need to go," I said. I crept across the trees toward the
turning that led to Hilmarton. From the edge of the copse I could
see the lights of a small town spread out at the bottom of a hill.

"Let's try here," I said, turning back to the others.

"Wait." Aaron pointed at Charlie. "I'm not going anywhere
with her. She *kidnapped* me."

"Whatever Charlie did, she was tricked into," I said, peering
back along the way we'd just come. Riley's men would surely be
here any second.

"I don't care."

Before either of us could stop him, Aaron had run out into
the road. He raced across the circle, toward the road that led to
the highway. I gasped as a car swerved past him, almost knocking
him down.

"Aaron!" Charlie called.

But Aaron didn't look back at us. He darted to the side of the road, then flung out his hand in an attempt to flag down the next car. It zoomed past him. So did the next and the next. I started to run toward him, but before I had even gotten across the road, a large gray station wagon pulled over. I watched as Aaron bent down and talked to the driver through the window. A second later he opened the door and got in. The car drove off toward the highway.

I ducked back behind the trees where Charlie was waiting, open-mouthed.

"I can't believe he just ran off like that," she said.

"He was scared." I blew out my breath, trying to control my own rising panic. "Come on, let's head for the town at the bottom of the hill."

"Okay," Charlie agreed. "We can find a police station. Explain what's happened."

I said nothing. Taylor's words about the police being sympathetic to Riley were echoing around my head. Could we really trust the police force? Could we trust anyone?

It took about ten minutes to reach the center of Hilmarton. We talked as we ran, telling each other everything we had found out this evening. Charlie was as shocked as I had been that Taylor and Riley had been prepared to let me die.

"Me and everyone else caught up in the bomb," I said. "Which makes the EFA just as extreme as any of the groups it's supposed to be against."

Charlie shook her head. "Even if my dad were alive, there's no way he could be involved with terrorists. My mum used to talk about him . . . I've seen videos of him. He just . . . he wouldn't be capable of bombing and killing innocent people. I mean, my mum died in the market bombing and he loved her, I *know* he did. Riley must have been lying about all that."

She sounded like she was trying to convince herself. I didn't say anything. After Taylor's and Riley's betrayal, anything seemed possible.

We kept a careful look out for EFA soldiers as we left the shelter of the trees and followed the signs to Hilmarton High Street. Neither of us had a phone and both of us were starving, so when we came to an Internet café offering five minutes free online with every pizza, we decided to grab some food and take the opportunity to work out exactly where we were. Charlie logged on while I went to the counter to fetch our pizza. When I came back to our booth, she was staring at the screen, her eyes wide with horror.

"What is it?" I said.

"Look." She pointed at the news website on the screen. It was a piece about the Parliament bombing posted ten minutes ago. I followed her finger to the third line.

In a statement issued earlier tonight, protest organization the League of Iron has claimed responsibility for the bomb attack, naming north London teenager Nathan Holloway as their "hero at ground zero." Holloway, 16, who attends a local private school, was seen leaving the scene by several members of the public. All witnesses claim Holloway was heard boasting of his successful detonation of the bomb.

I gasped. Why was the League claiming responsibility? And who on earth had come forward telling lies about me boasting I'd killed all those people? There was a video immediately under the text. I clicked to play it, the pizza I'd bought growing cold on its plate.

The screen showed the sights and sounds of the bombs aftermath: people running about, sirens going, lots of shouting and bright lights. I could clearly be seen, an intense look on my face, heading past the cordon, then ducking past the policeman who'd tried to stop me. The way the thing had been edited made me look as if I was trying to run away from him. The shot changed to a head and shoulders view of Roman Riley. He was standing on the street outside his own house.

"Yes, the boy, Nathan Holloway, came up to me," he was saying sorrowfully. *"I couldn't make out what he was saying at first, then I realized he was actually claiming he had set off the bomb. I led him away from the crowd. I was looking for a police officer. But before we'd gone very far, Nathan ran away again. I'm afraid he's a very troubled young man."*

I turned to Charlie who was watching the screen, open-mouthed beside me.

"I can't believe Riley's done this," I said, my voice hoarse.

Charlie refreshed the screen. A new post had already superceded the one we were looking at.

The police have issued an arrest warrant for Nathan Holloway, 16, who is wanted for questioning in connection with tonight's Parliament bombing. This follows their earlier arrest warrant for Charlotte Stockwell, 16, a friend of Holloway's.

A picture of both of us followed the post, with a warning to the public to approach us with caution and call the police if they saw us. Charlie's hands flew to her mouth.

"Why do they want to arrest me?" she breathed.

"Kidnapping Aaron Latimer, I guess," I said.

Charlie swore. "But he's free. We rescued him. Surely he'll tell them I was tricked into kidnapping him? *I'll* tell them. Let's go to the police ourselves. Right now. Surely if we explain they'll *have* to believe us."

I shook my head. Taylor's earlier words about how much support Riley had among top-level police officers echoed in my head. We couldn't trust the police, just as we couldn't be sure of what Aaron would say or do.

Right now, we couldn't be sure of anything except the need to hide. I let the reality of this knowledge settle in my stomach, a deadweight.

I turned to Charlie. "We need to get away from here and think it all through." I pulled my pants pockets inside out, showing her what was left after I'd bought our pizza. "I've got three pounds on me," I said. "You?"

"About thirty pounds." Charlie made a face. "It's nothing. Where are we going to go? What are we going to do?"

"I don't know," I said, "but thirty-three pounds is a start. We'll just have to work out everything else as we go along."

TWO WEEKS LATER

CHARLIE

I can't tell you where we are, but we're safe.

We're still together, Nat and me. Life is hard, but we have each other. We even talked about how we feel. That scares me. A lot. But the truth is Nat means everything to me. I don't know what I'd do without him. I certainly wouldn't have made it this far.

We're getting some help, though I can't tell you who from.

It isn't from the police. That's for sure. We are public enemies as far as they are concerned. Nat knew we would be, right from the start. I was all for turning ourselves in, attempting to prove our innocence in person, but Nat was more cautious. He suggested that we waited a bit, maybe gave our side of the story at a distance to see how the cops responded.

In the end we got ahold of a phone, made our own video, and posted it online.

The response was unbelievable.

And not in a good way.

Our faces were plastered across every news program and website in the country. Commentators were calling us "a Bonnie and Clyde for the iPad generation," whatever that means. Roman

Riley was widely filmed, shaking his head sorrowfully and saying how sad it was that young people like us felt so desperate that we turned to violence. Soon afterward CCTV footage appeared showing me shoving that gun in Aaron's face. He and Jas look terrified and I look like some mad, evil teen.

Just like Riley planned.

Nat and I waited for news to come out that Aaron was no longer kidnapped. But, again, it was all twisted. Two days after the kidnapping, the mayor of London did an interview with Aaron at his side. They both claimed that I kidnapped Aaron for the League of Iron and that he managed to escape without any help from either me or Nat.

"Why are they lying?" I asked Nat. "Aaron *knows* he wouldn't have got away if it wasn't for us."

"He's probably lying because his dad's told him too," Nat said. "Because they're scared that if they don't blame us, Roman Riley will come after them again."

The League of Iron posted another statement claiming responsibility for both the Parliament bombing and the kidnapping of Aaron Latimer—and naming Nat and me as the people they used to carry out the crimes. This post also included broadcast footage of us doing combat training with the EFA, though the way it was presented gave the impression we were learning to become the League of Iron terrorists.

At first we wondered why the League kept saying we had been working for them. And then we saw Riley on camera, telling the world about his stand against fraud. He looked right into the lens and said, *"I pledge to expose tax crimes wherever they take place."* It's the kind of thing you often hear politicians say but, when Nat heard him, he remembered the folder of accounts he sneaked a look at the League of Iron meeting.

"Riley must be using the accounts to blackmail someone in the League," Nat explained with a groan. "That's why they're keeping quiet."

It seems that Riley set us up from the beginning.

He ordered Taylor to make us break into his own house, even planting that photo of Aaron to make us believe we were discovering a League of Iron plot. And—again through Taylor—he fed us lie after lie about what the EFA stood for.

Riley lied. Taylor lied.

It was all lies.

Almost all, anyway. I often think about what Riley said about my dad being alive. I'm sure that was yet another lie. Well, 99 percent sure. There's always that little bit of doubt inside me.

But then, as Nat points out, that's how Riley operates: making you believe him, then shifting the ground underneath you, just as you start to feel secure.

We've been in touch with Nat's family. They've been wonderful, actually, really supportive, though Jas was wary of me at first until Nat explained how we'd both been tricked.

I tried not to let that hurt me. It wasn't Jas's fault. It was Riley's.

Everything is his fault.

My own family hasn't been anywhere near so helpful as Nat's. In the first week we went into hiding, one of the news stations did an interview with Brian and Rosa. Brian was clearly deeply shocked that I'd kidnapped Aaron. At least he kept saying I must have been brainwashed into doing it. Rosa, on the other hand, was happy to be digging the knife in.

"Yeah, Charlie's always been a bit odd," she said, a fake-concerned expression on her face. *"She's a loner . . . never made much attempt to get along with me or anyone else at school."*

The worst news of all we learned only last night. Parveen got in touch using the old draft e-mail technique. It was good to know she was okay—and her advice was helpful: she was adamant that we should stay in hiding, that we would never get a fair hearing with the League and the mayor of London and half the police force in Roman Riley's pocket. And then she told us the devastating information that George was dead, killed after acting as fake decoy down in the tube station.

The news has hit both of us hard. It's impossible to believe that George, with his powerful fists and easy charm, simply doesn't exist anymore.

At least Parveen also gave us some hope. She told us about a resistance movement based in a secret location, which is working against Roman Riley and his allies. We're heading to find it now. Neither of us has said as much, but we're both aware that becoming part of a bigger protest against Riley is our only hope for survival. We know that if we go home, the evidence against us will send us to jail—that's if Riley doesn't get us first.

And we are determined to resist and defeat him, whatever it takes.

It's going to be a battle. The latest polls show that the House of Parliament bomb has sent the Government's ratings plummeting. There's going to be an election soon. Everyone's predicting yet another coalition—with Riley's Future Party expected to win the most seats.

In a few weeks, Riley will probably be prime minister.

He's got everything he wanted.

Except us.

Except our lives.

And we intend to keep those for as long as we can.

ACKNOWLEDGMENTS

Thank you to Molly Harcourt and, of course, to Moira, Gaby, Julie, and Melanie. Particular thanks to brilliant author and feedback queen, Lou Kuenzler.